## LETHAL LURE

To me the open door meant an ambush and I reacted without thinking. I took a quick step into the room and turned to slam my full weight against the door, preparing to take on whoever was setting me up. The door didn't hit the wall. As I expected it squeezed back against the body of the man who was hiding behind it.

But he forced himself out of the space and came at me like a cyclone, crouched in the kung fu stance, whirling and kicking as I backed away. I reeled against a coffee table and desperately grabbed it and held it between us.

He sent a smashing kick at the table, tearing it sideways from my hands. Then he half stepped forward and hit me like a lightning strike over the right temple. As I somersaulted away from him into darkness, one detail filled my mind. He was small and deadly . . . and Chinese.

# LIVE BAIT

# LIVE BAIT

## Ted Wood

BANTAM BOOKS
TORONTO • NEW YORK • LONDON • SYDNEY • AUCKLAND

*This low-priced Bantam Book
has been completely reset in a typeface
designed for easy reading, and was printed
from new plates. It contains the complete
text of the original hardcover edition.*
NOT ONE WORD HAS BEEN OMITTED.

LIVE BAIT

*A Bantam Book / published by arrangement with
Charles Scribner's Sons*

*PRINTING HISTORY*
*Charles Scribner's Sons edition published April 1985*
*Bantam edition / August 1986*

ISBN 0-553-25558-4

PRINTED IN CANADA
COVER PRINTED IN U.S.A.

U   0 9 8 7 6 5 4 3 2 1

For Mary,
who has made me a happy man

# LIVE BAIT

*1*

THE short one had a two-by-four in his hands. The big one was swinging his arms, punching his right fist into his left palm like a ball player. They were standing in the shadows of the fence that went all around the construction site, waiting for me, the way they must have waited for the last security guard, the one they had put in the hospital.

I guess they had come from the van that was parked up the street when I came on duty at midnight, working on my Academy Award for best performance as a no-hoper. I had been slump-shouldered and shabby, my Bonded Security uniform baggy, the tie knotted the wrong way so the narrow end lay in front. They had probably laughed when they saw me drain the mickey of rye I was carrying and drop the bottle down the sewer. They didn't know it was only cold tea. They were expecting a loser, not a policeman.

I stayed in character, flashing my light over them, nervously, but beyond as well, checking they had no reinforcements waiting to join in the headkicking if they put me down.

"Hey, who's there?" I kept my voice tense. The short one chuckled and swung his four-foot length of timber, nice and easy. "You're not s'posed to be here," I said and straightened up, not dramatically enough to make them suspicious. My job was to hold them—both if possible, one anyway.

The big one came out first. He had shoulder-length hair that looked gray in the bluish light on the pole in the middle of the site. "Hi, Pop," he said, and then the little one charged me.

I paused one second to whistle a long clear note through my front teeth, then crouched to meet him. He was whirling his club, expecting me to cower or run. Instead I

1

ducked under his swing, catching him on the wrong foot, gripping his right wrist and sticking out my left hip. His own momentum took him up and over, flat on his back like a flopped mattress, three yards beyond me. Then the second one charged and I dropped into the classic boxing crouch my father had taught me twenty-five years before and shot out a straight left, only with the hand up, flat against his chest.

He ran on to it and his feet flew from under him, leaving him on his back almost under me. I knee-dropped in his gut and the air went out of him with a whoomph. Behind me I heard Sam barking as he galloped over the broken ground and I shouted, "Fight!" without looking back. The big man lay working his legs and sucking for air that wouldn't come. I turned, keeping low, in time to see Sam grab the short guy by the arm that still held the two-by-four. "Good dog," I told him and he snarled and clamped his jaws tighter until the man yelled and dropped the board. I picked it up and swung it across his shins, not hard, just enough to remind him that he had started all this. Then I told Sam, "Easy," and he fell back, panting.

I stooped and rubbed his head with the ugly torn ear. "You're worth a whole platoon," I told him. "Good boy." He whined with pleasure and I patted him again and told the man, "Pick up your buddy and let's go."

He swore and I swung the two-by-four the way he had, earlier. "Pick him up."

He did, cradling the limp body in his arms. "That's good," I told him. "Head for the shack."

He staggered, swearing but never letting go, over the forty yards to the trailer that the builder had placed beside the gate as an office. I ushered him up the three steps ahead of me and he stumbled up and lowered his friend to the floor inside. Sam was half a step behind me and I told him, "Keep," and we both stood looking at the pair of them as they lolled on the floor, against the wall.

I reached the phone off the hook and dialled, then grabbed the knot of that lousy necktie and wriggled it free. Fullwell answered the phone, repeating the number I'd dialled.

"Hi, Simon. Reid Bennett. We had visitors."

"Did you stop them?" His voice ran halfway up the scale to an anxious yell.

"Yes. They're here in the shack with me, behaving like good boys."

"Nice work, buddy. I'll be there in five."

He hung up and I followed suit. I flicked the tie a couple of times to get the creases out and retied it, properly. I've worn uniform enough years that I like to do it right. Not always as smartly as I once wore dress blues in the U.S. Marines, but as tidy as the copper I'd been in Toronto for nine years. Then I took my cap off and reached for my lunch pail. I had a thermos in there and I poured myself a cup of coffee and looked over the prisoners.

The small guy was watching me, puzzling. He had the thin, mean look of an underfed dog and the black tattoos on both arms that told me he had done time, probably heavy time, in the pen. He was in his late twenties, scrawny and angry.

The other one was the standard racetrack rough. You can see a dozen like him any night, making two-dollar bets and waiting for his luck to change. He was in his thirties and by the look of his check shirt and dirty green work pants, it hadn't changed yet.

The younger one spoke at last, a blurted question, almost embarrassed. "What happened to the old guy who came on at midnight?"

"I'm not that old," I told him.

"You? Christ! This guy was way shorter, a real rubbie."

I wanted to warn him not to judge books by their covers but he probably didn't read that much anyway, so I sat quietly, sipping coffee and waiting for Fullwell to arrive. I was looking forward to it. He'd asked me to do a job for him and I'd done it; I figured I could collect the cash he'd promised me and head back to Murphy's Harbour. Not a bad day's work.

IT began the day before. I was picking tomatoes from the vines I'd stuck into the sandy garden of my house at Murphy's Harbour a couple of months earlier when the only tomatoes you could buy were jetlagged with the trip from California. Now the store in town was full of fresh local produce, and I was stuck with the problem of disposing of enough Beefsteaks to feed the world. Plus I had the second worry of what to do with the remaining thirteen days of my vacation. That was when Fullwell pulled into the driveway in his Oldsmobile.

He waved and called, "Hi!" as he got out of the car and slapped his knee for Sam to come and get patted. He knew Sam from before but that didn't get him any favors until I told Sam, "Friend," and he wandered over to take his stroking. I followed and shook hands.

Fullwell looked at me approvingly. "That's one hell of a tan," he said.

"Easy to come by. I've spent the whole summer looking for lost kids, tagging cars, checking for stolen boats," I said.

He grinned. "Yeah, and solving homicides."

"That too. But now I'm on vacation, just like rich folks."

"I bet." He drawled it as if he were telling a joke, saving the punchline for later. He stretched his shoulders, extending both arms straight, like a scarecrow. "It's quite a drive up here."

"And you didn't make it to come fishing, did you?" I nodded towards the house. "Come in and have a beer."

"Good thinking." He tossed his openweave fedora through the window of his car and followed me into the house. I left the tomatoes where they were. The fruit flies would feel more at home in the open air.

My fridge was pretty well empty except for a case of Labatt's Classic. I hooked a couple out and took them through to the parlor. It's not a comfortable room, or house for that matter, but I don't need a lot to keep me happy. I spent two years in Nam, mostly in the boonies. Being in out of the rain is still a luxury.

Fullwell sat in the armchair. Because it faces the TV he probably figured it was the most comfortable chair in the house. He didn't know the set is dead and the chair dying. A spring twanged under him and he frowned.

"My ex-wife got the good stuff," I explained.

He managed a smile. He's a big, pale man, one of those paper-skinned redheads who never take a tan, even if they're in the sun for a week. And he never is. He's an office worker. He spends his time indoors at Bonded Security in Toronto. We'd met when he came up to Murphy's Harbour on a murder investigation after one of his guys got himself cancelled. Afterwards, Fullwell had offered me a job. I guessed he was back here to up the ante.

He took out his little tin of Dutch cigarillos and looked around for an ashtray. I got up and found him one I'd picked up in Hong Kong while I was on R and R there during my first tour in Nam. He nodded thanks, put it on his knee and lit up.

"I was wondering how busy you were, now the summer's over and your cottagers have all gone home." He let the question lie there on the air like the plume of smoke he blew out.

"I'm supposed to be on vacation. But I don't like to go too far." Murphy's Harbour is a one-cop town, up north of Toronto, a vacation spot. It had been jammed all summer, now it was emptying out for the long winter wait, but I still felt responsible. "The Provincial Police would take an hour to get here if somebody called for A Policeman Quick."

"How often does that happen?" He knew the answer as well as I did, almost never. He didn't wait for my reply but gave me the facts, fast and clean. "I need some help, the kind with muscles in it. I think you could handle it better than anybody else I've ever worked with."

"What's up?" I'm not hooked on risk or anything as neurotic as that, but policing Murphy's Harbour in the off-season is only a little bit livelier than counting sheep.

"Night before last, Friday night, Saturday morning, we had a disturbance on one of our sites. It's a construction site. Somebody slashed the tires on an earthmover. Client was madder'n hell."

"Where was the guard while this was going on? Off for a beer, asleep, what?"

Fullwell gripped his smoke between his teeth, eyes squinched up. "He was asleep, in the shack, which was lucky for him. We fired him, of course. Next night we put a young kid on, nineteen years old, keen, a real crackerjack."

"And?" I took a pull on my beer and waited.

"And this time, around two A.M. he didn't check in on schedule so the Field Officer made a hit on the property and found him with his head kicked in. Most of his teeth gone, internal injuries, he'd been gone over by experts."

I whistled. Toronto is a law-abiding city. Outside of bar fights that could happen anywhere, a man doesn't often get into that kind of jackpot.

"What do the police make of it?"

Fullwell made a little ceremony of tapping the ash off his cigarillo, not meeting my eyes. "We kept it quiet."

"An assault like that and you didn't report it? Why not?"

Now he looked up at me, out of eyes as pale blue as antique delft. "Not my idea, Reid. We've got a new VP Marketing. He's spent time in New York with the company, where this kind of thing happens more often. He figured the publicity would be bad for business. So he got me to keep it out of the hands of the police."

"What did the kid think about that? He must've been mad to know he's been ignored."

Fullwell shook his head. "No, that's cool. He's in hospital, all expenses paid, full salary, everything. We just want to catch the guys who did it to him. Meantime we put it around as a fall."

I sniffed. I've been a policeman for ten years now, nine of them in Toronto. To my way of doing business, this was all wrong. You don't sweep near-fatal beatings under the rug. You take them to the police.

"And you went along with this VP?" It didn't sound like the Fullwell I knew. He was always outspoken. I've heard him chew out their head office people for not caring enough about the men on the job.

"I didn't have a whole lot of options, Reid. This new guy is the blue-eyed boy. He's brought in a slew of new business and his word is better than mine at the company."

"Yeah, well that happens, I guess. Did you make the usual enquiries? Is the kid in hock to some loan shark? Does he have a jealous boyfriend, what?"

Fullwell took a farewell pull on his smoke and stubbed it out as if he were beating time to a record. "No, this guy's straight arrow. He's an engineering student at the U. of T., brings his books to the site and studies between making his rounds."

"And what did he tell you?" It was getting interesting, a big city crime instead of the petty thefts and traffic offences I had to deal with most of the time in my own work.

"He said it was two guys. One was short, had a two-by-four. The other was big. They cracked him over the head with the two-by-four and put the boots to him while he was down."

He picked up his beer bottle and measured the level with his eye as if he were a pharmacist, took a swallow and set it down again. He hadn't come all this way north to drink beer. "I feel bad about this one, Reid. It's never happened to an employee of mine before. I've had guys hurt, of course, but never worked over. I want to catch these bastards. That's why I came to you."

"You want to go trolling for trouble, using me as live bait?" The idea was intriguing. I wasn't scared of a couple of headbeaters. They were probably amateurs. They'd have a few drinks in them to toughen them up. They would be slow. With Sam's help I could corner them before they could harm me.

Fullwell gave me time to think it through before he went on. "The new guy asked me if I knew anybody who could handle it. He wants to keep it to one man, for the sake of security. He doesn't want anybody else to know. So, anyway, I told him about you, that you could probably do it standing on your head."

"Thanks a lot," I said. "I'm not into group encounters." I watched him, seeing the tension grow in his face until I said, "But what the hell. How much are you going to pay me?"

He relaxed, grinning first, then slapping his knee with his

hand. He raised his beer bottle to me. "Cheers. I knew you wouldn't let me down. I can't pay a fortune but we can spare five hundred bucks, for a night or two's work."

I didn't tell him that was exactly what my job in Murphy's Harbour paid me, per week. He probably knew anyway, they had good records at his company. "Well, that won't jeopardize my amateur standing, will it?" I said and he laughed.

"We're a lean, mean machine when it comes to paying out. Most of the guys get minimum wage. Five hundred is big money to us."

I shrugged and grinned again. It was big to me as well. This job doesn't pay well, but it's the best I could get after leaving the Toronto department when they didn't back me in the followup to a fight I was in. My wife couldn't take it either, and with her gone my expenses were light. All I had to buy was a few groceries, chow for Sam, and fishing lures and the occasional case of beer or bottle of rye for me. With five hundred found dollars I could replace the worn-out chair and stock up on books for the coming winter.

I set down my beer bottle. "You're in luck. My sister lives in Toronto. She's been wanting me to come down and spend time with her and the kids. This gives me an excuse to play happy families."

He beamed. "I didn't think you'd let me down."

"I'll need a uniform," I said.

"Forty-two tall was my guess. It's in the trunk." He winked at me and stood up. "I figured you'd bail us out."

"Yeah, well it's on one condition," I warned him and he stopped.

"What's that?"

"Stick a box of those tomatoes in the trunk when you leave. Otherwise the fruit flies will carry me away."

## 3

I sat and read the Toronto *Sun* and drank coffee and waited for Fullwell to turn up. Somebody once said of the *Sun* that it saves you from a whole lot of bad news. He was right. Except for the pinup on page three there was nothing in it. But I wasn't reading for news anyway. It was just a trick to isolate my prisoners so that neither one got the chance to do any talking before the interrogation began. It's standard procedure. It often pays off with a flood of talk when you finally turn on the tap.

The little guy spoke once but I hissed at Sam and he growled until the man got the message and sat back against the wall, legs drawn up to cover his testicles. The movement added to my suspicion he was an ex-con. He had the right mix of arrogance and fear.

After twenty minutes or so a car stopped outside the gate and a door slammed. Then footsteps and the door of the trailer opened.

It wasn't Fullwell. I assumed this must be the VP he'd told me about. He was stocky and held himself erect, the way short cops do, or guys with tall girlfriends. He was around five-nine and two hundred pounds, with a round face that looked friendly until you checked how close together his eyes were. He was wearing an expensive Haspel suit and a light straw hat with a wide green band that clashed with his suit. He flashed me a formal smile, his eyes receding deeper into the crinkles of fat, the teeth baring themselves a neat quarter inch in his mail-slot mouth. I decided I didn't like him. He had a little leather holder in his hand and he flapped it open and shut, giving me a half-second glimpse of the Bonded Security shield. "Inspector Willis," he said.

I stood up. "Reid Bennett. And these two are the callers." I indicated the guys on the floor. They were watching us, dull faced. It was more proof, if anybody needed any, that they had spent time inside. The first thing a guy learns in the joint is to stay cool, show no emotion at all.

Willis turned and smiled at them like Santa Claus. "Picked the wrong guy this time, didn't you?" he said cheerfully.

The bigger man cracked first. "Waddya mean, this time? I ain't never been here before."

Willis kicked him, an almost invisibly fast flick of the foot that landed up inside the knee where the nerve runs over the bone. The man writhed away and swore. Willis laughed and I said nothing. This was not my way. It wasn't police work. I would move the next time he played dirty. For the moment, he didn't. He stood looking at the big guy, his smile slowly draining from his face like dishwater going down a sink. "I want you to talk, I'll tell you. Otherwise, keep your yap shut, got that?"

The pair of them sat and watched him, not speaking, their eyes rolled up towards him. Now he backed off a pace and looked them over. "You make me puke. Two of you. Two of you, working over a kid on his own." He took a pace to one side and then back, the way a soccer player might to throw a defender off guard. They watched him like cobras watching a mongoose. "So now you figured you'd get some more kicks, right? Tonight you'd put some other guy in hospital, right?"

His voice rose to a shout and I expected him to kick again but he didn't. He lowered his voice instead and chuckled. "Only this time, no luck. This time you came here and found two of us working and the dog. And that's how come you both got your arms broken and the dog tore the crotches right out of you."

The big one blustered, waving his hands to keep away any blows. "Waddya mean? He didn't bite us. We didn't get hurt, not bad, anyway."

Willis laughed. "Not yet," he said. He turned and picked up the two-by-four from the table. I read the anger in his face and knew he was serious. It was time to take charge.

I picked up the phone. "Okay, Mr. Willis. I'll call the police to come and get these turkeys."

He whirled to face me, feet apart, the blustering bully's pose that is so vulnerable to the pre-emptive kick. He had the two-by-four in his hands and he looked as if he intended using it on me. "Forget the phone, sir," he said softly. "This isn't police business."

I dialled the police number. "Put the club down and relax," I told him calmly.

Instead he hunched himself like a bull, pushing his lower lip out, holding the board in both hands, the way you hold a rifle for bayonet work. I held the phone, listening to the ringing and watching his eyes for the flicker that would tell me which move to make. But the blow didn't come my way. Instead he spun around and brought the club back to smash down on the small man. I dropped the phone and caught the board at the moment he reached the end of his back swing, pulling down. He lost his grip and stumbled, swearing.

"Forget it," I told him, replacing the phone on the cradle. He straightened himself up, blazing with anger.

"You're fired!" he shouted and pointed at the door as if he expected me to bow my head and shuffle out.

I touched Sam on the head and pointed to the two men. "Keep," I told him, then jerked my head towards the door and told Willis, "Let's step outside, Inspector. We have to talk."

He glowered at me, the fury still white hot in his eyes. But he was pro. He had no cards left to play here so he went along with me, but first spoke to the two prisoners. "One move and he'll have your throats out."

We went out into the softness of the September night. I was in front but I moved to one side as soon as I was through the door, so Willis wouldn't feel tempted to take out his frustrations in a sucker kick. I'd seen how quick he was with his feet.

We stopped a couple of yards from the door and spoke in low voices so the men inside wouldn't overhear. He went first, the anger and words boiling out of him. "What in hell are you playing at? These guys beat up that kid last night. Don't you care what happens to the other guys you work with?"

There would have been more but it was all on the same note so I held up one hand and took over. "Maybe Simon didn't explain to you that I'm moonlighting on this job as a favor. By profession I'm a policeman. I know the rules better than most security people."

In an instant he was ingratiating. "I know that, for crying out loud. I know about you. But these are unusual circumstances and you're out of uniform."

"Look. We have no proof these two worked the kid over. It's likely, even probable. But no judge would convict them."

"Exactly." His voice took on the anxious whine you hear in used-car salesmen when the customer reads the price tag for the first time. "That's just the point. They'll get a slap on the wrist and sent on their way. I want them to know they can't push a Bonded guy around the way they did." I didn't answer and he bored on with the final argument, the one he thought justified all his actions. "Hell. If people can't depend on our guys to take care of themselves, how can our clients depend on our services?"

"If you work them over, you're no better than they are. And no smarter." I cut him off as he tried to interrupt. "Why not let me talk to them, try and find out who sent them. This thing is starting to look organized. This is the third night they've been here, it's not personal, it's business. Let's find who's behind it and go after him."

Willis drew in a long soothing breath that seemed to cool him down completely. When he spoke again his voice was pitched naturally. "These are the fellas who hurt the kid last night. It's them who oughta suffer. But I understand what you're saying."

"It's the only way," I assured him. "A few bruises won't mean much to these guys. But if we find out who sent them we can go after him full bore."

He sniffed again and then said, "I suppose it's the only way."

"The only way I'll go for," I promised him. "Just play along for a couple of minutes. No violence, okay?"

"All right." Like a schoolboy forced into an apology he stuck out his hand to me. I shook it, instinctively turning sideways to him first, clear of his feet. I still didn't trust him. "No hard feelings," he said.

"None. I can understand how mad you got, knowing your employee was hurt." I couldn't, honestly. If he was professional he should have been able to accept the realities of his job and do it by the book. A copper has to, no matter what his personal feelings may be. That's why so many of us end up with broken marriages or drinking problems.

We went back in, him in front. I took out my wallet before I followed him and was busy tucking imaginary bills into it as I came back in. "Okay, Inspector, I'll take the big one." I pointed at the man and crooked my finger. "All right, you, on your feet."

He squirmed and looked around, wildly, at his partner, at Willis, at me. "You said you was callin' the cops."

"There's been a change of plan." I smiled at him, trying to look like Willis. "If I call the cops, the next thing you'll be out on bail. The inspector just explained it to me." Willis snickered, right on cue. I reached down and grabbed the man by the collar. "Come on now, don't make it any harder on yourself." He came, awkwardly, trying to comply and stay out of my reach at the same time. I picked up the two-by-four and hissed at Sam to come with me. I didn't need him, except for his part in the charade but I didn't want Willis to have any unfair advantage if he tried to hurt the little man while I was outside. I still didn't trust him any farther than I trusted the prisoners.

I shoved the man down the steps and walked him ahead of me, steering him with little jabs on the shoulder until we were off in the middle of the site, out of earshot of the trailer.

The earthmover with its slashed tires stood there, a hulk of steel and shadows. I shoved the man up against it, face first, taking one wrist and holding it behind him, not applying any pressure except for the tacit pressure of fear. "What's your name?"

The question threw him. He was anticipating pain, not words. "Hudson, Charlie Hudson."

I lifted his wrist a fraction, not enough to hurt, enough to let him know I could, if I wanted to. "Which arm you want broken?"

"Hey! No! Hey! Come on, sir! I never hurt the kid."

I kept my voice bored. "You were here."

He still spluttered, trying to turn his face to me over his shoulder. "Yeah. We was here. Me an' Kennie. But it was Kennie done the kickin', not me."

"Your turn to use the two-by-four, was it?" Never acknowledge the usefulness of information as long as it's pouring out freely.

Hudson squirmed, trying to face me so he could look convincing. "Hey, no sir. You seen Kennie. He's meaner'n a snake. Like he was in the joint as a kid an' a bunch of guys gave him a hard time an' since then he's mean."

"And you're not. You're mister nice guy?" I lifted his wrist a millimeter and he responded with a short moan, fear again, not pain. I was ready to believe him. He and Kennie were the typical Mutt and Jeff pair of wasters. One big and dumb, the other small and smart. He'd been here with Kennie, no doubt of that. He might even have kicked the kid in the head a time or two, but not out of malice, just to be sociable. He wouldn't have wanted Kennie to think he was chicken.

But he was. He was a mass of fear and I used it, shoving him a little tighter against the dew-misted metal of the earthmover.

"Who sent you?"

He tried to turn, surprised at the question, but I kept the pressure on and he burrowed his face against the metal in front of him. "Who sent you to slash the tires and hurt the kid?" I repeated, tonelessly.

"If I say, will you let me go?"

"Talk fast," I told him contemptuously. "Right now I'm supposed to be kicking your head in."

"His name is Tony." It came out in a half scream. "Honestagod that's all I know. Tony."

I spun him by the wrist so he turned around with his back to the machine. I stood back a pace, clear of his feet. Sam growled, low and savage. "That's not good enough. Tony who?"

He shook his head, scrubbing the back of his skull against the metal. "I don't know, and that's the God's truth. He was just Tony. He knew Kennie. We was havin' a beer at the Millrace, down on Queen Street near the track. This guy comes in and him an' Kennie get talkin' an' he asks would we like to make a double sawbuck."

"Was that for cutting the tires, or hitting the kid?"

"For both. We was s'posed to make trouble." He paused a second and when I didn't respond he gabbled on. "But I never touched the kid. That was Kennie. You seen him t'night with that two-by-four. He would've killed ya."

It all rang true. This guy was just bluster and belly. He'd charged me because he'd thought I would catch him if he didn't. But he had no guts, and no deep meanness in him.

"Tell me about this Tony. What's he look like?"

Now his hands sprang to life, drawing a picture in the air. He sketched a height with his left hand, perhaps five-ten, then wide-apart hands for wide shoulders. "Biggish guy, dark, moustache, good dresser. Wears a suit. No bastard else in the Millrace ever has a suit on, never."

"How old?"

"Thirty, thirty-five, you can't never be sure with Eyetalians." This was a slip and he bit off the word as soon as he realized what he had said.

"Does he sound Italian?"

He shook his head. "No, Canadian as you 'n' me."

"Then what makes you say he's Italian?"

"He's got one of them, you know, Jesus on a crosses, on a chain round his neck. An' with bein' called Tony an' all."

I switched the questioning. I had what I wanted, now I needed some insurance. "Where're you living?"

"Around." He said it without embarrassment. "I been in a room on Shuter Street since Friday. Before that I stayed with Kennie at his mother's. She's in an apartment up on Woodbine, close to Gerrard."

"What number?"

He told me, and gave me her name and the fact that she was a widow and worked at a dry-cleaner's on the Danforth. Then he got fearful, covering himself against my following the story down.

"You won't say nothin' to her, eh. I mean, she don't know Kennie's up to nothin'. She thinks he's workin' at the car wash with me."

I got the name and address of the car wash and the fact that he and Kennie had just been released from Burwash where he had served most of two-years-less-one-day for rolling drunks.

"Okay, I'm going to let you go. We're going to walk to the roadway nice and easy and you're going to run to the corner. Run every step of the way or the dog will get you." I patted Sam on the head and he snarled, on cue.

Hudson nodded eagerly and I ushered him past me and walked him to the gate. I opened it and told him, "Run!" and he did. I didn't even stop to watch, just turned away with Sam, back to the trailer.

Willis was writing in a notebook. The little man looked up from the floor and licked his lips. I could tell he had been talking and didn't want his partner to know. He dropped his eyes and waited until Willis snapped his book shut and asked.

"You kick the other guy's ass good?"

"Good." I nodded and he grinned.

"Fine. I was just having a chat with Kennie here. Now it's his turn, just wait while I show him off the premises."

"That'll be my pleasure," I said. I still didn't trust Willis. But he didn't object. "Just don't put him in the hospital," he said and laughed. I beckoned to Kennie and he came towards the door, head down as if there were cameramen outside, ready to take photos and show them around the store where his mother was respectable.

We walked a few paces and I told him, "Stand there," and he did, as promptly as a Marine grunt under a drill instructor, except that he turned his head towards me, suspiciously.

"We can do this two ways," I explained. "Either you can talk or we can do what the inspector promised and get my dog to tear you up. Which way's it gonna be?"

"Waddya want?" There was a tight, frightened vibrato to his voice. I could see his buddy had been right. He had been brutalized in the pen and the memory lived with him, night and day. I kept my voice calm as I asked him, "Who sent you to hit the kid and mess up this site?"

He sighed a big theatrical sigh and said, "What kid?" but I hissed at Sam and he growled, moving closer, his teeth gleaming in the light from the roadway. Kennie covered his crotch with both hands, "Okay. It was Tony."

I went through the same routine of questioning but he knew no more. I wasn't surprised. Only cops and judges and hockey players have last names for guys like Kennie. Everybody else is known casually. Tony was Tony, no last name. The only extra information I got was that Kennie had done jobs for him before. "Takin' care of guys who owed him money," he said proudly. He was small for the job but maybe Tony's clients were even smaller, or maybe they rolled over when they came up against his mad-dog ferocity.

When I'd got all the information he had I told him, "The guy in the shack wants your head on a plate. So you yell, and you run, got that?"

He had and he did, leaving the gateway in a ripple of footsteps with a long, fearful yell. I watched him go, still unsatisfied. We should have gone by the book and charged them both with attempted assault. Maybe the Crown Attorney would have got information out of them in the morning, when the started plea bargaining. Or maybe they would just have gone back inside for breach of parole. Either way, the law would have been served.

I shook my head and went back in. Willis was standing hunched over the table, shoulders rounded as he studied the Sunshine Girl in the paper. "I just love that young stuff," he said happily. Then he closed the paper impatiently and turned to me, airing his smile again. This time it looked more relaxed and genuine.

"Well. Did your play-acting work?"

"Yes. I got the name of the guy who sent them, no idea why they were sent, just the guy's name."

I expected him to press me for details but he didn't. Instead he raised both hands to shut me up.

"Listen. I like your moves, Bennett. What I want is you should follow this guy up on your own. Don't mention Bonded Security. If there're any questions, tell people it's a criminal thing from your own jurisdiction, anything. But keep us out of it."

I must have looked surprised. He made a placating little gesture. "Yeah, I know that's not the way I came on when I got here but I've been thinking." He took off his hat and rubbed his hand over his slicked down black hair, then settled his hat back on, the way a soldier does, tipping it forward first, then easing it back. "I've been thinking. You're a pro at this kind of stuff. What I am is something different. I'm a guy who sells our company's services. You're the investigator, so investigate, and I'll do my job. Stick at it for a week and if you get results we'll double that five yards, make it a grand."

"How far do you want me to go?" It was a deliberately clumsy question. I didn't understand him or his offer. His mouth was talking peace and logic, but his eyes were still full of anger. I watched him for body English as he answered, checking for any convulsive movements, sublimated blows that would mean he wanted me to hurt people.

He put both hands flat on the grimy table. "I want you to find out who set us up, that's all. The authorities can take it from there."

I nodded, agreeing. "Fine. In that case, I'm going to need a few bucks for expenses."

"Our limit is fifty a day," he said instantly. "Come into the office in the morning and draw a hundred. But I want receipts or it comes out of my hide."

# 4

THEY don't give receipts in places like the Millrace. It's cash and carry. All your cash, if possible, for more beer than you can carry. That's why the floor is covered in gray vinyl tile that can be slopped over with a wet mop when the need arises. As Ontario beverage rooms go, it's close to the average. Until the 1960s it was illegal to allow the public outside to see into any place where people were drinking. This means that most old beer parlors are in windowless basements. And Canadian breweries aren't allowed to promote, so the gloom isn't cut with neon beer signs like they have in cheerful corner bars in the States.

Like most places in town, the Millrace had a cocktail lounge up on the main floor but I didn't bother going in there. When guys like Hudson talk about a bar, they mean the beverage room. Beer is cheaper down there, and that's the name of the game. They aren't looking for atmosphere. In any case, I knew Tony wouldn't be up there. His kind of operation goes on at the despair level of civilization, which is a pretty fair summation of the basement at the Millrace.

There was a casual crowd in there when I arrived at seven the next evening, most of them truckers or mechanics from the transport company down the block. They looked tired and dirty but were yukking it up before going home. I did the routine thing, holding up two fingers to the waiter and dropping a fin on the table. He dropped my two glasses of draft and three-eighty in change. I slid him a quarter and he stuck it in his tips pocket, all without a word.

I'd brought the evening paper with me and I folded it open at the racing page. The trots were being run at Greenwood racetrack just down the road and I figured Millrace patrons would be horseplayers and the paper would make good camouflage.

The names and data made no sense to me but I sat and looked them over and chewed a toothpick while my head played with the idea of who Tony might be. From the description I'd got, he figured to be a loan shark. Probably he had a circuit on race nights. First he would hit the Millrace and a couple of other bars where the hopefuls were gathered, dreaming of the big win. Then he'd go down to the track to lounge around in his suit with the crucifix gleaming while a stream of contacts brought more hopefuls to him. The only thing that didn't fit in was why he was hiring muscle for construction site sabotage.

The easy connection to make is to talk about The Mob, and it exists in Toronto, just like any other city, but most of the Italians in town are good people. They work like dogs and went crazy the day Italy won the Soccer World Cup, but aside from that they spend all their time at home making wine and turning their tiny gardens into showplaces. Maybe Tony was an import from Buffalo, that's where most of the heavies in this region hang out.

After a while the guard changed in the room. The workies went home and were replaced by gray-faced older men who had been back to their rented rooms and washed and changed and eaten TV dinners and were looking for beer and company while they watched whatever crud came in over the big TV at the end of the bar. As the tables filled, one of them came and sat opposite me, going through the same ritual I'd performed, then sitting staring dead ahead, smoking Export cigarettes. He looked as if he was replaying his day, giving himself all the zingers he hadn't delivered when the foreman chewed him out for being too long in the john.

It was quarter to eight before Tony arrived. There was no mistaking him. He was the way Hudson had described him, thirtyish, five-ten, running to pudge, wearing a pale summer suit. His crucifix had company tonight, a gold shark's tooth and a medallion on a gold chain that could have held an anchor.

He sauntered in, cracked a joke with the waiter who laughed fit to bust, then turned away stone-faced to served his next table. Tony went to a corner table. A couple of guys were already there but they took their beers and moved, leaving him the space. He sat down with his back to the wall and cocked one leg over a vacant chair. The waiter hurried over with a Perrier and twist. That surprised me. You can get anything in a beer parlor these days but Perrier in this end of town is a rarity. It seemed Tony was a big wheel in the Millrace.

He threw a blue five-dollar bill on the table and waved the waiter away. The guy bowed and disappeared the bill into his tips pocket. Tony lit himself a cigarette from a soft pack, an American brand, and sat surveying his empire. Half a minute later another man came in, heavy-set and surly. He sat halfway down the room where he could watch Tony, ordered a single beer but didn't touch it. I assumed he did the collecting on Tony's delinquent debts and spent the rest of his time making sure some disenchanted borrower didn't try to take an empty beer bottle up alongside his boss's head.

I watched for a while, over my paper. Men came to Tony, stood and talked and were waved away to the other guy who did tricks with a wallet. Then they left, confident that some horse was going to save them the problem of repaying six bucks for five on payday. After about twenty minutes Tony took a token sip from his drink and stood up. So did his partner. I made my move, dropping my paper on the table and scooping up my change. As Tony lounged towards the door I cut him off. I didn't have any formal plan. You can't accost citizens of any stripe and ask them how come they're setting up bashings. So I dropped into my most comfortable undercover role, the inarticulate French Canadian. I do it well. My mother was a Dupuis before she became a Bennett and I speak farm-country French like a native and can do a good "haccent" when I have to disguise my background.

"I guess you mus' be Tony," I said, leaning on the second syllable of his name.

He stopped to study me as if I were a noxious insect. Up close he was not handsome. His face was fleshy and his skin was cratered with ancient acne. "What's it to ya?"

"Yeah, well a frien' of me, he say Tony a good man to know."

"What friend?" His muscle had moved in behind me, not close enough for concern but only two steps away. I grinned vacantly. "Kennie. Little guy, dis big." I held one hand out, about five feet from the floor.

"I don' know no Kennie," he said and moved by. I fell in beside him. This was what I wanted, a chance to walk him outside. Muscles stayed two steps behind us as we left and walked up the stairs towards the street.

"Lissen, I don' wan' bodder you. This Kennie, 'e say 'Tony, 'e give me work some times.'"

He didn't looke at me, just mounted the stairs as slowly as if they led to a throne. "What kinda work you in, Frenchie?"

"Right now, no kin'. I bin away a while."

"Yeah, well when you ain' in the bucket, waddya do?"

"Drive a truck, work in d'bush. I strong like 'ell."

He paused at the top of the stairs, a little out of breath. "Yeah, well I ain' in the delivery business an' there ain' no bush around here." He paused to grin at his shadow. "Hey, George, you see any bush round here?"

They both laughed. I poured some desperation into my voice. "Yeah, well, it don' 'ave to be like dat. I do mos' t'ings." George had overtaken me and was standing a pace back, the ideal distance from which to sucker me. I moved ahead, opening the door for Tony. He stepped out and I waved at the other guy but he stayed put, a dumb half-grin on his face.

Tony had stopped on the sidewalk, still smirking at his last wisecrack. I followed him, then pushed the door shut behind me and stuck my heel against it, unobtrusively. As I expected, his bodyguard pushed it, then shoved, then backed off a moment to hurl himself against it. I timed it perfectly, jerking the door open so he rushed through and collided with Tony. They both swore, then Muscles turned and charged me. I ducked under his slow swing, caught his arm and twisted it up his back, pushing him face first against the wall. He swore but his arm was locked and he was powerless.

I turned to Tony, grinning at him, the big dumb ox of a bushworker. "I do dis kin' work pretty good, huh?"

Tony wasn't laughing any more. He narrowed his eyes and said, "Leggo o' him," in a bored voice. I pulled the man off the wall and gave him a little shove so he staggered over the sidewalk and lurched against the side of the car parked there illegally. It was a Cadillac, of course, Tony's car.

The guy turned to rush me but Tony told him, "In the car, George," in a voice that said there would be no performance bonuses that week. George swore and muttered but he got into the driver's seat.

Tony looked at me with more interest. "Why was you inside?"

I shrugged. "Two guys come at me in a bar. I fix dem good. Den dis cop come in, pull out his gun. He say 'come' I come."

"Two guys." Tony nodded approval. "How'd I get in touch with you if there was a job needed doin'?"

I shrugged, the gesture everybody recognizes as French Canadian since Trudeau became Prime Minister. "I come 'ere hevery night." I thumbed behind me, at the hotel.

Tony nodded. "See ya around," he said, flicked a finger at me and got into the rear seat of his car.

I stood and watched while he said something to his bodyguard and the car moved out into traffic and away down the street. It wasn't clear how much I'd accomplished. At best I'd made Tony consider me a possible recruit for his next leg breaking. But he wasn't about to take me into his confidence. My best bet was to stick around for a few days and see if he came back to me. At the same time I would try to get some help from my old buddies in the Toronto police department. I still had a lot of friends there. I'd been away in Murphy's Harbour for twelve months but the old connections were still in place, at Headquarters and in the detective office at Fifty-two division. Somebody would give me the scoop on Tony—whether he had a sheet, who his bosses were. Now I knew who he was, it could be productive.

I had parked my car about five blocks away. Ex-cons don't usually own a car for a while after getting out. I had wanted to look authentic so I'd hidden the car, leaving Sam in the rear with the window down. Five blocks is a long way but I knew he'd respond if he heard me whistle. And I knew, dealing with people like Tony, that I might need reinforcements.

I did. It happened about halfway to my car. Most of the area is residential, old homes with short lawns without fences or hedges. There's no parking on the street, not on race nights, anyway, when the traffic boys are out with their tickets and tow trucks. I was slouching along the right hand side of Queen, staying in character, when I heard a car squeal to a stop against the curb. I turned and saw the Cadillac at an angle, six feet from me. There were two men in the front seat. The one nearest me was Kennie.

He burst the door open explosively, but I beat him to it, taking a long vaulting kick at the door that slammed it across his nose as he leaned out. It slowed him but he was tough and he kept coming. I didn't wait. I grabbed his arm and flipped him eight feet, upside down on the edge of the nearest lawn. At the same time I whistled for Sam, high and shrill.

The driver was the same bodyguard, only this time he had a tire iron with him and he roared as he came at me, full of anger from his first humiliation. I took two strides to meet him on his wrong foot, ducked under the iron and sank stiff fingers into his stomach, not hard enough to kill him. He dropped without a sound and I turned to Kennie who was on his feet, pulling a "For Sale" sign out of the lawn. Then Sam arrived and I told him, "Fight!"

Sam grabbed his arm but this time he knew what to expect and stopped struggling at once.

"Good boy," I told Sam, but not, "Easy," and he kept his hold on Kennie's arm.

"This is getting to be a habit," I said and he swore. And then of all the dumb, impossible things I heard a voice behind me, pitched an octave low, the way young cops always pitch their voices at fights. "Okay. What in hell is going on?"

# 5

I turned to see a young motorcycle cop getting off his bike against the curb. And Tony was getting out of his car, making it look as if he had been driving by. "I saw the whole thing, off'cer," he said smoothly. "The big guy kicked the little guy and then set that dog on him."

I knew what was going to happen now. The whole Chinese Theatre of investigation was going to play itself out because a fact is a fact only when the policeman knows it. Hell, I knew. As a cop I believe only a tenth of what I hear, half of what I see.

The motorcycle copper tugged at his cap as if that would smarten him up and came to stand in front of me, pointing at Sam, still sounding like Paul Robeson. "That your dog biting this genn'leman?"

"Yes, and it's his 'For Sale' sign that he was trying to bend over my skull."

"That's a savage dog," Kennie whined. "I was jus' walkin' down the street, mindin' my own bus'ness 'n' it bit me. You oughta shoot it, off'cer."

This was the moment when the driver finally managed to get up on his knees in the roadway. He could move but he still couldn't speak. The cop looked at him and almost swallowed his chewing gum. "Another one. What in hell is going on?"

Kennie sang out a long sad song but I didn't bother interrupting. I've heard too many arguments in my time. Let one guy do the screaming, then tell your end of it, cool and rational, otherwise you look as bad as he does.

I told Sam, "Easy, boy," and he let go of Kennie's arm and came to stand beside me. To show him off and give myself some credibility I told him, "Sit," then, "Lie," and he did. The young copper was impressed.

"Quite a dog," he said, ignoring Kennie's monologue.

"He just saved me from getting my head kicked in by these two," I said humbly. But Tony wasn't letting it go at that.

"Lies. Lies. Don't you believe him, off'cer. He was robbin' the pair of them, using that dog instead of a gun."

The motorcycle man had never heard that story before and he decided he was out of his depth. "The three of you better come in and talk to the detectives," he said. "Stand there, I'll call for a car."

Kennie looked at Tony anxiously, and I saw Tony nod, a change in the length of the shadows under his eyes. So Kennie stayed quiet, and so did I. I kept my ID in my pocket. It wouldn't cut much ice here on the street. I was the chief of police at Murphy's Harbour but at this moment, in this place I was just another John Doe suspect. I stood silently and waited while two police cars came and took us to the station.

And that was where my luck gave out. The detective who was coming down the stairs as we entered was Elmer Svensen. He knew me. Once, half a dozen years before, he had let a couple of rounders get the drop on him. They took his gun and held him hostage and I'd been the guy who dived through a window and shot the one with the gun before he could use it on Elmer. I'd saved Elmer's neck but he had been angry with me ever since. Personally, I'd been bailed out enough times by the artillery or the cavalry in Nam that I just get on with my job, feeling grateful, but to a policeman losing your gun is more embarrassing than losing your pants. Svensen hated everybody who had been involved in the case.

He was wearing a fawn raincoat and a fedora with a little feather. He was the only guy in the department who still wore a hat. It was vanity. He was Scandinavian blond, his hair so thin he looked bald. He saw me and snorted. "Well, if it's not our goddamn hero."

I said nothing. He had venom to spit out before he made sense. The motorcycle man asked him, "You know this guy?"

Svensen walked up to me, looking me in the face, working his Doublemint with an angry thrusting of his lower jaw. "Doesn't everybody? This is Reid Bennett, the hotshot veteran from Viet Nam."

I said nothing and the motorcycle cop looked over at me with recognition dawning on his face. "Hey, I remember, couple of years back, you took on three bikers, empty-handed, killed two of them."

Kennie and Tony's bodyguard were looking at me with new respect. Now Tony had begged off and left them with nothing but their lies to protect them, they were fearful. They believed that all policemen are a band of brothers. It's nowhere near true, but fables help pass the time in the penitentiary.

"So what was he up to? Kung-fuing some poor bastard?" Svensen asked. I could smell rye on his breath and realized why he was pumping that chewing gum. He stepped over to Kennie and checked his bloody nose. "He do that to you?" he roared, thumbing back over his shoulder to me.

Before Kennie could answer the motorcycle man cut in. "He says he was walking along Queen Street and these two came at him." I had an ally here, he was looking after me with the respect men use on sticks of dynamite.

"And, strictly in self-defense, using only the minimum amount of force required, he pounded them both out, right?" Svensen snorted and turned away, then back, so abruptly that I thought he was going to swing at me and braced myself to counter if I had to.

He swung back, but I could see he was pulling it, not going to hit me, only trying to see if I would flinch. I didn't and he looked down at Sam who was curled obediently at my feet. "And this is Rin-tin-goddamn-tin the wonder dog," he said and laughed.

I said nothing but Kennie thought he could take advantage so he whined "Sonofabitch bit me. Lookit." He pulled up the sleeve of his windbreaker to show the unbroken indentations from Sam's teeth.

"Did he?" Svensen became solicitous. He pretended to examine the marks, then raised his eyes to me. "That dog's savage," he said softly. "He's a menace." He reached one hand back under his coat towards his gun which I guessed he kept detective-fashion, in the middle of his belt at the back.

"Pull that thing and he'll have your arm off," I said evenly.

"Will he now," Svensen sneered, but he didn't draw the gun. "So we can do it by the book. I'll charge you with having a weapon dangerous to the public peace, to wit a savage dog, and the Humane Society can electrocute him. Mission accomplished."

The motorcycle man spoke up, gravely. "Wasn't acting savage that I could see, he was just holding this guy's arm that was holding a board, looked like he was using the board as a weapon."

"Likely rabid," Svensen said. "I hear there's lots of rabies up in the sticks where this guy works." He was running down. He'd been squaring his old debts, now he was losing interest.

"You still working for the department?" I asked him.

He glared at me. "Yeah. Some of us can keep our jobs, you know."

I had quit the department in disgust but this was not the time for semantics. "Well, I want to charge these two with assault. If you'll have them exchange names and addresses with me I'll go swear out a warrant tomorrow. Okay?"

Svensen turned to the motorcycle man. "I know this joker." He pointed at me. "He's a royal pain but he's no criminal. This must be a personal beef. Have them exchange names and send them on their way."

Then he turned back to me, hungry for the last word. "And you, get in your car or on the bus or whatever and head the hell back where you came from. Next time him and you are in here, he's gone."

He gave the top of his fedora a gentle little pat to settle it more firmly and walked away with the knees-out swagger that some detectives cultivate after a few self-important years of coming in on crime scenes where people are eager for heroes.

I watched him go, out the door and down to his car, and most likely around the corner to the nearest blind pig for a couple of shots of free rye to put his Humpty Dumpty ego back together again.

The motorcycle man was quick. He made us all dig out our IDs and Kennie's eyes widened when my Murphy's Harbour police chief card came out of the wallet.

I smiled at him, extra friendly for the sake of the shiny-faced policeman. "That's right. I'm a chief of police," I explained. You could see the wheels whizzing around behind his eyes as he tried to work out what I'd been doing in a Bonded Security uniform and how far I was going to press my complaint. But like a smart little ex-con he said nothing. He just listened while the policeman made a note of all our names and addresses, including mine, at my sister's in Toronto, and Kennie's, with his mother. Nobody would have guessed, watching the ritual, that ten minutes earlier the other two had been trying to put me in hospital.

One of the uniformed men from the station drove me back to my car. I debated going home. It was thirty-six hours since I'd slept but my adrenaline was running so I went down to the Bonded Security office to see what Fullwell had.

The answer was, not much, except for a cup of their machine-brewed coffee that tasted like a boiled book. We sat and sipped a cup each while he went over the things he'd done.

"I first of all checked out all the contractors on the job, to see if any of them were shady. They're not."

"Are they all Toronto companies? Nothing from Montreal with mob connections?"

Fullwell nodded and went on, ticking them off on his

fingers. "All based here, but they're a mixed bag, like, on any building project in town. I checked that out too. We've got a couple of Italian outfits, including the earthmoving people whose stuff was hit. Two others run by old-country Scots, a couple of Greeks, and a Jewish electrical firm."

"But they're all Canadian?" It sounds a dumb question but for years our government was so big on multi-culturism that people push their heritage without reminding you that they're Canadian first.

"All of them, except for the people putting up the money for the building. It's a Hong Kong outfit." He checked his notes. "The Heavenly Lotus Corporation." We grinned at that but he gave me the hint that made some sense of the attacks. "They're a very businesslike outfit. They've already got the building rented for occupancy next July and their major customer has got a penalty clause in the construction contract. If they're late it's going to cost them around twenty grand a day."

I whistled. "Then they don't need any aggravation this early in the construction cycle. Maybe they're getting shaken down by somebody."

"Makes more sense than anything I can think of," Fullwell said. We discussed the possibilities for a while, then he asked me, "Did you come up with anything?"

I told him about Tony and he called a contact at Police Headquarters and asked for information, giving my description of Tony and the license number of the Cadillac. It all took about a minute, during which he said, "Uh-huh," a few times and scribbled over the complete backs of two envelopes. He thanked the person at the other end and hung up.

"Tony Caporetto, age thirty-eight, lives at a fancy apartment in the West End." He gave me the address and I wrote it down on the back of a parking slip I had in my wallet. "He's never done time but he's been arrested four times. Twice for bootlegging, once each for assault and trespass. Got off every time. The witnesses wouldn't press charges, said they couldn't identify him properly. That's all. Oh, and his car is registered to Calabria Enterprises, same address he lives at."

"Well, on the face of it, I'd say he was trying to squeeze

some extortion bucks out of these Hong Kong people," I suggested. "Maybe I should go lean on him some more."

"Good idea," Fullwell said, "but not tonight. Why'nt you head home, start again tomorrow morning after some sleep."

I yawned and nodded. Right now I was winding down. It would be better in the morning, when both the world and me were brighter. Fullwell stood up and led me out to the reception desk. Sam scrambled beside me, his nails clicking on the vinyl tile. "It could pay off. Tony will've heard more about you by then, he may be scared enough of what he hears to talk a little."

I shrugged. "From what I've seen of him, he's too small a fish to be running anything so complex as an international racket. He's a nickel and dime loan shark. Maybe I can get the name of the next guy up the ladder from him. Then we can go to the boys in blue."

Fullwell cocked his head, doubtfully. "That's the way I'd like to do it, but this guy Willis outranks me here."

"Then don't tell him, just go by the book and call the police. I would have done that last night, left to me. I figured that's why I was here, to catch these slugs. Then to let them go like that, that was crazy."

"Agreed," Fullwell said. He dropped me at the front desk and I walked out past a pretty little Bonded Security guard. She was sitting with a pile of schoolbooks in front of her but she was reading a paperback with a cover that reminded me of the boonies in Nam.

I went out and drove up north to my sister's house on one of the side streets full of sixty-year-old maples, the kind of place you see only in Toronto or in Andy Hardy movies. She used to be married and lives there with her two kids. She insists I stay with them when I get into town and doesn't mind the odd hours I come and go, but she woke up when I got home and called out, "Reid?" in a voice that was only a little nervous.

I called back to her, "Okay, Lou, it's me. See you in the morning," and headed for bed, grateful not to be standing around the construction site again. I guess I was there an hour before the phone rang in her bedroom. Louise answered and called me. I padded down to the kitchen, pulling on my pants as I went. It was Fullwell, sounding wide awake. "Can you come back in, Reid? We've been hit again."

# 6

THIS time it wasn't the construction site. It was a warehouse out on the northeastern fringe of Metro Toronto where new subdivisions and industrial land gradually gave way to fields of cattle corn. By the time I arrived there were five cars inside the front gate and a uniformed policeman was keeping people out. He made an exception for me when I explained my connection with Bonded Security, pointing out the timekeeper's office where Fullwell and a couple of detectives were talking.

Fullwell did the honors. I shook hands, then nodded and followed him out under the overhead conveyor system to a green wall where the fire alarm stood.

The wall was blackened with blood still fresh enough to show red on the concrete floor where it had dribbled down. There was a lot of it. I asked, "Will he make it?"

Fullwell gave a respectful little flick of his head. "He's a tough old East Indian guy, used to be in the army out there. Lemme show you what he went through."

He meant it literally. Around the corner was an internal office with a frosted glass wall that had been shattered. Fullwell stopped and pointed. The trail of blood started on the floor inside the ruined window. "The police say he was run down by a forklift with the platform raised half way. He ducked under it and the whole thing went through the wall, pushing him in front of it."

I whistled. "Any idea what happened then?"

Fullwell led me back, pointing out the blood trail. "They think the attacker left him there and went back to the loading ramp in bay 12. It held a trailer of liquor for shipment south. It's gone now."

"How much was that worth?" I was beginning to think this job was unconnected with the hits on the construction site. Liquor is a prime prize for any thieves.

"Haven't seen the manifest, but the detectives guess around a hundred and fifty grand, retail. Maybe a quarter of that sold illegally."

The bloodstains on the trail we were following became smears instead of splotches. I bent to examine them. Fullwell said, "Yeah, they figure he collapsed here and dragged himself to the fire alarm. The department called us and the police. When they arrived the big doors were open, they came in, gave our guy oxygen and hustled him to Scarborough Centennial Hospital. I got here about ten minutes after."

"Is anybody standing by him at the hospital?" I've seen a lot of bloodstains in my time and by the size of these I didn't give much for the guard's chances.

"Willis, from our company, he's up there, along with a member of the police ethnic squad. He speaks Urdu and this guy's language is Hindi but he's got a recorder so if he says anything at all we can get it translated later."

"Good thinking. He must be in poor shape. He won't be saying anything in English, if that's his second language, not for a day or two, if ever."

We walked back to the timekeeper's office where one of the detectives was talking on the phone. The other one asked, "Find anything we missed?" He smiled, but there was an edge to his voice, cops anywhere have no time for amateurs.

"Didn't expect to," I assured him. "But we have a policy." It relaxed him enough that he told me, "Looks as if the guy, or guys, came in through the washroom window at the back. For some reason it's not wired with the alarm. I guess they thought it was too small for a man to get through."

I snorted a sympathetic laugh along with his. "Anything bigger than a mail slot, right?"

He nodded, wearing his smile like yesterday's carnival

mask. "Yeah, so anyway, they came at him with a two-by-four, we found it alongside where the forklift is kept at night. Then he must've gone for the phone and the guy started the lift and ran him down with it."

"Could turn into a homicide," I said. "He lost a hell of a lot of blood."

The detective sniffed and dropped his smile completely. "I sure hope not. I'm s'posed to be taking my young lad fishing tomorrow."

Fullwell had names to take and other rituals to perform before he was free of the police. I spent the time going over the scene again. Whoever had done this was small enough to get through a window no bigger than the jacket of an LP. I wondered if Kennie, perhaps with Hudson alongside him, had earned some more of Tony's money tonight.

There was nothing else to check and when Fullwell was free I took him outside to my car and we worked out our next move. He had already given the police the names of Kennie and Hudson. There was a parallel in the choice of weapons that suggested they might be involved here. But he had not mentioned Tony. His involvement was all too nebulous. Tony was our suspect, not theirs.

"I think the best thing we can do, is for you or me to have a word with Tony, see if we can find out what's going down," Fullwell said. "Although, he's already made you for a plant, you'll have to do something more direct than just chat with him."

I thought about it for a minute or so, sniffing the good country smells of the cornfield that backed on to the warehouse parking lot, listening to the rushing roar of the traffic on the 401, even at this time of night, glad to be back in Toronto and working on a real case again after the quiet months at Murphy's Harbour. At last I said, "The only place that guy would feel pressure is in the pocket. I think I know how to apply some, without even bending the law."

"That's a relief." Fullwell exhaled his tensions in a big, gusty sigh. "I don't need to know anything except what he tells you."

## 7

FULLWELL'S comment bothered me as I drove back to Louise's house. Was he really expecting me to get rough with Tony? Had the fear of Willis robbed him of his good nature? I know how business pressures can bend a man. But I hoped he was just tired. I had liked him from the first time he came to Murphy's Harbour on the investigation. I'd taken to him as I might have done with another policeman, but now he was coming on like Willis. I put it down to the fact that he had two of his men in hospital, one of them perhaps terminally. He was operating out of weariness and anger.

I went back to bed but got up in time to have breakfast with Louise and the kids. They're boy, girl, with the same age difference there is between me and Louise. I guess there's not much glamour in sharing bowls of cornflakes with a ten- and eight-year-old, not for anyone with a pair of their own to worry about, but I like it. My wife was too busy selling computers and building herself the kind of career they write about in *Cosmopolitan* to want children. I was her one indulgence, the ex-Marine policeman too restless to finish university. We got on almost excessively well in bed but the rest of the time we mostly wondered where the other one of us was coming from. She left when the going got tough, when I was acquitted of manslaughter in the death of a couple of bikers. The media wouldn't let go of it, and Amy just let the thin little thread that bound us together snap under the pressure, so I'm a bachelor uncle and it's no hardship to get up after two hours' sleep for the kind of action most men my age walk through every morning.

Once the others had gone, I called my connections in the police department. None of them had anything to add to the dope Fullwell had gotten the night before. Tony just wasn't enough of a wheel to have any legends sprout up around him. That made it certain to me that he was not the guy behind an intercontinental extortion racket.

At seven I was back in the Millrace, sitting in front of the same two beers, not bothering to read the racing page this time. Tony was on to me. All I wanted was contact, not cover. I sat and watched a game show on TV. The sound was too low but it didn't matter, you could tell who won by the way they jigged up and down and kissed the MC, who looked like a lecherous cadaver.

At seven-thirty the door opened. I was primed to expect Tony but this wasn't him. It was Svensen and a younger, smaller guy whom I took to be his new partner. Svensen came in, swinging his shoulders like the cop in an Agatha Christie play, looking around with the kind of amused superiority that gets policemen a bad name. Then he saw me.

He ambled over, swinging his legs and laughing out loud. "Well, goddamn. Not you again." He sat down across from me, not taking his hands out of his coat pockets, still chewing his gum. "How's it going, hero?"

"Not bad, Elmer, yourself?"

He dropped his smile, letting the corners of his mouth sag for a couple of beats before he took up his chewing again. "Okay, until you turned up." His partner came over and joined us. He was young and dark and eager but he looked embarrassed by Svensen. I guessed he'd smelt the rye, too.

I nodded to him. "Hi, I used to work with this guy. My name's Reid Bennett."

He stuck out his hand, serious. "Tom Lenchuk. I've heard about you. I hear you kicked a lot of ass."

It wasn't true. Except for one episode in my Toronto career I'd never done anything violent. Then I won a fight in which I might have been killed, staying alive by using a lot of Marine Corps tricks that most Toronto policemen never learn. But I had no chance to explain; Svensen took over, beaming like the game show host on the silent TV screen in the corner. "Right on, Tommy. Reid Bennett, the one-man destruction team." I could feel the other customers turning to look and I felt the anger creeping over me. What was Svensen trying to do? "So, who're you here to clobber tonight?" He cocked back on his chair, tilting the two front legs off the ground. He looked like a rodeo rider on a Brahma bull.

"Just these two beers and a little time," I said evenly. "How about you?"

"Business." He slapped one hand down on the table, making my beer glasses jingle. "Just here to talk to a citizen about some hassle out at Finch and Warden last night."

"Just a hassle? That guard didn't die?" I kept my voice low. It seemed that everyone in the place was listening to us, straining as they had never strained for the TV show.

Svensen laughed another of his showbiz laughs while he did his best to stare me through. "No, he's gonna be all right. He'll live to punch more time clocks." When I didn't comment he bored on. "Naah, that's not the problem. Thing is, the outfit he works for hired some nickel and dime investigator from the sticks to follow up on it." He stopped and had a laugh, looking around to check that everyone was in on the fun with him. "Like, I mean. Some guys are fine for putting the blocks to bikers. But investigation, that takes brains."

His partner cracked a brief, pained smile but said nothing. I could tell he was new to plainclothes work. Life was still a game of cops and robbers. He hadn't realized yet that most of the time the robbers have all the laughs. He should have grabbed this opportunity.

Then Svensen rocked his chair forward and leaned over the table, his eyes cold as pebbles. "Get the hell back to Hicksville. We've been put on to Tony. It's a police case now, so leave it to the professionals."

He leaned back on his chair. With a lift of my toe I could have sent him sprawling but I didn't dislike him that much. "You go ahead and investigate," I told him. "Me, I'm having a beer."

He stared at me. I could see the pores in his nose, smell the mint on his gusty breath. "Good." He almost whispered it. "On account of this is a departmental investigation. If you get underfoot I'm going to have your ass for obstructing police. You got that?"

I said nothing but after a reasonable wait I lifted my beer and took a good sip. Svensen breathed hard, through pinched nostrils and said, "I don't want you bothering Tony."

"It's no bother. This is business. I'm all tapped out and payday isn't till next week."

For a moment I thought he was going to laugh again. His mouth winced at the corners but then he pushed away from the table and stood up. "Just remember what I've told you."

I put one hand on my heart. "Forever," I promised and turned my eyes to the TV where a pretty blond girl was hanging around the MC's neck, jumping with both feet off the ground in rapturous little hops.

Svensen nodded to his partner and they left, lightening the mood of the whole room. I drank my beer, ordered another and sat waiting and watching "M*A*S*H" where all those cute enlisted men fed straight lines to the doctors. I wondered what Alda and his men would have done in some of the field situations I'd been in. But meantime, I waited and finally, half an hour later than the previous day, Tony showed up.

This time he saw me at once and didn't bother with the visiting statesman entrance. He and his bodyguard went together to the corner table. The waiter rushed them their drinks but there was no tip. There were a few words— about me, I judged, from the hissing the waiter did—then they waved him away and opened their store.

The first customer was a mechanic by the look of his fingernails. They had that mourning band around them that handsoap won't touch. He was around forty, a little heavy and lost-looking. I'd seen him soak up six beers in half an hour and he had the paper under his arm, folded to the race page.

He spoke to Tony and was handed over to George, who paid him and made out a note. He took the cash and was heading for the door when I stood up and intercepted him. "You wanna watch that guy," I said conversationally.

He wasn't expecting anybody to speak to him before the clerk at the betting window took his money. He stopped, openmouthed. I pushed on. "If you're behind with your six for five, he'll have his goon slam a car door on your hand a time or two, with the fingers in the hinge side."

He jolted his head around to look at Tony, then back at me. "Wa'd you say?"

I repeated it word for word and added, "You won't be able to fix cars so good after that, will you?"

He soaked it in, then narrowed his eyes and asked me, "You a cop?"

"You might say. Put me down as a friend." I grinned at him, a narrow-mouthed, vaguely threatening grin. I could see Tony and George bending their heads together but I'd been prepared for that.

The mechanic moved from foot to foot, uncertainly, then turned back to Tony and laid the money back on the table. The bodyguard started to bluster but he just pointed at me and said nothing. Then he gave them a quick shrug of apology and went out. I could hear him taking the stairs, two at a time. I sat down again. I was in the middle of the floor, not the best spot for security but my hearing was trained in a tougher school than this. I figured I'd hear anybody sneaking up on me.

Another man borrowed money and I went through the same routine. This guy was younger and more sure of himself. "You ain't scaring me," he said. I shrugged and sipped my beer. "Suit yourself. I can just tell you there's two guys in hospital now over them. One of them had his throat cut with a piece of window glass."

That convinced him. He swore, short and ugly, then turned around. "There's other places to get money," he said. He replaced the money on the table and left. Tony snapped his fingers for the waiter, the same one who had earned the fin the previous night. He bent over to listen, then went back to the bar and put his tray down. He came up to me as tough as he could manage. He didn't like this work one bit. "You gotta leave, you're drunk."

"I'm cold sober and I'm staying. Call a cop if you've got a problem. Or maybe your fink friends don't want any cops in here."

He licked his dry lips. "Look, I don't want trouble any more'n you. But I gotta tell you there's a sawed off pool cue behind the bar."

I nodded to the bodyguard who was sitting hunched, to ease the tension on his sore stomach. "Ask your buddy what happened to the last couple of guys who tried that." I don't like playing Clint Eastwood but there wasn't any other way of getting at Tony.

The waiter hesitated. I could see he was pricing out the chance of a beating. Would it be worth the big tips? Would they stop anyway? He decided against doing anything rash. Instead he called over his shoulder to the man on the taps. This was the typical beerhall bouncer, six-foot two maybe, but thirty-five pounds heavier than me, most of it under his apron. I guessed he'd made himself a name for sorting out fights. But I also guessed he did it carefully, waiting until a few swings had been taken and the battlers had decided it was all a mistake before he moved in. He was no menace.

"You. Out." He hooked with his thumb, like a baseball umpire. I ignored him, except for bringing my feet up in front of me, ready to dig in and move on him if he tried anything. I didn't have to worry. He made the predictable move, digging a stiff forefinger into my breastbone. I caught it in my left hand and rolled the heel of my hand down on the knuckle joint, bringing him crashing to his knees.

He swore but knelt still as I spoke quietly. "I'm just sitting here having a beer. If I choose to talk to the other customers, there's no law says I can't. Tell that to your complainant."

I let go of his finger and he stood up, backing off a pace. The word "complainant" had triggered him.

"You a p'lice off'cer?"

"Yes." No need telling him my patch was two hundred miles north, he didn't need to know.

"Why'nt you say so, off'cer. That's different. Can I send you over a beer?"

"No thanks. But I'd like to buy you one."

Give him credit, he was quick-witted enough to be the gracious loser. "That'd be good," he said and shook his sore finger. "That's quite a trick. Where'd you learn that?"

I could have told him Parris Island, from a crop-headed veteran of Iwo Jima. Instead I just laughed and said, "Yeah, it works, eh. Remember it in case some smartass tries prodding you."

He walked back to the bar, giving the waiter a minute

head signal to follow him. That left me alone with my beer. Tony watched in pure hatred. After another minute he got up, making a point of spilling his drink so it ran over a couple of chairs. He and his bodyguard marched out, and I fell in behind them, close enough to annoy, far enough away to be out of reach of a kick.

Tony stopped at the head of the stairs inside the main door. His bodyguard stopped beside him and turned to me, holding his coat far enough open that I could see he was carrying. I clomped up beside them, angled so they couldn't kick, ready to sweep George across the collarbone if he went for his equalizer. "I hope your date has a license for that thing or he could end up inside," I told him.

"All the license he needs, workin' for me," Tony said. "Now are you gonna take a hike or are we gonna hurt you?"

"Tell you what . . ." I slapped my hands together explosively and the muscleman flinched. "I'll be happy to leave you to take care of business in the usual way, if you'll spare me one minute of your time."

Tony swore and I shrugged. "Suit yourself, but you won't make much money unless you do. I can tag along wherever you go."

The bodyguard pulled his coat open again but I ignored the movement, he wasn't going to use a gun in public. Private, probably, but not here, where witnesses could come in any time. "Get rid of him," I told Tony. "This isn't going to take long."

He dismissed the bodyguard in a low hiss. "Go warm up the car, George. I'll be out in a minute."

George looked at him, then me, then lowered his head like a schoolboy caught cheating on his exam and went through the door.

A couple of new customers came in, middle-aged men in tweed jackets with cloth caps and mufflers. Limeys, I thought, keeping my eye on Tony who had his hands in his pockets and was acting bored. The men went down the steps talking about the Blizzards, the local soccer team, in accents that reminded me of my father. But my mind stayed on business.

"Right. I want one answer to one question and I'm through bugging." Tony just stared at me and I went on.

"Who got you to send those guys to beat up the Bonded Security guards, Kennie and Hudson?"

He responded as I had expected. "I dunno what you're talkin' about."

"Think hard," I told him easily. "Kennie is the little waster who came after me last night. Night before that, him and some other gorilla went for me on a Bonded Security construction site on Shuter Street. The night before that they beat up another guard. It doesn't matter why, I just want to know who asked you to send them."

He didn't answer but he didn't move away. I put some more pressure on. "I don't care about your part in it. I don't care how many six for fives you kite out. I don't care how many thumbs you break collecting. But I want that name and I'll stick to you like snot to an army blanket until you give it to me."

Like a lot of smalltime hoods he was not a smart man. I could almost hear the wheels cranking over in his head as he considered the alternatives. He already knew I wouldn't scare off. He was probably under pressure to keep his loan volume up. On the other hand, you don't give free information to a cop, not about men who pay to have other men smashed up. At last he spoke. "Now, I don't know what in hell you're smokin', thinkin' I got anything to do with some guy's head gettin' kicked in, but if I happened to hear somethin' and let you know, that would be it, right?"

"That would be it, dearheart."

"Yeah, well, I did hear some talk." He leant forward as if to whisper but I didn't bite. He was looking to headlock me and knee me somewhere sensitive.

"We're all alone, you can speak right up," I said.

He sighed and his shoulders dropped. It looked studied, as if he had picked it up watching those interchangeable heroes on TV. Finally he said, "Okay, asshole. The guy you're lookin' for is a lawyer, name of Cy Straight."

"Is he in the phone book?"

"Should be. He's got an office on Bay near King, one o' them bank buildings."

"Did he give you any reason?"

Tony drew himself back and held up his hands, the way Pontius Pilate must have done, palms outwards. "Our deal was a name. You got your name, right?"

"Right," I told him. "See you around."

He stood for perhaps a minute, waiting for me to walk away back downstairs but I'd seen enough of him to be careful in his company and I stayed put until he sighed and did his shoulder-drop again and left.

# 8

I didn't follow him. George could have been waiting outside with his tire iron and I was sick of getting swung at. Instead I went the other way, into the cocktail lounge on the main floor. I ordered a bottle of Labatt's Classic and asked if I could use the phone. The barman nodded to the end of the bar. "Help yourself."

Fullwell's wife answered and I introduced myself. She told me, "Simon's asleep, he's going in at midnight, is there a message?"

"Tell him, please, that I have a name for him. And I'll see him at his office a little before twelve, thank you."

I finished my beer before leaving. I was still up from my small victory, it took us another step closer to finding out what was going on. I knew it would be harder to get this lawyer to open up but we could play that as we found it. Maybe Fullwell's boss had connections we could use. In the meantime, my work was done until the night shift started.

It was dark when I left the bar, going out of the side door, carefully. Tony's car was nowhere around and I walked to mine and got in. Sam was in the back seat and I spent a moment patting him and telling him he was a good boy. He's all the family I've got up at the Harbour, but tonight I was heading home to my sister's place and I felt cheered by the prospect of a family evening.

She lives in the north end of the city, one of those cross streets that run off Yonge, where bankers and insurance brokers used to live thirty years ago. Since then the district has been taken over twice, first by upwardly mobile Greeks and Italians, then by a new generation of WASPs who bought up the old houses and painted them pastel colors and planted magnolias in the front yards.

Louise was watching TV when I got to her place. She looked tired. Her ex was a TV producer for the advertising agency where she used to work as a copywriter. After eight years of marriage he had taken a tumble for some model he'd met while filming a brassiere commercial. After a year of wrangling that ended when I had a nice brotherly talk to him about responsibilities, he had given Louise the house and moved in permanently with his girlfriend. Louise had gone back to copywriting, and with long hours at the agency and playing single parent she had her hands full.

She got up when I came in and clicked off the set. "Hi, Reid, can I get you a beer?" I guess I can say it, even though she's my sister, she's a looker. She has Mother's black hair and Dad's blue eyes and she's two years younger than me. I didn't figure she would be alone for too long but she tells me straight guys willing to take on a couple of kids are a rarity in Toronto, she's not having any more luck with relationships than I am.

"Cup of coffee would do me more good. I have to go out again later."

"Okay, I'll put the kettle on." I followed her out and sat at the counter while she brewed up, enjoying the domesticity. She nagged me gently as the kettle boiled. "You don't get enough sleep," she said. "You ought to take a whole night off sometimes."

"Maybe I will. I made some real progress today. I just have to fill some people in and then I'll come home, unless they want me to prowl around their sites for them again."

She put the coffee in front of me. "Yeah. Well take care. Nobody can live forever on nerves and work. Okay?"

I winked at her and after a while we watched TV and then she went to bed and I drove down to the Bonded office.

Fullwell was there with a coffee and a map of the city with flags on it at the points that Bonded Security was covering. He waved and blew smoke. "Hey, Reid, Barbara told me you got a name."

I sat and put my size elevens on his desk which was war-surplus oak veneer, like the one in my police station. He winced and pushed a coaster at me. I stuck it under my heel. "Tony opened up like an oyster. Tells me the word came from a high-priced lawyer down on Bay Street, man by the name of Cy Straight."

Fullwell frowned. "Just like that? Or did you have to play rough?"

"Just handed it to me, on a plate, just for being underfoot while he was trying to do business." And as I said it I realized what had been in the back of my mind the whole time. "It was a touch too easy," I added.

We sat and looked at one another without focussing, wondering why a slippery character like Tony would break Rule One of the jungle he lived in and talk to the law, in any form. "You thinking what I'm starting to think?" I asked.

Fullwell said, "Well, I hate to rap on a free melon, but you wouldn't expect anything for nothing from a loan shark, would you?"

I yawned. "No, I wouldn't. He must have something of his own in mind—he's sure not doing it because he likes me. Anyway, do you have any idea who Straight is?"

"Never heard of him." Fullwell coughed and beat his butt to death in an ashtray that already held too many of them. "He could be a partner in some big outfit downtown. I'll get on the phone in the morning."

"It wouldn't hurt to go and see him, feel the vibrations," I suggested.

"No, it wouldn't. But I'll brief the boss first. We're skating close to the edge on this one. If this guy's a wheel he can shout harassment and cause trouble. The boss has to know."

"Why not, he draws the big dollar." I was wondering what else Fullwell had in mind for me. I was enjoying the investigation after a leisurely summer at the Harbour. It was good to be part of a team again, even an unofficial team like this one. He filled me in.

"I'm worried they're going to keep the pressure on," he said. "And there's too many security companies in town for us to be able to keep on taking falls. It'll put us out of business if we can't do our job properly."

"So you want to run some surveillance?" It wouldn't be hard, I figured: a night spent driving from one site to another, finishing around four A.M. Punks like the two I'd caught don't work really late.

He stood up and indicated his map. Toronto is split neatly in two by Yonge Street, which is pronounced "young" and is in the *Guinness Book of Records* as the world's longest street. It happened that the Bonded sites were divided almost equally, east and west. Fullwell indicated the colored flags. "We've got forty-seven full-time sites, plus a couple of casuals that we hit once or twice a night. If we divide the sites we might just get around them by morning. Are you up to it?"

"Sure, you can take the extra one. And, because I'm a nice guy, I'll let you take Sam with you, he'll run interference in case anybody wants to play rough."

Fullwell looked at me gratefully. "I'd appreciate that. I'm not handy like you are with your karate or whatever."

I didn't correct him but I don't know karate. What I am is a well-trained scrambler, versed in the unarmed combat techniques they teach in the U.S. Marines. I can hold my own against any untrained brawler but I'm no match for a classically trained martial artist. But most people don't understand subtleties. If you hit anybody hard enough they call it either karate or kung fu. I've given up arguing.

"I left him in my car." I stood up. "Come on down with me and I'll turn him over to you, and give you the proper words of command. He's one hell of a good dog, but he's not a machine. You need to know the rules."

"Great," Fullwell said. "I'm not chicken but I don't like this." He picked up his hat off the top of a filing cabinet and placed it on his head as carefully as if it were a crown, then opened his desk drawer. "This is a list of the addresses, I had it typed up ready. You take the East end, I'll take the West, some of the spots out there are hard to find first time."

We went out, past the same girl, reading a new paperback with openmouthed concentration. I ordered Sam to go with Fullwell. He wasn't happy about it, but he's perfectly trained, if I do say so, and he went without a whimper. Then I briefed Fullwell thoroughly on commands and left, driving out to the first of my sites.

I had a hunch that any trouble that occurred would be on their in-town sites. Most of the other locations were remote enough that a lone car cruising up and stopping nearby would be conspicuous. If the guard was alert he could see it and call for support right away. The exceptions were a few warehouses, like the one that had been hit the night before. The car could arrive out of sight of the guard and an intruder could come close without being noticed. I decided to concentrate on these spots, plus in-town places where someone could walk up without being seen. Towards morning I would take a quick pass at the others.

I went first to the plant where the Sikh had been hit. The guy inside was a middle-aged loser, happy to have any kind of job. He sirred me to death so I figured he'd been in the army at one time. But he was fine. So were the next couple of guards I visited. I told them all the same thing. Watch for action on the perimeter, cars driving up, lone men coming close to the fence. And keep alert! Most of them had access to weapons of some crude kind, crowbars or boards, and I advised them to have something handy. They're not much use against a trained fighter but they would deter the kind of cheap hoods I'd collected on the construction site.

And then I went to that site. By now it was after two. I was listening to Charlie Pride on the country music station and was relaxed, but when I got to the gate and left the car the cool September air woke me up properly as I let myself in.

The patrol hut was empty. There were two lunch pails there so I realized that Fullwell had doubled up the coverage this night. I went and stood outside for a moment but nobody challenged me, so I took out my big flashlight but didn't turn it on and started around the circuit I'd made the first night.

While I was in Nam I learned about night patrols, the hard way. As a result I can move like an Indian, with no sound. My eyes snap into night vision quicker than most people's so I don't need the flashlight. And that's how I came up on the two guards before anybody heard me. I heard them first, one of them anyway, he was groaning. I stopped in my tracks and checked all around, at ground level and above me, on top of the machinery and shack that stood there. I couldn't see anything or hear anything else. So I flicked on the light and saw the two men, muddy and bloodied, lying in the frozen, accidental postures of corpses or the critically wounded. Then I heard a sudden padding of feet, running. I followed the sound on tiptoe, around the end of the shack in time to see a couple of men at the fence, scrambling up it hand over hand.

That was when I missed Sam. He would have covered the thirty yards between me and the fence in time to jump and hold on to the leg of one of those men. But I was too slow. In the four seconds it took me they had rolled over the wire and dropped cleanly to the other side. They didn't look back but I got an impression of neatness, of suits and white shirts and dark hair. Then a car, a late model Olds Toronado, pulled up and let them in without putting on the inside light. I was at the fence by that time but the light was out on the rear license plate and I swore and threw a rock after them. It landed twenty yards behind them. If they were bothering to look back they probably had a laugh over that.

# 9

I didn't waste time climbing the fence and racing down the street after the car. I ran back to the guards and checked them over. They were alive but they both looked bad. One of them had a walkie-talkie and I blipped the button and called but the girl at Bonded must have been turning pages on her thriller, she didn't respond, so I belted back to the shack and called the police emergency number. "One-fifty-one Shuter Street, construction site. Two security guards assaulted. Suspects escaped in dark Olds Toronado, no light on rear license, likely an eighty-two model." Then I gave them my name and asked for an ambulance.

The dispatcher made me repeat it but he was on the air as he spoke and within a minute a scout car was at the gate. I was there to meet them. They wanted to come in but I told them to drive west towards Church Street, then on to

Yonge, north-south streets where they might have caught a glimpse of the getaway car.

They left and I went out to the injured guards and waited for the ambulance. They seemed to be bleeding from the nose and mouth, from internal injuries, not the usual kind of cuts and bruises men get in fights, the kind you can give first aid to.

When the ambulance crew put them on gurneys they were alert enough to moan in pain, and I tried again to ask them who had done it but they were beyond talking. They were stunned, the way most people are by sudden violence. It changes your whole perspective of life. You can be four years old or forty, it makes no difference. In that first vivid flash of deliberately inflicted pain all your previous experience is cancelled. You realize the darkness is out there waiting to take you in and all this time you've been a baby, ignorant and lucky.

I thought they might be able to talk by morning, with luck, but that was all. I went back to the shack when the ambulance left, reaching it as the phone rang. It was Fullwell, who had been called on the radio when I turned in the alarm. "I'll come down there and check. You stick around on the site and I'll head to the hospital and check what I can find out from Bates and Cornish."

"Fine. But it's locking the stable after the horse is gone, I don't think those guys are coming back."

"I know," he agreed. "But it's all we can do. I'd like you to check the site carefully, maybe one of the attackers dropped something."

He hung up, just as the detectives arrived from 52 division. This time I was lucky. One of them was Irv Goldman, my old partner from two years before, when I was one of Toronto's finest. He recognized me under the big worklights at the site gate. "Well, hey, Reid Bennett. What in hell are you doing here? I thought you were the marshal of Dodge City on the Lake."

"Irv, you still peddling the same fish?" We shook hands and slapped one another on the back like a couple of visiting dignitaries. He was a good buddy and we'd been through some adventures together. The other guy cleared his throat and Irv introduced us. "Reid, this is my partner, Jack

Robinette. Jack, this is the famous Reid Bennett I've mentioned a time or two."

Robinette laughed, a friendly chuckle. "A time or two! I'll say. Tell me Reid, did you and Irv get up to all those stunts he's always blowing about?"

"Trust him," I said as we shook hands. "He's good people." I didn't feel like clowning but it doesn't pay to get steely-eyed with policemen. They see enough mayhem that they're impervious to suffering; they like to kibitz.

Irv said, "So what's with this security crap. I thought you were working steady, keeping the peace up at Mouse's Armpit somewhere north."

"Murphy's Harbour, and I still am. I'm just lending a hand to one of the Bonded Security guys. He helped me out once, this is tit for tat, plus a little coin."

"Nothing for nothing." Irv wrapped up the last of the kidding in one sentence. "Now what happened here?"

I told him quickly, mentioning the previous assaults and Tony. Irv sniffed. "I think I've seen that guy around. He's small-time. You figure he set this up?"

"Could've. But I think it's over his head. This looks as if it's an international job."

"Anybody in dutch with the Mob?" Robinette asked. "This is about their speed, although so far we haven't had much of it in town."

"If anybody is, they don't know about it at Bonded," I told him. "They went through the list of contractors; the only thing we found was this penalty clause in the finish date. Everybody seems clean." I didn't tell them about Cy Straight. That was a lead I wanted to follow personally; a bunch of detectives sitting in his office would turn him off like a tap. I'd have more chance to get the feel of the guy if I went there alone.

"And these guys you saw. They look Italian?" Irv asked.

"No, they were short, shorter than most Italians are these days and they were slim. They could have been fly-weight boxers, the pair of 'em. They just didn't look Italian to me."

"You sound pretty sure of it," Irv said. "And they weren't Jews. I'm the only Hebe in the city working tonight. It's the High Holidays."

"Could they have been Asians?" Robinette wondered.

He was anxious, wriggling the tiny knot in his tie, eager to make a useful suggestion in front of a couple of old workhorses.

I looked at him and whistled. "You know, they could have been." They had run with the same fluid energy I'd seen in the children in Nam. "What makes you ask?"

He shrugged. "One of the guys hurt, the man at the warehouse, he was East Indian. I wondered if these were some of his people. The Sikhs have got all kinds of feuds going, what I hear."

"They weren't Indian," I said, "but they could have been Orientals, maybe Viet Namese or Koreans or young, fit Chinese, before their feet go."

"Lay off the racial discrimination." Irv said. "Some of my best friends are in the laundry business."

We laughed, just keeping everything friendly, and I explained. "You know what I mean. A lot of Chinese have a kind of uncomfortable walk. These guys were pounding along to beat hell. They were fit."

We took a look around the site, debating the idea of having Orientals involved in the case as we poked over the ground. It was littered with the rubble of construction and we couldn't see anything worthwhile in the light of our flashlights but we were still at it when Fullwell arrived. He had not stayed long at the hospital. Both men were undergoing surgery for abdominal injuries; they both had ribs broken. We listened and I introduced him to the detectives and he gave us the details.

"The doctor at St. Mike's sees a lot of beatings. He says this one isn't typical. There are no facial cuts or contusions like there usually are when guys go at one another with fists or clubs. They'd been hit in the gut, by experts. Both of them the same."

Irv took a toothpick from the top pocket of his double-breasted suitcoat and stuck it in his mouth before saying, "Like maybe they'd been worked over by somebody who knew karate or kung fu."

Fullwell looked at him long and hard before he started to nod. "Exactly. That's what must have happened."

"It figures," I agreed with him. "That matches the two suitcoats I saw going over the fence. It looks as if the threat to the owners of this place is coming from some Hong Kong heavies."

Robinette sniffed. "Great," he said disgustedly. "That narrows it down to about two million guys."

Irv looked at him thoughtfully. "Look on the bright side. It crosses whole continents off the list of suspects. We could crack this one before I reach retirement." We all chuckled but we knew Robinette was the closest to the truth. Hong Kong violence is a new commodity in Toronto. The Intelligence boys are only beginning to start a file on them. We were looking at a blank sheet.

Fullwell left with the detectives, and Sam, leaving me to make sure there were no repeats. We figured I had scared them off before they had time to do any damage to property. So I stayed, hiding in the shadows waiting for something to move. Nothing did until a quarter to seven when the first of the workmen arrived for the day and the foreman relieved me. I drove back to Fullwell's office through the thickening rush hour traffic.

Sam was waiting in Fullwell's office. One of the office girls had brought him some milk in a coffee cup but he wasn't buying until I turned up and gave him the go-ahead. I thanked the girl, got myself a java, and sat with Fullwell, talking over the case.

We were still working at 8:30 when the company president came in. He was a big, meaty man in a blue pinstripe suit. He looked like those actors who used to play ruthless railroad executives in Roy Rogers movies. His name was Thomason. Fullwell introduced me, talking to him with the same degree of respect a beat copper would give an inspector. Thomason called us into his office and ordered coffee. His came in a cup and saucer, ours in Styrofoam cups. We sipped while Fullwell brought him up to date on our findings.

He sat and stared at Fullwell until he'd finished. It's an old trick for inducing suspects to feel guilty. It made Fullwell uncomfortable, but he's a pro and he stayed cool.

At last Thomason spoke, so quietly that we had to lean forward to hear him. It's another trick they teach you in management courses to make people feel insecure but I was only the part time help so I didn't bother resenting it. "If you remember, I was against our following up the first beating on our own."

"So was I," Fullwell said sturdily. "But on the advice of our marketing man, we did it."

Thomason let him finish then went on without acknowledging the interruption. "Now it's time to stand back and let the police take over."

"Fine," Fullwell said boldly. "They've already got the details, I'll contact them and ask them to proceed normally."

Thomason sipped his coffee, making a slightly pained face. He was staring at me over the top of his cup. "I think we misjudged badly," he said. I could guess what was coming but kept quiet. Thomason let us suffer a moment longer then set down his cup. "Think about it. We have one beating, a fairly conventional attack. Then we bring in Mr. Bennett, an expert in martial arts." He paused again but I didn't say anything. He went on, his voice rising with every word. "And then we have three more men hit, all of them by some fairly sinister person or persons unknown, two of them by some kung fu expert."

He let the suggestion hang in the air and Fullwell grabbed it, laughing angrily. "You're not suggesting that Mr. Bennett is responsible, that a sworn peace officer has been thumping our guards?" He stood up and took an angry step away from his chair and then back again. Thomason watched him like a schoolmarm supervising a kindergarten. "I'm not suggesting anything at all," he said primly. "But I am stating that the connection between Mr. Bennett and Bonded Security has ended, this minute, for all time. Is that understood?"

Fullwell was tough, too tough. I didn't need it, but maybe his pride did. After all, he had suggested me. "I find this line of supposition very offensive," he said. "I've known this man for a year and know him to be of impeccable character."

"You're not the personnel officer," Thomason said. "So there is no need to take this personally. I am paid to make executive decisions and I have just made one. Please pay Mr. Bennett exactly what we owe him and escort him off the premises forthwith."

"Send it to me," I said. "See you later, Simon. Thanks for

the coffee and the vote of confidence, Mr. Thomason. I wish
you luck."

I got up and walked out, whistling to Sam who came
bounding happily up to me. Fullwell said something final to
his boss; it sounded angry, but I could tell by the tone that
the war was over. I was through with this case.

Fullwell followed me into the elevator. There were other
people in it, a pretty girl with too much makeup and an
elderly file clerk with a wheeled tray of letters. We said
nothing as we rode down to the ground floor. Then, as the
others left, Fullwell blew up. I patted him on the arm.
"Don't take it personally, the guy's only covering his own
ass. I'm cool."

"The high and mighty sonofabitch. What in hell does a
business degree teach a man about security work? Or about
people for that matter?" Fullwell jammed his hands into his
pants pockets. "After all the risks you've taken for his
goddamn office."

"I owed you," I said. "And anyway, I'm not through with
the investigation. I've still got eleven days of vacation left.
Here I am at loose ends in Toronto."

Fullwell turned and grinned. "You serious?"

"Absolutely." The thought of proceeding alone was
appealing. I had a lead to follow and time to kill, and a
family to visit with when the day's chasing around was over.
"Yeah, I'm going to get myself some sound legal advice
before I go home."

Fullwell laughed out loud, a relieved laugh. "Nice going.
I hear the best man in town is a lawyer called Straight, Cy
Straight."

"I've heard that as well. Maybe while I catch a few hours
zuzz somebody would check the legal list and find out
where he works."

"I think that could happen right here in this building,"
Fullwell said. "Don't give it another thought. Just ring my
office later and ask for the address of the mortgage company.
Tell them it's Mr. Case calling."

"Certainly will, Mr. Fullwell," I said.

"I'll be waiting for your call, Mr. Case," he said and
bowed and we both laughed. It wasn't very funny, but
compared with the stuff we'd seen the last couple of nights,
it was at least light relief.

## 10

THE first thing I did was sleep six hours. When I'd got up, showered, shaved, and taken Sam for a walk I called Fullwell, using our Mickey Mouse code. The girl told me Mr. Fullwell had remembered the address. She gave it to me, along with the name of the law firm. Howe, Stark and Payne, an establishment WASP outfit rich enough to have a floor to themselves in one of the goldmines in the sky down at Bay and King streets.

I left Sam in the car, in a lot that charged by the microsecond, and rode up thirty-eight floors to their office. I'd decided what I would do is get a reading of this man, for his reactions. If he acted suspiciously I would tail him for a day or two and see if he made any contact with Tony or other known hard cases. It was thin but I didn't have many choices. Tony's record prevented me from trusting him right off. I needed some kind of confirmation that Straight was our man. After that I could follow him up. The police might have done it differently, but then they had more manpower to spare than I did. So I forged ahead.

Their office had oak double doors with a discreet brass plate with the partners' names on. I opened them and went through into the kind of plush-carpeted hush you associate with bank vaults full of old money. The receptionist was an anorexia victim in the middle of a desk that resembled a flying saucer. From a quick glance I couldn't tell how she got into it, there was no flap or visible hinge. I imagined she put it on like a crinoline.

I could see she was weighing me up. The tweed jacket was good, from the days when tailors gave discounts to Toronto detectives, but I had the kind of tan you don't get sitting in offices riffling piles of other people's money. She smiled a smile she had perfected about 1945 and said, "Good afternoon, sir."

There was a ten-second pause between "afternoon" and "sir" and a long hungry pause while she waited for me to whisper my request. By then she was beginning to realize that I was not one of their usual business clients. I was a special case.

I looked at her for a few more seconds without speaking. She was waiting for deference. Once she got it she would kiss me off without a prayer of seeing the man I'd come to visit. So I did what had to be done. Speaking curtly I told her, "I've got a message for Cy Straight."

She was startled. I could tell that everybody in this place was a Mister. She fiddled with her neckline. "Mr. Straight is busy."

"Yeah, well I'll wait then." I looked around for a chair and moved to it, my feet honestly swishing through the depth of that carpet.

She was in full flight now. "Sir," she called. And when I didn't respond at once, "Si-irrr!"

I sat down and picked up last month's *Fortune*. "Me?" I asked.

She waved both hands in a tiny, anxious motion, like a kid smoothing down her ruffled dress. "I must have your name. People can't just walk in off the street and expect to see Mr. Straight."

"Yeah, well okay, tell him a friend of Tony's is out front." To someone like her, used to the hushed whisper school of conversation, I must have sounded like a drunk in church. She stared at me with her mouth open. "Tony," I repeated, and flipped the magazine open to a piece on commodities.

She still didn't answer. Her mouth was working but her brain hadn't taken up the slack. I flopped the magazine back on the glass-topped table and mimed picking up and dialling a telephone. "A friend of Tony's is here to see you," I said and grinned.

The grin woke her up. She picked up the phone and dialled. She spoke into the phone, rapidly. "Yes, Sue, there's a, a gentleman out here to see Mr. Straight. He won't give his name. Says he's a friend of Tony's."

She made Tony's name sound like a conundrum. There were mouse scratchings on her line and she looked up sharply. "Mr. Straight's secretary says she can't interrupt him unless she has your name."

"Why not?" I stayed in character. It was not my favorite role but it was the only way I had to cut through the usual protocol and come face to face with Straight.

She repeated my comment into the telephone, then hissed a few words and hung up. "I'm afraid Mr. Straight's secretary says he can't entertain any business exchange without a proper introduction."

It was too good a chance to pass up. "I don't need entertaining, I'm here with a message." She opened her mouth to speak but I wagged a finger at her. "I'll just wait right here until he comes out."

She pursed her lips angrily, dialled again and informed the person at the other end of the line that they were stuck with me. So far as I could tell there were no other exits from the offices, except through this lobby. I had him cornered and we all knew it.

She hung up again and said "Mr. Straight's secretary will see you."

"Good." I nodded approvingly. "Now we're starting to get somewhere." I was expecting a clone of the receptionist. With just the same degree of pressure I was sure I could get by her and in to see Straight. Instead, the inner door opened and an elegant woman of about thirty walked out. She was Chinese, taller than average, dressed in a creamy silk blouse, tied at the throat, and a silk skirt. Her hair was bobbed in a cut that must have been intended to look practical but which was more strikingly feminine than waist-length curls. I looked at her and rose to my feet as if I'd been hooked. Any man would have found her beautiful. In my mind she brought out some echoes that made her irresistible.

She came over and held out her hand. "Good afternoon, my name is Yin Su. I work for Mr. Straight." Her English was unaccented but had the slightly metallic quality that let me know it was her second language.

Even a storm trooper would have taken her hand. I did it, working hard not to eat her up with my eyes. I stayed in character to say, "Yeah, well, a pleasure, Su, Tony sent me to talk to your boss."

She remained charming, the princess with the barbarian.

"I keep Mr. Straight's calendar for him. If you'll give me your name, and perhaps an idea of what this is about, I'll arrange an appointment."

"Yeah, well, that'd take too long." I was growing disgusted with myself. I had checked her hands and they were free of rings. Had we met under any other circumstances I would have been concentrating on getting to know her, not the man she worked for.

"He's very busy," she explained patiently. "He's one of the senior partners here and I have to be very careful of his time." I said nothing and she pressed on, losing just a touch of her smoothness. "His time is very valuable."

I was melting under the gaze of those cool brown eyes but I did what I had to do. "Yeah. Tony told me that. But he gave me a message for him."

She tried again, still calm. "Perhaps it would help if you could tell me who Tony is."

"Cy knows."

She smiled again, a polite tightening of the corners of her mouth. "Well, we seem to have a problem. Mr. Straight can't take time away from his work to see you and you won't make an appointment."

"So I'll just sit here until he comes out. He'll see me then," I said. "Thank you for your trouble, but this is private."

"Very well." She nodded, smiling one last time, and left. I sat down again and reached for the magazines. All the others were law journals. I sighed. This could turn into a long afternoon.

The woman at the desk made a point of being busy, glancing at me slyly over the notes she was typing. I ignored her.

A lot of my life has been spent waiting. Sometimes beside a twelve-inch Cong trail in Viet Nam, in monsoon rains that beat you half senseless, sometimes in the back of unheated vehicles in laneways outside fur warehouses in a Toronto January. I can handle the kind of discomfort most civilians never understand. By comparison, this was heaven. The couch was soft, there was Muzak, bland wallpaper music from the early sixties. I could have sat there all night. All I needed was patience and a forgiving bladder.

The receptionist made a couple of calls out and I listened

carefully. I hadn't seen any security people in the building when I arrived. Most Toronto offices don't bother with them, except for government buildings and the major corporations. A place like this wouldn't have anybody on the door during the day time. And I hadn't done anything that warranted sending for the police. It was all cool. All I had to do was sit tight.

Slowly, the afternoon drew on and the office emptied. Young men in blue suits and a few women, one of them pert and pretty, carrying a squash bag, came through the foyer and wished the receptionist goodnight. Some of them looked at me and back at her. She was embarrassed, as if I were something her dog had brought in, something she would be held accountable for. I just sat and looked at all the people. I wasn't sure whether Straight was amongst the men who left but I was gambling that he would think I knew him and would not come marching through, past a potential source of trouble.

The receptionist made one last attempt to shake me loose. "I'm going home now, the office is closed," she said. She stood up, touching a switch that unsnapped a catch on her desk and let it tilt like a halo around her blameless head.

"I'll let myself out when I've seen Cy," I said.

She snorted something that could have been "Really!" and went away behind the closed door of the inner office. She came out a minute later with a string bag containing three library books and left without looking my way.

It was shortly after that the Chinese girl came back. She had the jacket that matched the skirt over her arm. "Mr. Straight says he can spare you two minutes," she said.

"I thank you, ma'am." I didn't make a mockery of the ma'am. It didn't have any bearing on the investigation but I really wanted this woman to like me.

She led me back through the rear doors and across an open area to a windowed office. The door was open but she rapped on it with her knuckles and said, "Mr. Straight, the gentleman from the lobby." He motioned to me to enter and I nodded at her and went by. She stepped away and closed the door. Straight was at the desk. I wasn't sure what I'd been expecting, but this wasn't it. He was a hunchback, a small man in a dark suit which had been beautifully cut to minimize the fact that he was folded, halfway between shoulders and waist, with one shoulder thrust high. He was about forty, darkhaired and had incongruously pale gray eyes.

There were books on his desk, a couple of them closed with place markers in them, another open and a foolscap pad of yellow paper with hentracks on it in green ink. He put down his pen and looked up when I came in. "Su said you won't give her your name." His voice had the rigid vibrato of a man with a bad heart condition. He looked stern but not angry.

"Yeah, well, you know how it is." I sat down opposite and looked into his eyes. He stared back, his intensity defying me to acknowledge his handicap.

"No, I don't think I do. How is it?" He was unafraid. I guess a lifetime of weakness had made him strong. He knew I could have reached out and snapped his neck with one hand, any healthy man could have, but he acted as if I were the frog and he the magician.

"Look, I was talkin'a Tony. He said he knew a guy who knew a guy who needed some bones broke. I need a job."

Straight looked at me flat-eyed for about fifteen seconds and then laughed, without humor, opening his mouth and letting out the sounds as if they were vomit. I said nothing. He was acting, the way a D.I. will act with a bunch of raw recruits he wants to intimidate. He was bloody good at it, but he was acting. This was where the original call had come from.

I allowed the corners of my mouth to lift as if I were amused but sniffed loudly instead of laughing. He stopped and wiped his eyes with a handkerchief, although they didn't need it.

"When did you get out?" He was reaching for his back pocket with his right hand, canting his already raised shoulder painfully higher. I let him get the wallet out and open it. He took out a fin. "When did you get out?" he repeated, making a Clark Gable grin and holding out the five bucks. I said nothing and he waved the five at me. "Out of prison, the joint, the slammer, the bucket?"

"Yesterday," I said, eyeing the money the way he expected.

"And I'll bet you haven't had a drink since, have you?

Here. Go have a beer on me. Or will you go and tell the same story at the next lawyer's office you pass. Let me see, five dollars an hour, that's better than you'd make working."

I reached out for the bill. "Thanks, does this mean I'm hired?"

He tugged the bill a fraction of an inch from my outstretched fingers, his voice as scratchy as fingernails on a blackboard as he hissed, "There is no job. There is no Tony, none I've ever heard of, anyway. And there is no point in your remaining here. If you want a drink, take the five dollars but don't come here again, you frighten my help."

I flipped the bill out of his fingers. "But I don't frighten you, right?"

"Go," he said savagely. "This is the sum and total of my charity towards unemployed hoodlums. Understood?"

"Yeah. Thanks again." I winked and waved the bill at him and stood up. He was furious at me and at his own restrictive body that prevented his coming around the desk and throwing me out with his own hands. I might have felt sorry for him but too many of my own buddies had ended up in worse physical shape than his. Men I had served with had wound up in wheelchairs, in life-support systems. They had lost hands, feet, sexuality, life itself. He was whole— twisted, but whole—and I had an instinctive policeman's feeling that he was into something ugly, headfirst.

I touched the five to my forehead in a salute that was only a shade too slow to be formal. "Thanks for the fin, sorry'a take up so mucha your time." I nodded and backed out of the door.

The bullpen area outside was deserted. There were four desks and a number of typing stations and filing cabinets and one computer terminal. Earlier it had been a beehive. Now it was empty except for me. I folded the bill up tight between my fingers as I glanced around. On top of one of the cabinets there was a glass jar with no top. It had coins in it. I stepped out of my way towards the door and stuffed the five dollars into it. Behind me I heard Yin Su say, "Just a minute. What are you doing?"

She came over and looked into the jar. It was courageous, I thought. She was alone except for her handicapped boss. If I'd turned ugly she would have been helpless. She looked up, pulling out my five dollars. "You really put money in here?"

"Surplus to requirements," I told her and she grinned at me as if we were old workmates.

"That's the office swearbox," she said, "a nickel a word. You have a hundred curses owing to you now."

"I guess I'm already over budget in your books."

"No." She shook her head firmly. "You never said anything bad. If you want your money back, I will understand." She was still acting out her role as employee, office faithful. The link between us was as fragile as the first line of a new spiderweb, a breath might break it.

"I want to apologize for acting like a slob. I had a job to do." Maybe Cy Straight was listening, I didn't care. I already had enough of a feeling to know I would be following him later. The anger he had shown was a whiff of fear.

"You must have an unusual job," she said. She had the ability to talk straight but disarm me with a smile that wasn't even a smile at all.

"It's done now. I was wondering if I could ask you to share a cup of coffee, something, and give me a chance to explain what I do normally."

She straightened up, suddenly formal. "Really, I understand. You don't have to explain," she said.

"I'd like to. My name is Reid Bennett and I usually behave much better. I'd like the chance to demonstrate for you."

She laughed, one quick pure note. Behind her the door of Cy Straight's office clicked shut. He had been listening. I wondered why, running the possibilities through my mind. Did he really need privacy to work or had he closed the door now that he knew my name? Was he going to make a phone call to Tony? I watched the telephone console on the nearest desk and sure enough a light came on. I read the number next to the button, 4301. It must be Straight, nobody else seemed to be in.

The girl said, "I think I must go straight home, I have a lot to do tonight."

"That would be understandable but not charitable," I said. "I already hate myself for being surly to you and the lady in the flying saucer. I'd like to make amends, carry your books, lay my cape in a puddle, something."

She laughed with genuine amusement. "I'll walk out with you," she said. She slipped into her jacket and picked up a purse from beside one of the chairs. Then she tapped on Straight's door and leaned in. "Goodnight, Mr. Straight. Have a nice trip to Montreal. I'll expect you back late tomorrow."

Montreal? I was pleased to hear it. It meant he wouldn't be around to be followed. That would leave me time to follow this woman instead. I liked that idea a lot better.

"He's going out of town?" I asked innocently.

She said yes before catching herself and cocking her head to look at me quizzically. "Why do you ask?"

"It probably means you don't have to work late," I said. I opened the door and she went ahead of me, through the lobby and out to the elevators. She pressed the down button and stood looking at it, ignoring me. I was feeling drained, as if I had been in a fight. When the elevator came she got in and pressed the lobby button. I stood opposite but she didn't look my way, just glanced up at the lights indicating the floors we were passing. Other people got in at the thirty-second floor and she relaxed a fraction until we reached the ground.

I stood back to let the others get off and caught up with her as she walked away, briskly, only half checking that I was behind her. We went out through the revolving doors on to Bay Street. The sidewalks were crowded with hurrying people and the rush hour traffic sat all along the block, congealing in exhaust fumes and noise. She headed north, towards Queen Street. I crossed to the outside of the curb and walked beside her. I felt as awkward as a schoolboy. Maybe I should have ignored her, walked off to my car without looking back. Other men might have, but other men had not spent the last year up in cottage country, alone most of the time, or seeing women only casually. And other men had not been affected as deeply by a woman so much like this one that I was almost in a trance of memory.

"If you're heading for the subway, you're walking into a mob scene," I told her.

She turned to glance at me but kept walking. "It's the same every night. I am used to it."

"It would be lighter in another twenty minutes or so," I suggested. We had reached the corner, the light was against us and she waited, turning to look me square in the face.

"You are very persistent," she said.

"If I'm annoying you, I'll leave," I promised. She said nothing and when the light changed, started across the street. I added, "If I'm not, maybe you could spare fifteen minutes for a coffee or a Perrier."

She walked another four or five steps then grinned at me in a way so un-Chinese that I was startled. "Why not?" she said.

# 11

WE went to one of the transplanted English pubs that have sprung up in Toronto. This one sits close enough to the stock exchange to be able to get away with charging four bucks for a pint of Worthington E.

She had a Perrier with a twist; I took a pint. It was the only English thing my father missed in all his years in Canada. That marvellous first swallow always reminds me why. She watched as I enjoyed it.

"You look as if you've done that before."

So I explained about my father, the ex-commando from Lancashire who had come here in 1946 and found work in the nickel mine at Coppercliff, Ontario. He met my mother, a French girl from Callander, the town where the Dionne quints were born, and they married and lived happily ever after. It's not the most exciting story in the world, but because she asked the right questions I found myself telling it to her, and of the ending, for them, six months apart, during my last year in high school. My father's death, in a preventable cave-in at the mine, had soured me on my home town. I'd sent my kid sister to stay with our mother's sister, later on sending money for her to go to university, and I had dropped my own plans for more education. I joined the U.S. Marines instead and did my sociology and political science studies firsthand with an M16 in my fists, while I boiled the anger out of my system.

It wasn't a monologue on my part. I'm old enough to know that war stories are the origin of that old line, "I guess you had to be there." Nobody cares how close you came to not being wherever you are now, bending their ear with yet another retelling of your adventures. They may even get to wish you hadn't been quite so lucky. Fortunately, in a way, for us Viet Nam vets, the whole social structure was slanted against us from day one. Talking about Nam is like discussing the state of your psoriasis. Personally, I'm proud of the fact that I was there and came under fire without flinching and fired back and did the job I'd been trained to do, even though the politics of the war still confuse me and I wouldn't want to defend its principles. So when I mentioned Viet Nam, without drawing any pictures, and Su took a careful sip of her drink and said nothing for a moment, I figured she was another of the anti's I've met. But the war was not her prime concern. She lifted her eyes to me, over her drink and asked, "Did you know many women there?"

The question startled me. It's what men ask, with a smile and a nudge if they're young, a wistful look if they're older. But Su was straight-faced.

"One in particular." As I spoke I could remember Li's face. She had been more delicate than this woman, slimmer even, almost translucent in her beauty. And I remembered that last night. We were in a bar in Saigon. The terrible band was playing something they thought the Beatles had written, requested by some homesick grunt who was wearing a Dear John letter like a purple heart. "Yesterday," just slightly off key. And then the shoe-shine boy's cleaning box blew up. It killed him of course but they, perhaps even he, had known it would. It also killed seven Americans, wounded eleven others, and punched a piece of the brass footrail from the bar cleanly through Li's chest. I carried her out to the ambulance when it came, adding my shouts to all the others clamoring for aid but the big black medic just looked at me. "She dead, man. Git, there's PEOPLE inside an' they need me." And when I tried to stop him he had pushed me over and shouted, "F" crissakes. She dead, man. 'Many times you gotta be told?" He ran back into the bar and I was left, sitting there on the ground holding her until the young guy she had called her brother came for her, as angry at me as if I had personally set the bomb. I suppose he had to work for a living after that.

"She was killed by a bomb," I told Su, and reached for my beer but noticed that my hand was unsteady and changed my mind.

Yin Su looked at me, closely. "I'm sorry. I did not mean to remind you of something hurtful."

I waved one hand, wishing that I still smoked and had something to do with myself for a minute until the memories stopped chasing one another through my mind. Soon Li had been a bargirl, maybe the same as all the others but never to me. I had known her only weeks when I was nineteen and she maybe two years younger but she was a part of my life that would never leave me.

"The reason I asked is selfish," Su said. "I have met men who think that women like me are exotic. It seems demeaning."

It gave me a chance to change the subject. "Then allow me to apologize for the collective bad manners of all rednecks. Please excuse us for acting attracted. You're very attractive, and not just to us typical Kwailos."

"Kwailos?" She laughed, surprised, "You are not a typical foreign devil, not if you know the word."

"I try not to be. That's why I was sorry to have to act like one this afternoon. I didn't see how to cut the usual law office red tape any other way."

"Well, it worked," she said. "Mr. Straight never sees people without an appointment. I was surprised when he said he would make an exception for you."

"I thank you for that. I didn't really expect to get through to him."

She shrugged and smiled. "That's what I'm there for."

I was all out of things to say. She reminded me so strongly of that vanished portion of my life that I couldn't see the day, the golden quality of the light that poured through the low window of the pub, as mellow as English ale. Instead I was standing in the smoke and noise of that bar in the long seconds when I could have said, "Let's go some place else?" and we could have headed for the door, in time to move out of the path of that shard of brass. It was the thought that had filled my whole head for months afterwards, leading me into crazy risks as I did my best to join her. I guess I would have if the mortar shell had landed a meter closer to me. Instead I woke up in bed in a hospital, among round-eyed nurses and guys who had lost so much more than me that I slowly climbed back out of the crater Li had left in my life and rejoined the world.

All of this went through my mind in moments, but not quickly enough to be invisible to this strangely familiar woman. She had the same fragility I had loved in Li, overlaid with a Western assurance, in place of the artificial hardness Li had put on with her makeup. Now this one cocked her head, twisting her mouth in a wry grin that forgave me everything. "I seem to have touched a nerve."

I tried out a tight little smile of my own. "Sorry, ma'am, I was just woolgathering."

She twisted her wrist towards her so she could see the pretty little gold watch with no numerals. "The subway has to be empty now, except for me, and you, if you're heading north."

I had a car but this was not the time to offer her a ride; already I felt grubby, the redfaced recruit making googoo eyes at the pretty city girl. I could almost feel the straws in my hair.

"No, I have some things to do before I head home. I don't get into the city very often."

She stood up, picking up her purse, rehearsing the usual politeness. I was anxious to hold on to her, somehow. I said, "I'm sorry this has been such a crazy first meeting. I'd like a rematch, so you can see that I'm not usually this much of a turkey." She said nothing, but she was smiling, so I asked, "Are you busy later this week?"

As I spoke I was aware that I had not yearned like this for any woman, including my wife, in fifteen hungry years. Maybe she was right, maybe there are some men who are intoxicated by Oriental women. If there are, I'm one of them, for life.

She did me the courtesy of looking at me, squarely as she thought about my words for perhaps ten seconds. Then she smiled and said, "I think I'm free on Thursday," in a serious tone that collapsed in helpless laughter. "Try me," she added.

"Thursday?" I echoed. We both laughed and she told me where and I suggested when and that was it. I walked her to the door and up to the corner. I don't know what I was thinking or expecting. I'd known a lot of women in those years, some of them important to me. Hell, I had even been married. But I was still breathless around this girl.

We parted at the corner. She walked through Simpsons to the subway and I went back to my car, paid five dollars ransom and drove off with Sam, baleful and mistrustful, in the back seat.

Louise was in the kitchen, tearing lettuce. She smiled at me and said "You look like you just won the sweep."

I waved one hand, elaborately casual. "Nothing so grand." She pulled the "Oh, yeah" face that kid sisters grow up with and then stopped her work and dried her hands on her apron.

"This package came for you, about ten minutes ago, in a cab."

It was a manilla envelope, eight by fourteen, legal size. There was no monogram on it, just the plain white typewritten label addressed to "Mr. R. Bennett" and the address of Louise's house.

I took it and looked it over, wondering automatically who could have sent it to me. If it had come from Fullwell it would have carried the Bonded Security crest and I couldn't think of anyone else who knew where I was staying. I hadn't even left the information with George at the police station in Murphy's Harbour.

I must have looked mystified enough to prompt Louise to say, "Why not open it, then you'll know who it's from."

I tore it open and tipped it out. It held a sheet of paper, folded around a bundle of other papers. I opened it and whistled with surprise. I was holding a solid wad of twenty-dollar bills.

I counted them, while Louise watched. They added up to one thousand and eighty dollars and I frowned. People who send unmarked envelopes full of cash usually have a good reason. You don't expect them to make mistakes in arithmetic. The figure must have some significance, but not for me. There was another paper enclosed. I pulled it out and looked it over. There were four words on it, typed in a sans serif electric typewriter face. They were: *Wait for our call*.

"Curiouser and curiouser," Louise said. She was looking at me over the bowl of salad, wondering perhaps if I was going to go bright red and confess that I was on the take from a bunch of hard cases.

"Makes no sense to me," I told her. I didn't let her read the message. I was worried by it. My benefactor, whoever he was, knew where I was staying. The knowledge made me uncomfortable. I've had my share of adventures, in and out of the service, but they were always one-on-one affairs that affected me alone—not my sister and her kids.

We ate supper and I kibitzed with the kids, and worried. They were young and fragile and precious, like all kids, and it seemed I had turned over a stone that hid some ugly kind of creature. I decided I would wait in for the call, no matter who or where it came from.

It happened at seven-thirty. I had just piggybacked Katie up to bed and was heading downstairs for a last game of snap with Jack when the phone rang. Louise picked it up, in the kitchen, then called me, her voice yodelling up cheerfully, "It's for you."

"Thanks." I took it in her bedroom. She hung up down below when I picked up the receiver and for a long moment there was nothing on the line but the faint electronic sighing as if this were an overseas call. Then a voice said, "Yeah, Reid. Some friends of mine asked me to give you a call."

"About what?" There was nothing distinctive about the voice, no accent or tone that would have helped me pick it out again. It was just a plain, businesslike telephone voice, a little slow but not loaded with menace or anything that might have made a normal person suspicious. But then, not many normal people get care packages containing over a grand in unmarked bills.

"Le's jus' say about the way you been spending your nights lately."

"Man's gotta work." I tried to make myself sound petulant, not intrigued. I wanted him to volunteer more information.

" 'Preciate that." The voice was toneless, like a tired grade-school teacher in the last period. "Question is what he's gotta work at. I mean, there's people would say you're pushing kind of hard on something that don't matter a hill of beans to you."

"I'm just helping out a friend."

Now the voice took on an edge, exasperation at my stupidity. "Bullshit. You're jus' playing a game o' cops'n'robbers. Hell, if you wanna do that, why come down here? You wanna kick ass an' take names, you can do that up in Murphy's Harbour."

"Why's it upsetting your friends?" I knew why. The money alone would have told me, the call was spelling it out. I had gotten too close to somebody. Automatically I thought of Cy Straight with his unstraight back and his law office, where a man would be able to stretch out his hand and pick up a legal-sized envelope without any trouble at all.

"I don' have to draw you no pictures, 'kay?" The voice was showing signs of stress. I had obviously had my quota of kind words, now it was time to wrap up, to take the money and run.

"Why'd you send me the cash?"

"Token of good will. A man shouldn't have to work two jobs to make a living."

"I appreciate the thought. What if I tell you I like working two jobs?"

There was a heavy rasping, like a man rubbing a file over a spade. "Yeah, well, my friends think you should retire."

"And if I don't."

Again the rasp and then the words I had dreaded but expected. "Yeah, 's up to you. But, in case you forgot a'ready, we know where you live." There was a short pause, as if a man with a long arm were reaching out slowly to the cradle, and then the phone clattered down.

## 12

I replaced the phone at my end and stood looking at it and worrying. I'd seen these people at work. If someone ordered a guy like Kennie to come over here and play handball with the kids' heads, he would do it, no questions asked. And he would enjoy doing it, picking a time when I wasn't there and counting every blow a direct pain to me. There was no question. I had to change my way of working, or give it up altogether. I couldn't put them at risk.

I went downstairs and played a game of cards with Jack, then put him to bed and went back to the living room where Louise was sitting listening to background music and fiddling with a note pad on her lap, working on some problem she had brought home from the office. She looked up when I came in. "Hi, who called?"

"A guy from Bonded. They want me to go out tonight and check on their properties again." Lying doesn't hurt a bit, compared with the real thing.

"When will you be going?" she yawned as she glanced around at the clock. It was close to eight, dark outside.

"I think soon, then I'll head back early, I'm not going to put in any more nights than I absolutely have to." As I spoke I was making a plan for my night's work.

With Straight out of town, I would go and find Tony and see what sparks flew when I told him some cock and bull story about Straight. In the meantime, I would give Louise and the kids the best protection they could have.

"I'd like to leave Sam behind tonight. He's fed up with driving all over Toronto in that crummy car. I'll give him a night off." I was fiddling in my pocket for car keys, not meeting her eyes.

"Is something the matter?" She wasn't scared, her

question was for my safety, not hers, she couldn't guess at a world where women and children were in danger because of the things their menfolk did for a living. That happened only on television, not in North Toronto among the wisteria and divorces.

"Not really, but there are some real creeps mixed up in this thing and I'd feel happier if Sam were sleeping on the rug down here than if he were off with me somewhere."

She snorted a quick little laugh. "You don't expect someone to come here?"

"No, but Sam's staying here would make me happier as I toddle on my weary way. What do you say?"

She laughed. "As Dad always used to say, anything for a quiet life."

I leaned over and gave her a quick kiss on the forehead, then I walked Sam out into the garden to get him comfortable for the night and brought him back in. I showed him through all the rooms, one after the other. "Guard!" I told him, and raised my left index finger to let him know I was serious. It was my own signal for the ultimate defense against prowlers; it kept him silent, charged with knocking an intruder down and standing over his throat until I called him off. He settled down on the hall rug with a thump and I patted his head and went back to Louise.

After that there was nothing to stop me going out. I asked her to come out to the stoop and wave to me as I left, and I carried an empty suitcase with me to the car. Anybody who was thinking about my life-style would have known that Sam would have been with me if I were leaving, but it was dark by now and I figured it might fool a casual observer. Maybe they would think I had taken the hint and gone home. And maybe they wouldn't, but at least Sam was on duty for me.

I had left too late to catch Tony at his circuit so I drove right to the racetrack, bought a ticket and went looking for him.

The usual crowd was there. Most of them are the mugs—working stiffs who work at lousy jobs because they think of nothing but the track and the modest little wins they make that pay for steaks and bottles of cheap rye once in a while. One time you found nothing but Cabbagetown natives there, guys born and bred in Toronto's only real slum.

Tonight it was different. I guess the world has changed in the last ten years. Many of the horseplayers were black, West Indians by the sound of their singsong voices, and from the strong whiff of marijuana that hung over the area. And there was a good smattering of Chinese, gambling the Caucasian way for a change instead of sticking with their endless games of fan-tan in Chinatown.

The real regulars were still there, the guys who work at nothing but racing. You see the prosperous ones in the clubhouse, sipping Scotch on the rocks and eating lobster while the girls come to their tables to take the hundred-dollar bets. But most of them are down at the two-dollar windows, scraping change to get a bet together. They wear shiny suits and threadbare shirts and usually a raincoat, summer and winter, and they hustle for cash like pelicans diving for fish off the Florida Keys. Nothing's too murky to draw them if the money is there.

I recognized one of them when I walked through. He's a thin guy in his fifties, five-nine around one thirty. He's deep enough inside himself to disguise his endless poverty and bad luck by improvising a little dance with every few steps he takes. Some copper called him Bojangles once and the name stuck although he's white, or would be if he took a bath. He'd finked for me a few times when I was a detective in Toronto and he recognized me at once as the source of a possible fin, maybe a sawbuck if the world was looking after him. He bobbed over to me and stood, ducking his shoulders, smiling his toothless smile. "Hey, Mr. Bennett, waddya say?"

"Hi, Bo. What's new?"

He sketched a few steps. "Aw, hell, shoulda had the six horse in the third race. He paid thirty-seven eighty."

He was set to give me a summary of all the horses he had bet in the last three years if I hadn't cut him off. "Listen, feel like doing me a favor? I wanna see Tony. You know, Tony with the loans, he's generally here by now."

He glanced around in surprise. "Hey, yeah, gen'ally." Then he turned back and peered at me, shielding his eyes with his hand, as if I were hot. "You mean you're flat, Mr. Bennett?" He lowered his voice conspiratorially. "Hell, I wouldn't go to Tony for a bet on the only horse in the race.

He's ugly, y'know? That guy as works for him broke my buddy's thumb one time."

I shook my head patiently and took out my wallet. I still had my vacation pay from Murphy's Harbour. It looked like Eldorado to him. "No, I just got paid. I wanna see him about something personal." I tugged on the corner of a ten, pulling it as gently as a good stripper working on her first glove. Bojangles cleared his throat, his voice cracked like a teenager's.

"I could ask around for you, if you wan'ed."

I gave the bill a decisive tug and handed it to him. "Do that, eh, I'll be over by the rail."

He grinned and vanished the bill into his dirty pocket. "Fer sure, fer sure, Mr. Bennett. Be right back."

He didn't come back until after the next race, shaking his head angrily. "Sonofabitch broke," he started, but I waved him down. "It's about Tony . . ."

"Oh, yeah." He cleared his throat again. "Well, I met a guy, see . . ." He paused, waiting for me to bring out my wallet again but I looked at him calmly and his nerve gave out and he rushed ahead with his message. "Yeah, well, I was talkin' to a guy, said Tony's stayin' home tonight. Said if a feller wanted to see him, he'd have to go over his place." He stood looking at me, licking his dry lips. I took pity on him and pulled out another ten. Before he could grab it I said, "There's a horse called Baby Lou running in the next race. Put me a deuce down and spend the change."

His emotions were split right down the middle. Gratitude for the extra cash was almost outweighed by the certainty that my horse would end down the track. How could anyone as rich as I was be so dumb, he wondered. But he bobbed a nervous thanks again and took off. I watched him go, then reached in my pocket and pulled out the note I had made when Fullwell mentioned Tony's address. Good. It was in the West End, I could cut across the Gardner Expressway instead of ploughing through the traffic lights and stop signs to head north or east.

I went back out to my car and drove away, down the Woodbine extension that swings around the bay, south of the racetrack, and then climbed on to the Expressway. It was pleasant, driving past the lights of the downtown area, chest-high to the big office buildings. I cut off at Jameson and headed north through the Italian area. It as a warm enough night that a few people were out on their porches, drinking homemade wine and spraying their neat front gardens with casual hoses. It made me feel a little homesick for somewhere I've never been, a place where there was company and conversations about things I'd never had a chance to talk to anyone about. And I wondered about Yin Su. What would she be doing now? Laundry for the next day, perhaps, maybe just listening to music. Whatever it was, she was most likely not brooding on me, I decided, and I shouldn't waste any time daydreaming about her.

Tony's apartment block stuck up out of a row of good two storey houses in a way that let you know the builder had a lot of clout with the local zoning authorities. I wondered if Tony, or his family members, owned the place.

Calabria Enterprises had a penthouse. I pressed the bell and immediately it buzzed in response, without anybody's asking who was there. That surprised me. Guys like Tony don't casually admit strangers. Even if he were lying around in a dressing gown, waiting for a call girl to arrive, he would have checked. When you employ men to break limbs for you, you have to be careful.

I rode up seventeen floors, listening to Muzak and wondering what kind of person defaces the walls of elevators. From the height of the scratches on this one it was somebody short. That let Tony off the hook.

His apartment was located at the far end of the hall and I stood for a moment to check that there was nobody around. An apartment corridor is a bad place to be ambushed.

Nobody jumped out of a doorway at me and I came to P6 and tapped. I could hear rock music playing; it sounded like a party, but somebody heard me at once and the door swung open inwards, almost slickly enough to be automatic. But I don't believe in magic. To me the open door meant an ambush and I reacted without even thinking.

I took a quick step into the room and turned to slam my full weight against the door, flinging it back another foot as I faced away from it, preparing to take on whoever was setting me up. The door didn't hit the wall. As I expected it squeezed back, against the body of the man who was hiding behind it.

I tried to hold it against the wall, but the man was too

small to be trapped. He forced himself out of the space and came at me like a cyclone, crouched in the kung fu stance, whirling and kicking as I backed away, reaching for anything I could throw. I hit him with the Princess telephone but the cable checked it, preventing it from hurting him. Then I scrabbled a lamp and dish of fruit at him, but he was winning, backing me away from the door. I reeled back against a coffee table, scooped the ashtray off it and sent it at his head but he ducked under it and came on. Desperately I grabbed the table and held it between us. It was only a delaying tactic. My arms would tire before he did. So I did what all the manuals advise rape victims to do. I began to shout. "Police, here! You back off. Police! Police!" It wasn't very dignified, but neither is lying in a hospital bed with your arms and legs tied to the ceiling, and that was the only outcome I could see to this situation.

And then, almost contemptuously, he ended it, sending a smashing kick at the table, tearing it sideways in my hands as he half stepped forward and hit me like a lightning strike over the right temple.

As I somersaulted away from him into darkness, one detail filled my mind. He was small and dark and deadly, and he was dressed in a suit that was too wide in the lapels, too long in the skirt to be fashionable, unless you happened to be Chinese, which he was.

## 13

I thought at first I was in the belly of a chopper, my body jouncing awkwardly against some spar that was digging into my chest. But as I opened my eyes I found I was looking at the soft, fawn broadloom rug of Tony's apartment. The jouncing was coming from the shiny toe of a big shoe that was sticking out of the leg of a polyester suit, the kind that comes with two pairs of pants for ninety-nine ninety.

Painfully, I rolled on to one elbow, my head threatening to snap right off my neck, and peered six feet away to the happy moon face of Elmer Svensen. "Nice try, asshole," he said and dug me again with his shoe.

Normally I would have caught his foot at the ankle and thrown him on his back but my body was playing old man games on me.

"Did you get him?" I heard my wheezy voice ask and the big face split into a grin.

"Let's establish the rules of this game," he said. "I ask the questions, you do the answers. Okay?" I had heard him use similar routines a dozen times on investigations we had shared. It was his method of letting the suspect know there was no chance of getting away with anything. He was caught, dead to rights.

"Did you get the guy who hit me? He was Chinese, dark suit, maybe five-three, around 120."

Svensen laughed the bigger than life laugh of the schoolyard bully. With his big meaty face hanging open he turned and called to his partner, "Hey, guess what, hotshot got all messed up by some Chink pygmy."

There was no answer and Svensen dropped the laugh and prodded me again with the same shoe. I reached up and tapped him on the shinbone with the point of my middle finger. "Don't do that," I cautioned him. He drew his leg away with a yelp of surprise and I got up, first to my knees and then to my feet.

"Did you see the Chinese guy?" I asked again, politely. There is nothing like being hit on the head to heighten your sense of the importance of politeness.

Svensen snarled now, all pretense at humor and amusement gone. "I didn't see any Chinaman because there wasn't any Chinaman."

I sat down on the arm of Tony's chesterfield. "I was here," I explained mildly. "Take my word for it there was one tough little Bruce Lee of a Chinese kid, and he was good."

"Okay," Svensen said, suddenly hearty again. "Let's go along with this fairy story of yours. Only I want all of it. First of all why were you in this apartment? Second, everything that happened while you were here."

I gave him the outline, leaving out all reference to Straight. I had come back to talk to Tony because the people at Bonded had asked me to follow up on the investigation, not in an official capacity, just to see if I could find anything out in a casual way. When I got to the apartment, I suspected something tricky and had been right, painfully right.

Svensen listened, not saying anything, just glancing at me and then around, to his partner, who seemed to be waiting outside the door, as if afraid to come in and embarrass me with his presence.

When I finished, Svensen said, "Won't stand up, none of it."

"Why would that matter, I haven't done anything wrong, I come to visit a guy, somebody jumps me and hits me in the head. Except for one hell of a headache I'm in no trouble."

Svensen turned to look me full in the face now, his grin starting to show, like the edge of a woman's slip. He backed off one pace and beckoned me with his index finger. I got up and followed, holding my head in both hands. It felt as if it might drop off if I let go.

He led me down the short hallway beyond the living room. It had three doors in it. One went into the bathroom, the second was closed, the third was open and led to a bedroom with an enormous round water bed in the middle of it, covered with a silk embroidered counterpane. On the counterpane lay what used to be Tony Caporetto. He had blood oozing from the corner of his mouth and his eyes were open, rolled back in his head, just the whites showing.

Svensen sniffed, unwrapping a fresh stick of gum. "You do real neat work," he said.

# 14

"GET real. He was taken by the same guy who hit me." I managed to keep my voice level, with no trace of pleading in it, but I had been at too many incidents with Svensen as my partner not to recognize how thin my story sounded.

Svensen put his gum wrapper neatly in his pocket. Anywhere except a crime scene he would have tossed it over his shoulder. "Cute," he said, folding the gum into his mouth as if it were part of some complex technical process. "The guy ices Tony. I'm not sure how many times he was hit, but there's all kinds of bruising I can see. We'll know better when the coroner's been here. So, anyway, he beats Tony to a bloody pulp, then he comes out and gives you a neat little lovetap on the head so you can just come out of your sleepybyes as the big bad policemen get here."

"You were watching." I said it mockingly but I was worried. On the evidence in front of him there was no other conclusion he could have reached. I tried to brazen it out. "Why aren't you looking for the kung fu kid?"

"Because there isn't one." He took three quick angry chews at his gum with his front teeth, like a squirrel. "You and Tony were on the outs from the first time you met him. First off that phony deal, you fighting a couple of his boys on Queen Street. Then, next thing you're in his hangouts looking for him. He caused you trouble and you wanted to square him. Well now you have, kiddo, and you're going inside for ten years."

I said nothing. He had a case, but not much of one. I concentrated on telling myself that story. I didn't want to think about getting sent to one of the penitentiaries where men I had arrested were doing time. The last policeman that happened to ended up cutting his own throat one night, rather than have it done for him in the exercise yard.

The next hour went by like the first act of a play I'd seen too many times. The homicide squad arrived, then the coroner, then the local inspector. The media people gathered outside. It would have been tedious, except that this time I was the prime suspect.

The homicide men took me back to the station when they had finished their preliminary investigation and sealed the apartment.

Normally they would have spent four or five hours going over the place, digging through the last pocket of the last suit in the closet looking for information that might point to Tony's killer. But this time they didn't have to. They had me.

There were two of them, both equally tired and gray-faced, even now at the tag end of one of the hottest summers in years. One was heavy and worried looking, the other was thin and a little short. By one of those department coincidences that can sometimes wreck a career they were named Hooper and Cooper, close enough to cause a lot of confusion in court. Somebody in the department had rhymed it to give them their nickname, the supersnoopers.

Hooper was the lean one. He took me through my story again, listening without comment. When I'd finished Cooper jumped on me.

"This is the second time you've been busted for murder, right?"

"It was manslaughter. And you know what happened. I came across three bikers and a grocery store clerk. The guys came at me and I put two of them down."

Cooper sighed. "Yeah, I know the story. It's part of the goddamn folklore of this department. Lord knows why. A lot of guys have done the same thing."

Hooper interrupted him, waving his cigar. "Not so, Coop, this guy was in the U.S. Marines." He made a joke of it, then snarled at me. "I was in Korea for crissakes, what's the big deal."

"Look, send me home, it's been a long day. I've been hit in the head. I don't need any more war stories," I complained.

Hooper waved his hands, like a grade-school music

teacher conducting the Christmas pageant. "You're missing the point, like how come you could take out two bikers, big sonsabitches with leather boots an' sweatstains an' all that. Yet you walk in on some dinky little Chinese kid an' he puts you down?"

"Don't you ever watch TV? This kid was a skilled kung fu fighter. The only surprise to me is, why he didn't finish me off while I was down."

"Yeah," Cooper nodded. "That's exactly where Hoop an' me start to wonder what gives."

And so, as I had known I would have to, I told them all that had happened to me since leaving Murphy's Harbour. They listened, noncommittally, smoking. Then Hooper said, "So let's go over to your place and pick up this envelope that came to you today, if it's there."

Cooper nodded. "Good idea. How much d'ya say there was in it?"

"Just over a thousand dollars."

"How much over a thousand?" Both of them had become suddenly more interested. Hooper took his cigar out of his mouth to wait, as if smoke might interfere with his reception mechanism.

"Eighty bucks. There was a thousand and eighty dollars in it." I looked from one to the other, wondering what I had missed so far. Neither one spoke. They just looked at one another with beams of satisfaction. I waited and when they didn't speak I asked, "Well, aren't you going to let me in on it?"

"Sure." Hooper gave a dry little cough. "Ever hear of the Triads?"

"Sounds like a college football team."

He shook his head. "No, these guys are for real. They're the closest thing there is to a Chinese Mafia."

I said nothing. It was all news to me but I was wondering how they had gotten on to the subject. Cooper explained as he led me out to the elevator. It was still very relaxed, they hadn't charged me, didn't put the cuffs on. "Seems like there's a temple, monastery, something, in China. It was full of kung fu monks. This was, what, Hoop, four hundred years ago?"

Hooper nodded. The elevator came. We got in. Cooper went on. "So the king got mad at these guys for whatever reason makes kings mad. And he sent his soldiers to wipe 'em out."

"And there were a thousand and eighty of them?" I was excited. The men I had surprised at the job site had been Oriental; now I was sure they were kung fu experts. It was starting to fit.

"No, it was a hundred and eight of them, left after the crap cleared," Hooper explained. "And that's the figure they use in all o' their negotiations. It's always some factor of a hundred and eight."

"The guy who spoke to me on the phone didn't sound Chinese." I was replaying the memory, trying to make the voice conform to a physical type. I remembered forming the image of a heavy middle-aged Caucasian, blasé, bored, casually cruel. "No," I said slowly. "The guy who called me was a Canadian. A used-car dealer type."

We came to ground level and they went out with me to their car. I wasn't under arrest but there was one either side of me, they weren't sure how much to trust me. If I'd run away, they would have shot without hesitation.

I went into the back. It wasn't a cage car, for which I was grateful. But I didn't try the buddy-buddy trick of leaning forward ingratiatingly. Policemen spend so much time in cars that they have relaxation down to an art form. Hooper drove and Cooper carried on with the conversation, not turning his head, just cranking up the volume on his growl.

"So it gets kinda mystifying to me," he said. "You got somebody makin' like he's Chinese only he isn't, sending you Triad money. Then you got some little gook kickin' you in the head."

"Or . . . ." Hooper said. They looked at one another like an old married couple and grinned happily. "Or," Cooper continued, "you got a vivid imagination and a lot of things you want covered up."

There was nothing to say. I'd sat in his place enough times, next to a partner who had heard all the pathetic lies with me a thousand times and we had laughed and looked for the obvious answers, the ones that are almost always right. There's an old saying that some doctor dreamed up, talking of diagnosis but applying equally to crime: When you hear hoofbeats, think horses, not zebras. These men were thinking that way, and that meant that I was due to end the evening in a cell at headquarters. It was the only answer that fit all the facts they had.

The lights were out at Louise's house. The two detectives came out with me quietly. There had no mention made to me but I guessed they had a search warrant. I hoped they wouldn't execute it. I didn't want Louise's kids woken up and frightened.

And that was what reminded me of my previous fears. I had put them out of my mind once Sam was in charge. If anyone came into the house he would be pinned to the floor. I didn't think a kung fu background would help against Sam. He was quicker than any man he'd ever been up against. And besides, if there was a fight, surely Louise would call the police station right away.

If I had been alone I would have walked the perimeter of the house before going in, but with the two detectives along I just unlocked the front door and switched on the light.

In a low voice I called, "Sam!" and from the back hallway I heard his savage working growl.

"My dog's pinning somebody," I said quietly. "There's no tricks, I have to walk through and see what's happening."

I sensed the detectives glancing at one another but didn't turn back. I went carefully through the door that led to the basement. Sam was on guard, standing over a man who was lying face up on the short stairway, his eyes bulging with fear and congestion from being kept with his head lower than his feet for a long time. The detectives came and stood at the doorway, gazing down at the man for about fifteen seconds before Hooper asked, "This the same Chinaman who jumped you at Caporetto's place?"

# 15

I told Sam, "Easy," and he sat back on his haunches, beside the man's feet. "He's yours," I told the detectives.

Hooper walked down the stairs past the man, looking down at him as a civilian might look at an accident victim. When he was four steps below him he said, "Okay, on your feet and against the wall."

The man didn't move, just rolled his eyes first at Sam, then at me. I motioned to him with one hand, hooking him up. He stood, carefully. I took a step back, making it look casual, but making sure to be out of range of those hands and feet. I was still shaken from the blow I'd taken earlier. I noticed that Cooper had his hand under his suitcoat, at the back of his belt, on his gun I judged. He was being careful, too.

Hooper said, "Hands on the wall, feet well back," but the prisoner didn't respond, just glanced at Hooper as if he wondered where the noise was coming from.

"Sonofabitch don't speak English," his partner said. They stared at one another in growing wonder. "Hey, Bennett, show him what to do," he told me.

I did it, carefully not making the mistake of letting them know I spoke a few words of Mandarin. I knew that if I as much as ordered Chinese food for the next month I'd be linked to this case inextricably.

Keeping Sam between us, I pressed both hands on the wall and gestured with my head for the prisoner to do the same. He did. I shuffled my feet back until I could barely support my weight and gestured again. This time he was very slow to move. He had been counting on breaking away but could see the limitations of the posture. I straightened up and wagged my finger at him until he did what we wanted. I wasn't happy about his position. Because he was standing on stairs, his uphill leg was bent. If he were as good as the man who had jumped me at Tony's place he could bound up from that leg like a jack-in-the-box. "I wouldn't trust him, he looks a lot like the guy who hit me," I warned.

Cooper was ready for him. He came down the stairs, squeezing past me and Sam and stood his full weight on the toes of the man's uphill foot. I saw the little man flinch in surprise but he did not cry out. Then Hooper came up the stairs the other way and snapped the handcuffs on his left wrist, then pulled him upright and neatly snagged the other arm behind him.

"Okay, Coop, you can leggo o' that foot now," he said amiably.

Cooper stood back and his partner gave the prisoner a little shove up the steps. I turned and went ahead of them, stooping slightly so that I could rub Sam's neck as I told him what a good dog he was. I didn't let myself think what might have happened if I hadn't left him here tonight.

The detectives didn't say anything but I could tell they were no longer interested in me as a prime suspect. It would have been possible, I guess, for me to have set up this whole thing as a charade to prove my innocence. But policemen know that people don't play clever tricks like that. Most of the lying and cheating is done after the fact and is clumsier than this.

So we had a quiet little talk in Louise's front parlor. I brought out the envelope and note I'd been sent. They took it, giving me a receipt. And then came the hard decision for me to make, whether or not to lie.

"Is this the guy who clobbered you in that apartment?" Cooper was patient but insistent. "I know they all look alike to most guys, but you were in the East, you should know."

I struggled with the urge to lie. The prisoner had said nothing, done nothing, simply stood as if rooted to the spot. He might not be the man who had jumped me, but I know the Bail Reform Act. If I didn't say he was, he would be charged with Break and Enter and would be sprung before the arrest report had been typed. He could return, this time not trying to get into the house. Instead he might just toss a Molotov cocktail at the front door.

"He could be the other guy's brother," I said. They were both too experienced to buy that and I didn't bother trying any harder. "The clothes are wrong. The one who hit me was wearing a dark double-breasted suit. It's unlikely he's been home and changed before he came here."

Cooper picked up a pear from the bowl of fruit Lou keeps on the side table. He went to bite it, then turned to me and held it up as if asking permission. I waved and he bit the end off, sensuously. "I know what's on your mind. Him or his friends may be back to carry on where he left off. Right?"

"That's what I'm thinking," I said quietly. "My sister and her kids live here."

"Yeah, well, of course, we won't be able to get him bail overnight because he doesn't understand English and he wouldn't know about showing up for his court appearance." Cooper took another bite of the pear, filling his whole mouth, talking around the edges of his pleasure.

"Yeah, so we'll keep him in until morning, when we can get the interpreter in to see him. Meantime, I'll get the scout cars to come by here and keep an eye on things. And you can stay."

It was the line I'd been waiting for. I nodded acceptance, as if giving them credit for seeing the light at last. "Good. I guess they're awake upstairs now, I'll go up and tell them not to worry, I'm staying here."

Hooper waved his forefinger at me. "You're free, but you're not clear. Don't leave town, we'll be in touch again before this thing is sorted out."

I thanked him and then took Sam outside as we showed them to the car, the prisoner walking awkwardly between them, paying no attention to anyone. They put him in the back, face down on the seat and got into the car, closing the doors quietly. "Don't leave town," Hooper told me, mock-serious, and wagged a finger as he drove off.

I took Sam around the house, telling him, "Seek." He ran through the alley, probing under the verandah, checking the garbage cans, but he found nobody. "Good boy," I told him and headed back inside. It was obvious where the man had entered. Louise had a clothes dryer in the basement. The vent went out through the glass of one of the windows. He had removed the outside cap, shoved the pipe away from the window inside, then reached down to open it. I was very thoughtful as I ordered Sam through the house, making sure that there was no more problem. Not for the first time since leaving Murphy's Harbour, I wished for the comforting weight of my gun. I'm a Marine Corps style scrapper and know lots of tricks you don't learn in the Boy Scouts, but up against a qualified kung fu exponent, I was next to useless.

Louise had come downstairs while I was in the basement. She had plugged in the kettle and was standing, not watching it, pretending that she wasn't scared. "What happened here?" she asked quietly.

"We had a prowler. Sam pinned him and the detectives came and locked him up." I tried to make light of it but couldn't. This was her house not mine. I had no right to bring her or the kids into any kind of danger. "I'm sorry, Lou. If I'd known the case would have blown up into this type of situation, I'd have stayed in a motel."

She looked at me, the way our mother used to. "Is it all over now, was that the only person involved?"

I shook my head. "I don't think it was. I think you and the kids should leave here for a few days, until this business has settled down."

"Oh, great." She reached for the tea caddy and pulled out a couple of tea bags. "That's just peachy. You come visiting for a couple of days and the next thing I know we've got men breaking into the house, presumably to get even with you." She stood very straight and tall, proud as a lioness defending her cubs. "How do I know this is going to end here? How do I know these people won't come back after you've gone home?"

She hadn't raised her voice, but her questions were all the more worrying for being pitched in such a reasonable tone.

I tried to soothe her. "Look, we've got the guy in custody. In the morning the detectives will talk to him, through an interpreter. They'll find out who sent him and this whole thing will be over." It wouldn't be that simple, even if we could keep the guy in custody long enough to give it a whirl; I knew that but I lied. I was sick with worry about Lou and her kids and I didn't want it to show.

She wasn't convinced, but she's not a person who worries

over nothing. She did what our mother would have done in a time of crisis. She made tea and we sat and talked about it. First of all she threw cold water on the idea that there were Chinese people involved. "I've heard you say yourself, when you worked in Toronto, the Chinese people are the most law-abiding in the country. Now you're suggesting they're trying to attack me because they're mad at you. It makes no sense." Her voice was calm but her eyes were cold blue sparks.

I tried to soothe her. "I know what I've told you. And it's true. The Canadian Chinese population has always been great. Look at Mr. Luck, the guy who ran the restaurant in Coppercliff. His eldest son is a doctor, his daughter is a dentist, his other son is over at IBM showing them how to build computers. They're the typical people we're used to here. They work hard and they succeed and they're honest as the day is long."

"Exactly," Louise said. She shrugged deeper into her soft housecoat. It wasn't cold and I could see she was afraid, looking for reassurance wherever she could get it.

"Yes, exactly," I agreed. "But funny things are happening these days. The makeup of the Chinese population is changing. There's a whole bunch of newcomers from Hong Kong. And it's already been shown that there's a fair proportion of grifters among them. You read the newspapers. What about that guy found with his throat cut in Chinatown, that big square down on Spadina Avenue. The murderer was never caught. And you've heard the same whispers everybody's heard, about enforcement things going down in the Chinese population. Times have changed, and the losers are the majority of Chinese people, the good ones."

She looked at me soberly and set down her teacup. "You think you can put a stop to this business?" I nodded and she went on, looking for the definite answer. "You can do it before you head back up north?"

I nodded again. If it became necessary I would quit at the Harbour and stay with her and the children until this business was ended. "I promise," I told her.

"Okay then," she said softly. "We'll do what you ask."

We talked about that while we drank tea. The children would stay with their father and his girlfriend. She was doing her best to be nice to them, hoping to get the guy to marry her. The kids had been over there before. Louise would stay with a girlfriend from the advertising agency. I would stay here with Sam to help keep the house safe, and I would carry on with the investigation until we had wrapped the case up.

"Some crummy line of work you picked for yourself, big brother," she said.

"I know. But somebody's got to do it and I'm not much good at anything else."

She smiled a tight little smile and said, "Okay. Just make sure to water the begonias for me." Then she walked away without looking back.

I set Sam to guard the downstairs and went on up to the landing above. There I sat with my back to the wall and my legs along the top step and slept until first light. Nobody disturbed me.

I went to bed before anyone else was awake and got up when I heard Louise moving. Sam was on guard downstairs but nobody else had attempted to come in. I took him outside for a quick check around the yard, then spent a few minutes roughhousing with him, putting him through his attack paces a couple of times to make sure he remembered all I'd taught him.

He had, and I took him back into the house for breakfast, scratching behind his torn ear, the memento of his biggest-ever battle.

At eight o'clock I phoned Fullwell and gave him all the news. He was beat but insisted on coming up to talk things over. It didn't take long. The police had all the information I had. They had warned me to wait in town. Bonded Security had warned me not to work on the case any more. "The only think you can do and stay legal is watch game shows on TV," Fullwell said.

"Except for one thing. That Chinese guy will be in court. It might be interesting to see what happens there, who comes to bail him out." I stood up and grabbed my windbreaker. "You go home and sleep. I'll check the court."

# 16

I left Sam on duty and drove to the old City Hall. It has twenty-six courts, most of them dealing with city and provincial offenses, the petty stuff that makes money for most cities and helps make policemen so unpopular: parking, speeding, drinking infractions, everything except federal offenses. They're handled out of court twenty-six, so I went straight to it and checked the calendar. There was a Yin Chang on it. Bingo!

They don't list the offenses any more, but Chinese people don't get into trouble often enough for this to be a different man. I peeked inside but he wasn't there. Only the bit players, witnesses, families, and weary policemen were sitting in court. The accuseds were either on bail, stretching their legs in the last moments of sure freedom, or standing in the bullpen below the court, waiting to be brought out when their name was called. I didn't wait. Instead, to fill the last few minutes I went down and got a cup of the lousy coffee they sell at the stand inside the back door. It tasted like old times, not good, just old times.

An elderly sergeant was on duty in the court and when he came out to shut the door I squeezed by him and sat at the back of the room. Three lawyers were sitting at the table in front of the magistrate. I didn't recognize any of them. We rose for the magistrate and sat while a number of remands were arranged. Two of the lawyers left after this and the hearings began. It was the same old snake dance I'd attended so many times, high drama for the people charged, boring to the police and legal staff.

And then they called Yin Chang. He was brought up the stairs under the courtroom from the bullpen below. I got a good look at him. In daylight he did not seem very menacing. Not to the average North American, anyway. We equate menace with size and demeanor. This skinny little immigrant in his shiny suit and the soiled white shirt looked harmless as a flea.

The Crown Attorney asked for a remand, on the grounds that the arresting officers were in High Court on a homicide trial. That might have impressed some magistrates. This one only sniffed and asked about bail for the accused. I was hoping that the homicide men had informed the Crown of the facts but they hadn't. He commented that it seemed like a fairly minor episode. The householder had found him cowering in fear from the family dog. Everybody laughed, except me. I was wondering why nobody was making a proper presentation to the court, giving an idea of why the man was inside. Then I wised up. The homicide guys had guessed I would be in court. They were giving me the opportunity to do some of their work for them by following Chang for the rest of the day. This evening they would drop by my place and pick my brains, taking the precaution of warning me I had been a bad boy to follow up, that this was not my bailiwick. Like hell it wasn't.

The magistrate and Crown agreed on bail of two thousand dollars, a fair sum given the Crown's view of the case. If the man was a vagrant, he would have to stay inside, if he wasn't, he would be able to find the money somewhere.

The interpreter was called. He explained it all to Chang who stood without moving or speaking. Then, just as they were about to send him back down the stairs to the holding pen, a young woman stood up in the front of the court. "I would like to pay the money," she said, and although I could not see her face, every hair on my head tingled. It was Cy Straight's secretary.

In a tiny voice she asked where she could pay the bail. They told her and she turned away, heading for the door and the bail office. I got up and followed, not making it obvious, waiting until she was out of the door of the courtroom before I left. I caught up with her as she clip-clopped over the old stone tiles. "Hi," I breezed. "Fancy meeting you here."

She turned, saw me and looked away again, quickening her pace as if she could shake me off. I walked alongside her. "Hi, remember me, Reid Bennett, we met yesterday?"

She stopped now and smiled an apologetic smile, as formalized as a boxer's handshake. "Of course. Pardon me. I was rushing."

"To the bail office to spring Yin Chang," I said, smiling just as wide. Anybody looking at us would have assumed we were sharing some joke and that she was waiting for me to deliver the punchline.

Her smile grew fixed but did not leave her face. "You were in the courtroom?"

"It was only fair," I said. "He was in my house last night."

Her smile flickered as a light bulb does when the current cuts in and out. A Caucasian girl would have gasped. "That's just an allegation," she said slowly.

"To the court, maybe. Not to me. It was my house and it was my police dog who pinned him. So I've got a special interest in the case. I wondered who retained Mr. Straight to spring him."

Now her smile grew wider, more natural. "Oh, but you know I can't tell you that. That is a legal confidence."

"It's a legal coincidence too." I beamed. People passing would never have sensed the tension that was building between us like lightning waiting to strike. "I came to see Mr. Straight because of his connection with some other bad people. Next thing I know my house is raided and Mr. Straight is paying the bail of the guy who did it."

"He is a lawyer. He has many clients. Not all of them are ethical." She allowed the smile to fade down to a polite creasing of the cheeks. I was starting to become a pain. Any ideas I might have harbored of getting to know her better were out the window. This was turning into a freeze.

"Then I will have to go and sit in his office all day again, all night if necessary, and ask him why he has such bad clients, and why he is so quick to come down and bail them out."

"He will have you thrown out of his office," she said.

"What makes you so confident?"

She turned and began walking again, towards the bail office. "He told me, never to allow you to see him again."

"Just like that? How often does he lay down those kinds of rules?" I was still smiling, though my jaw was aching with the effort. "And what prompted him to say it? I guess he just walked in this morning and said, 'Don't let that man in again,' and you didn't say 'which man' because you knew intuitively that he meant me."

"He told me last night," she said angrily. And the words stopped me like a bullet.

"How?" I asked. "You left the office with me, and he was heading out of town. How did he tell you anything?"

She stopped now and turned to face me. "You are causing me a great deal of irritation, Mr. Bennett. If you don't leave me alone, I'm going to call a policeman."

"I'll head back and wait at your office, then," I said. This was the one building in town where it would not do to get into a shouting match with anybody. Besides, I really wanted to get back in front of Straight. He had to be the missing link between the broken heads at Bonded Security and the money that came to me at home, and the death of Tony. A couple of questions was all I wanted to ask him.

And then the most curious event of the whole night and day happened. The girl stopped walking away and turned back to me, even walking a half step my way. "I must ask you very politely not to do that," she said.

I nodded, a reasonable man, ready to do anything that made sense. "Can I ask you why not?"

She took another half step towards me and the brightness in the corners of her eyes washed away any professionalism I had. "Because this man Yin Chang is not my employer's client. He's my brother."

# 17

I said nothing for about fifteen seconds. Then I said softly, "I'm sorry that your brother has brought you this shame." She nodded but didn't speak. She was a Western girl, but six thousand years of Chinese upbringing don't disappear in one lifetime. She had already lost all the face she could spare and she was resenting my knowing and my presence both. I didn't think I could make any amends for it but I wanted to try. It was my best chance for getting a word in private with Yin Chang. Maybe he could shed some light on what was going on, but I would have to get on her good side first.

Then she said, "Mr. Bennett, you must excuse me. I have to go and pay the money."

"When you do, he is your responsibility. If somebody makes him do something bad and he doesn't come back to court, you will lose your two thousand dollars."

"I work for a lawyer, thank you. I understand simple points of law just as well as any policeman," she said, icily.

"I appreciate that. And I appreciate your feelings about my staying here. But I have to ask you to let me speak to your brother. Once I find who sent him to my house in the night I will be able to help him stay out of prison for good."

She looked at me expressionlessly and I waited. She was within her rights to tell me to go to hell. If she did I was in for a long, boring day outside her house, watching to see where her brother went. But if she decided she owed me, perhaps for my confidences the day before, perhaps out of shame and protectiveness for her brother, I might be lucky.

"Wait here," she said at last. "I will bring him here and tell him you wish to speak to him."

"Thank you."

She walked away briskly and I stood against the wall, trying to be invisible and scratching my head about what was going on. If Yin Chang was her brother—and they had the same surname, so it was a possibility, although I hear there are only a hundred names in the whole of China—then how come he spoke no English while she sounded like a Canadian-raised girl? I didn't have an answer for that one. I figured maybe she had been sent out from Hong Kong earlier, perhaps to go to one of the visa schools here. But her English and her Western manners were so deep that I couldn't imagine she had picked them up in a few years. No, it was a puzzle. And I thought about her brother. There was always the chance that he would cut and run if he saw me. I guessed that if she was going to keep her promise she would not tell him I was here.

And as I waited, I thought about the night before. These

Chinese were too good for me. If her brother was as fast as the guy who had fought me in Tony's apartment, I had no chance of besting him if he chose to get ugly. I would need an advantage, something to buy time. It would have been better if I could have been carrying my .38 Colt but it was two hundred miles away and I was not licensed to have it in Toronto anyway. Besides, if I had to kill a man who was a foot shorter than me and fifty pounds lighter, I'd end up in the penitentiary for sure. So after a minute's thought I went back down to the cigar store at the back door and made an innocent little two-buck purchase.

I was back in my place, half sitting on one of the old hot water radiators against the wall when she returned with Yin Chang. He saw me and did a doubletake but she said something very quiet. He ripped back at her, loud enough for me to hear but too fast for my meager knowledge of Mandarin to keep up. I beamed at him and ambled towards him, losing the required amount of face by making the first move. I figured that if I sat on the radiator and waited he would never swallow enough pride to take the ten steps on his own. "Hello," I said and then, "Nee jeng ying wen ma?" which means "Do you speak English?"

He and Su were both suitably startled but she answered for him. "We speak Cantonese, not Mandarin and Chang has no English."

"Perhaps your brother would permit you to interpret for me," I suggested. Butter would not have melted in my mouth but I could feel his hostility coming off him like the smell of sweat. She spoke quickly and he made a brief answer.

"Chang says he will talk to you," she said simply.

"Thank you. Tell him, please, that I bear him no ill will for coming to my house. He was doing a job of work."

That did not convince him but it sat well and he spoke a little less harshly to her. I continued, "I am a policeman and yesterday a friend of mine was killed by someone who knows kung fu. I saw the man who did it and know it was not Chang."

She rattled, he listened, then looked at me, without words.

"Tell him that the police detectives who took him away last night have set men to follow him all day. They want him to lead them to his friends. Then they will arrest his friends."

This wasn't even close to the truth but it sounded plausible and it put a whole bunch of pressure on his narrow little shoulders. He listened and said nothing but he looked at me with new interest. Su tried again to make him respond but he cut her off with a word and she said, "He understands."

"So, to spare him the shame of bringing dishonor on his friends, I will get him out of here without being seen and will take him to a place where he can hide until dark."

This time he answered at length. "He says to ask you why you would do this thing for him?"

This was the test and I took it slowly. "I do it because I once had a Chinese wife. I have great affection for the Chinese."

Su looked at me keenly as she spoke out of the corner of her mouth to her brother. As I listened I silently begged Li's pardon. We had never been even close to marriage, but she had changed my life more permanently than any piece of paper could have done.

Chang said nothing and I added the last piece of the speech, the payoff for me. "Also I do not believe that any Chinese sent a man to harm a woman and children. I believe he was sent by an evil Kwailo. If I can find that Kwailo's name I will go and punish him, man to man."

Let's hear it for six thousand years of culture. I bowed like a Mandarin and waited, watching his face as Su seesawed through the syllables. Her own face was a study. She was trying to be impassive but the animation of her speech made it difficult and I could read the tension in her eyes in case he were to name her employer.

For a long moment he said nothing. She began to repeat herself and he cut her off with an impatient gesture. I've been in enough interrogations to recognize what was happening. He was ready to talk. And then, of all the damnfool crazy bad luck I heard a hearty voice shouting across the hallway. "Hey, Reid, how are you?"

I tried to ignore it. All I needed was one minute. Nothing else mattered to me except finding out who was behind this. But there was no avoiding this man. It was Willis from

Bonded, with Fullwell, and they were heading straight for me like a couple of overfriendly drunks at a convention.

Yin Chang shut up like a door. Su glanced at me and at the men in distrust. I swore under my breath. "I'm sorry, Su, these men are people I used to work with." I held up one hand to the security men and they both paused, ten feet away. Digging into my windbreaker pocket I found a ballpoint and a piece of paper and scribbled Louise's phone number on it. "Please, call me later. Even if your brother is not with you. I must talk to you."

Fullwell spoke first. "Sorry to interrupt like this but I've been looking all over for you. Had to ring your sister at work to find out where you were." He paused and turned to nod and smile courteously to the two Chinese. Su smiled back and she and her brother turned and walked away.

"What was that all about?" Willis asked casually. "Got a taste for that yellow meat have you?"

"What was so important?" I asked Fullwell. He was looking embarrassed about Willis, the way a child would be embarrassed if his mother said something outrageous to a schoolmate. My question did nothing to set him at ease.

"It's Thomason, our company president," he said awkwardly. "He's pretty exercised about our going behind his back yesterday and going to see Cy Straight. He sent me to warn you off, completely."

I said nothing and he waved one hand, embarrassed. "I'm sorry, that came out kind of clumsy."

"That's not what bothers me," I said. "I was just wondering who in hell told Cy Straight where I came from."

We stood and looked at one another like the three wise men outside the stable door. Willis spoke first. "I never even thought to ask him." He laughed, a short snarl of a sound. "Not that there was any damn talkin' to the guy. He wants your ass, buddy."

"He's free and clear of me," I said. "But as of last night when a hood turned up at my house, this isn't his case any more, it's mine."

I turned and saw Su and her brother going side by side down the wide steps to the big front doors of the building. I was angry to have missed my chance to talk to Chang but it made no sense to follow them. For one thing they were probably going to take the subway, which meant I would stand out like a totem pole if I tried to tag along, and for another thing, I had built up about two cents' worth of trust between us and didn't want to lose it by acting like a flatfoot.

"So what was Thomason's message?" I forced myself to attend to the two men.

"Quite short and not sweet," Willis said. "He says you are not in any way connected with Bonded Security. If you attempt to visit any of our locations or to use us in any kind of excuse for anything at all, he's going to have you arrested for impersonating a company employee."

I snorted. "Then I'll get three slaps with a wet noodle and we all go home. What is it with that guy? Doesn't he know any law at all?"

Fullwell ducked his head, awkwardly. "I know, Reid, the guy's a moron. The only thing is, he's put the responsibility on me. If you don't lay off, he's going to fire me."

# 18

WHAT I felt like doing was sitting somewhere and having too much beer. But the bars don't open in Toronto before eleven and I was too long off the force to know where there was a friendly bootlegger to visit. Instead I went back to Lou's house, stopping on the way home to buy a bottle of Black Velvet and a case of Labatt's Classic. I'm not normally a solitary drinker but I had some thinking to do. I invited Fullwell to come with me but he was stuck with Willis and there was no way I was pouring booze into that oaf, so an hour later I was sitting in Louise's living room moodily finishing a beer and wondering what to do next. It would be easy to pull my horns in and head out of town, but I couldn't leave without making certain that the threat to Lou and her children left with me. And I wasn't sure how I could guarantee that would happen. What's more, I was running out of places to look for answers.

In the meantime, I gave up on drinking and made myself a sandwich. I was about to eat when the phone rang. I picked it up not knowing what to expect. This was still a surprise.

Her voice was soft as wind chimes. "Hello Reid. This is Yin Su. I was wondering if you could spare the time to come and see me."

Spare the time? Would eleven days be long enough? I wondered. "I'd like that very much. Would you like to meet for lunch somewhere?" I was glad I'd only had a couple of those beers. And her call had killed any interest I had in solving the case. Bonded could take care of it themselves. I would sooner spend time with Su.

"I have told Mr. Straight I will be at home," she said. "If it's not too much trouble, perhaps you could come over here."

"Fine, where do you live?"

She told me, and added, "Please hurry. I will be waiting." I hung up the phone and shook my head in wonder. She didn't sound like the same girl I'd spoken to an hour earlier. Maybe it was having sprung her brother but the tension had gone right out of her voice. She sounded appealing. And girls as beautiful as she don't have to go out of their way to appeal.

I felt like running out and jumping into the car. Maybe her brother would be there, maybe not. I didn't care. This was becoming personal. But, pleased as I was, I have been a copper and under fire enough times to be careful. I spent a few minutes making sure that nobody would surprise me while I was away. I opened all the doors downstairs and gave Sam the run of the place, telling him to guard it. Then I cleaned my teeth and checked my shave and went out to the car.

I was full of different emotions. This was not Soon Li I was going to meet. There was no logical reason to be pushing the speed limit, anxious for a sight of that exotic face of hers. She was a witness to an aspect of a criminal investigation, and I was a copper looking for guidance. I knew that, but all the same I had to convince myself not to stop the car at the corner of Eglinton and Yonge, where the hippie girl with the long skirt sells the rosebuds. I decided against it. She was smart enough to recognize the impact she had made on me. And I wasn't really sure that her brother wouldn't be waiting behind the door. I'd need something more substantial than a posy if he was.

She lived in one of those classy older apartments on a side street, the kind they would have used as a setting for the car in a Pierce Arrow advertisement. It had art deco numerals and a driveway barely big enough to wheel a bicycle through. I parked on the street, noting that the green hornet had made his rounds earlier, tagging the entire block. If I was lucky I'd make it without owing the city five dollars.

When I found her number on the directory and rang the buzzer she answered, "Who is it?" in an attractive upward lilt that reassured me this wasn't an ambush. I went in and rode up to the fourth floor. She had opened the door and was waiting for me, cradling a bluepoint Siamese cat in her arms.

She might have chosen the cat as a contrast to the pale blue silk cheongsam she wore. It flattered her and made all the compensation she needed for being small in the breast. She looked good enough to nibble.

I said, "Hello, thank you for asking me over."

She ushered me in, backing a pace to make room. I took a microsecond to glance through the crack of the door. There was nobody behind it. "My brother would not stay," she said.

I digested that while I looked around the apartment. It was sparely furnished with lean-looking chairs and a table that had not come from any of the city's bargain stores. The wallpaper was Oriental grasscloth and the few pictures were delicately drawn Chinese flowers and mountain scenes.

"You have a lovely home," I told her, and wondered where the hell her low-life brother had gone.

She nodded graciously and poured the cat down into a chair.

"Thank you. Some of my friends think it a bit too ethnic."

She played the word like a trump card and we both laughed.

I glanced around. "You brother doesn't live with you?"

"No." She shook her head vigorously. "I don't think we are, what's the word? compatible. Not since he grew up. Would you like some tea?"

"That would be great." I stood up as she moved to the kitchen and went with her. I have been in too many booby-trapped places to relax until I've scouted the ground. And I knew what kind of person her brother was.

She sensed what I was doing. "I assure you, Chang has gone," she said and smiled awkwardly.

I shrugged. "No matter. I'm glad of the chance to talk to you. Your brother isn't important." Nor would he be, unless he came whirling out of one of the back rooms, swinging a cleaver.

Then I relaxed and watched her as she prepared tea, moving with the same grace that had delighted me in Li. She filled the kettle and brought out a tiny pale blue porcelain teapot with a handle held on with raffia. She put a few pinches of green tea into it and turned to face me.

"The reason I called you was to talk about him," she said. She was standing foursquare and it seemed to me there was an unusual toughness in her face. I wasn't sure if she had hardened herself to discuss her brother, or just to keep me at arm's length.

"What did you want to discuss?" I tried to keep my voice conversational. We weren't talking about the angry little punk she had sprung that morning. We were talking brothers, period. No harm in that.

"He wouldn't tell me what he had done," she said. The kettle began to steam and she turned the gas off with a faint pop. "I wondered why he would do anything so bad as breaking and entering. Nobody in my family has ever been arrested before. But he wouldn't tell me. He said that I was a woman and he was a man and I had no right to ask him any questions."

"A whole lot of men feel that way, not just your brother," I assured her. "I guess it's worse in the Orient than it is here but it's a common enough answer."

She poured the water into the pot. "That is not an answer, Reid." Her accent whispered on the edge of the R sound, almost transmuting it into an L.

"You didn't ask a question," I said, just as softly.

She put the teapot and two little handleless cups on a

tray and picked it up. "Now you are being evasive," she told me, firmly. "I wanted to know what he had done at your house."

I told her. She stood there with the tray in her hands, looking into my eyes. Then she nodded and ushered me through to the sitting room, pointing the way with her chin.

"Do you know where he works? Who his friends are? Where he lives, anything about him except that he's your brother?" They were hard questions but I had no way to make them soft for her.

She set the tray down on a low bamboo table. "I do not know much about him. He works for an importer."

"What's the company name?" I asked.

She paused, her hand halfway to the teapot. "Is this an interrogation?" she asked politely.

"Forgive me. It's a long time since I had tea with a girl. I've forgotten my manners." I sat back and said nothing and after a pause she poured tea for both of us. I took it and said "Daw jeh," and she laughed with delight.

"I thought you spoke Mandarin," she said.

"I'm a man of many surprises." I didn't bother to explain that I had learned the Cantonese for "Thank you" while eating a fried egg sandwich in the back of the Jade Pagoda in Murphy's Harbour. I could also say "Please" and had made Chong's wife collapse in helpless laughter by asking for a translation of "You are very beautiful." Aside from that I knew nothing that wasn't on the menu.

Su didn't follow it up anyway. Her mind was too much on her brother. She sipped her tea and said, "I do not know the importer's name. He has never told me. He doesn't tell me anything unless he has to."

I started to probe, more gently. "Is there any way I could help?"

She looked up, then down at her teacup, demure as one of the painted figures on the wall behind her. "You would help me?"

"I would try." I knew enough about Oriental etiquette to leave it at that. I must give her no reasons, pay her no compliments. The whole business had to be dispassionate, no trouble to me, no value to her, otherwise she would be indebted and that would make the situation untenable.

She was more Western than Li might have been. She

looked me straight in the face and said, "That would be very kind of you."

"Pleasure." I waved a hand. If I was going to be doing any favors for her, it was good that they would bring me closer to this case. I might find out who was behind it all and celebrate its end back here when all the shouting and chasing and locking up were over.

"I only know that he has a friend who works in a restaurant on Dundas Street," she said.

"Didn't he tell you anything more? The friend's name? The name of the restaurant?" Interest in the case was taking over again. I guess I'm a better cop than I am a ladies' man.

She spoke quietly, not looking at me. "His friend is called Wing Lok. He works at the Palace Gates." Her voice sank to a whisper. "I don't think this friend is good for him. He loves to gamble."

I didn't call that a hot newsflash. All the Chinese men I've ever met, in Canada, or Saigon, or Hong Kong where I spent some R and R time from Nam, they lived for their gambling. It made their eighteen-hour workdays more bearable.

"I'll go and talk to this Wing Lok and find out what I can about your brother." I would try anyway, if he spoke any English; it would be good to get an understanding of the nasty little hood Su's brother seemed to be. It might just open up the whole case and then I could finish with it and devote the rest of my time to calling around here.

Su was seated across the table from me and she put her cup down and looked at me, her eyes spilling over with gratitude. I stood up and set down the tiny cup. "No time like now," I said. She got to her feet, the cheongsam opening gracefully to the thigh. She had good legs, I noticed, without even realizing I had looked. And she was tall for a Chinese girl, perhaps five-three, her forehead reached my chin. On impulse I stooped and brushed her hair with my lips. And of all impossible imaginings she tilted her face to me, eyes closed, lips moist and I bent further and kissed her mouth.

I don't know what I expected, perhaps the dry scared kiss of a high school girl on a first date. I knew that she would not have the same intensity of emotion that Westerners did when they kissed. She was different, exotic, shy, scared, whatever. But when our lips met, I melted.

My arms went around the smoothness of her shoulders and I held her close, lifting her to tiptoe height as we clung together. And when our mouths at last parted, she did not open her eyes. You can tell me it was wrong, it was too soon after meeting, that our coming together had been full of too many old memories. I knew all that but I was disarmed entirely. I kissed her again, holding her to me until she opened her eyes and said, "I think you are a bad man, Reid Bennett," and giggled.

"What can I say?" I tried to chuckle but my voice was harsh with longing. This was not just a woman, something to take into the bedroom and make love to, this was the reincarnation of all I had longed for when I still was young enough to be innocent.

"I do not think my brother is very important to you," she said, her words formal but her eyes dancing.

I crossed my heart with a quick sketchy flourish. "Believe me, Su, he's the second most important thought in my head right now," I said, trying not to match her chuckle.

She laughed out loud and stood at arm's length to look me up and down. "You are very bold," she said. "But I think I know what to do."

She turned, still holding my hand, and led me through to her bedroom. She had a queen-sized bed covered with a down quilt in some smooth fabric the color of her golden skin.

She stopped beside it and turned to look me in the eyes, seeking what? I didn't know. I was intoxicated by her nearness. I raised my free hand and stroked her cheek. She rolled her face towards my hand, pinning it softly against her shoulder. Then she pulled her hand free of mine and reached over her back to unfasten the top of her cheongsam.

We undressed, in pace with one another, not speaking. Her body was lithe and hard, reminding me almost unbearably of the beauty of Li but I pushed that memory out of my mind. This girl was living and strong and lovely and I had survived those old scars.

I lifted her in my arms, bending my neck to kiss her firm little breasts, feeling the nipples ripen under my lips. She groaned, so quietly it was almost an assault to have heard her, and softened in my arms so that I lowered her on to the bed like a bundle of clothing. I caressed her concave little belly, gently exploring further until she stiffened and clung to me and climaxed.

"Quickly. Now," she hissed and pulled me down on to her.

Afterwards we lay, looking at the ceiling. I was out of touch, remembering the straw thatch that covered the mat where Li and I had loved. "You are very quiet," she said gently.

"That's what beauty does to me," I said, rolling up on one elbow. I bent down and kissed her nose. "If you were ugly I'd be talking your head off now as I grabbed my clothes."

"I am not beautiful." She smiled a tiny smile. "I know what I see in the mirror. I have a Han face, like five hundred million other women."

"There is nobody in the whole world who looks like you," I promised her. "You're special." And then she kissed me and we were back where we started.

Later we showered together and then she made tea and finally we embraced one last, sated time and I left, feeling as if I had just been handed an Olympic gold.

# 19

THE Palace Gates was a middle-brow restaurant new enough to serve Szechuan cooking instead of the traditional Cantonese food that used to be the only game in town. It had a double frontage and about fifty tables inside. Most of them were empty at three in the afternoon, just a couple of kids who looked like students from the Ontario College of Art around the corner and a pair of good-looking matrons discussing plans for the Bar Mitzvah of one of their sons.

I seated myself in a corner, remembering the way I'd been outfought the night before. I didn't want efficient little warriors coming at me from behind if Wing Lok decided he didn't like the look of me.

The manager was a well-dressed man in his fifties. He was Chinese, of course, but close to six feet tall, which was rare, and dressed in a dove-gray three-piece suit. It was a little out of character for the quality of the restaurant and I wondered if he was one of the big wheels in Chinatown. I knew the Chinese had their own internal organization, as rigidly defined as the city council and mayor. I wasn't sure what the significance of the authority was, but it mattered enough for men like this to dress as if they worked the Stock Exchange instead of a restaurant.

He came across to wait on me personally so I guessed that most of the help would be off duty. Probably Wing Lok with them, but I would try to make sure. I ordered a beer and pretended to be looking at the menu while I waited for the manager to come back.

He brought it and beamed as if it was the most fun he had had all week. I smiled back and asked, "All alone today, no help?"

He smiled some more and allowed that there were very few people working, just the cooks preparing for the dinner rush.

"Is Wing Lok working?" I asked him politely. He did not quite start with surprise but I could tell it was unusual for a stranger to be looking for the help.

"Wing Lok is your friend?" The smile went on but I dropped mine now.

"Kind of," I said. "Is he here?"

The smile became even more urgent. "No. He not here until fi' o'clock." I wondered what made him so anxious. Had other foreigners been ahead of me asking for the kid? Was he the boy's father? What?

"Then I'd better wait." I said, "Maybe I could get something to eat, if the kitchen isn't closed."

"Of course." He handed me the menu but I just laid it in front of me on the table again.

"Have you seen him today?"

He was serious now. "Not today. He not in today. His day off until fi' o'clock."

"Yeah, well I have to see him. I'm with the government."
His concern increased and I guessed I'd hit a nerve.
Perhaps the boy was here illegally. There are around twenty
thousand visa students attending boarding schools in Toronto. The city is popular, especially with Hong Kong
Chinese. Most are legitimate but the occasional one gets in
as a student and goes underground. Mostly it means only
that they don't want to go home, they find opportunity in
some restaurant or laundry but some of them end up in
crime. At least, that's the word I heard once, when I
attended a Provincial meeting on law enforcement.

The boss was smiling again, trying to avert whatever evil
eye I represented. I put him at ease. "Not Immigration,
Revenue Canada, it's about his income tax."

The sun came out on the boss's face. Income tax was no
crime. He would pass my message. But I didn't let it ride
there. "Where could I find him? I'm supposed to be off duty
at four-thirty and I don't want to wait around after that."

He didn't know of course. Chances were that if the boy
was illegal he was living beneath our feet on a cot among
the supplies in the cellar, but this guy would never admit it.

I nodded, dropped money on the table for the untouched
beer and stood up. The boss nodded and smiled some more
but I didn't leave. Instead I walked over to the big double
doors leading out to the kitchen. There was a glass panel in
each one so the waiters could see who was coming the other
way. I glanced through. Inside was the standard steaming
monochromatic room, white walls and stainless steel tables
and the big black stovetop hot enough to turn water to
instant steam as the cook cleaned it.

There were four men there in addition to the cook. They
were younger, fit, talking together at a table in the back.
Two of them had tea, one had a bottle of Coke.

The boss called something but I ignored him, opening
the door and taking four strides towards the table before
speaking directly at the one with the Coke. "Wing Lok," I
said. "Remember me?"

He spun around and dropped into a kung fu crouch. The
others backed off, startled. The show of violence surprised
them as much as it worried me because I knew what he
could do. In that first instant of recognition I felt like the

dog who caught the car. This wasn't what I had planned. I'd wanted to find Su's brother, not go up against a guy who had bested me once. If I had recognized him earlier I would have called the police. The only way to take him out was to shoot him.

He had recognized me, too. As I watched, the confidence grew in his eyes. I was a pathetic Lofan, big and clumsy, the typical "backwards-man" that hostile Chinese people find so offensive and ridiculous. He was going to put me away, for keeps. And he could do it. I kept our eyes locked, waiting for the first flicker that would warn me he was coming. Out of the edge of my vision I noted that he had his hands clawed. He was a tiger style fighter and he could kill me with one hand if he chose to.

Slowly he advanced, along the edge of the long stove. The cook said something to him, but backed away, terrified. There was now nothing between us, no place for me to hide. The stove was on my right, a long countertop on my left. Instinctively I reached out, not looking, and picked up the first thing that came to hand. I heard it gurgle and flashed it a microsecond's worth of attention. It was a can of peanut oil, wide open at the top for easy pouring.

In the same second his crouch tightened and he began his stalking move towards me. Without waiting I hurled the oil at him, not in his face but in an arc that leaped from him to the stove. It erupted in flame and as he flinched I stepped in and kicked him. I didn't go for the groin. A trained man might have his testicles retracted safely into his abdomen, instead I hit him solidly in the only place that would stop him, under the kneecap.

He collapsed, blazing and screaming, holding both hands on his broken leg. The other men were all yelling. I looked around and found the fire extinguisher and played it, first on him, then the stove, then the walls. Then I upended it and hit him firmly on the collarbone with the canister.

I find Chinese ugly to listen to, and with five men screaming at once, the kitchen was bedlam. But they all stayed back, doing their best to keep furniture between themselves and me. I was afraid one of them would go for the meat cleaver, but nobody did. They were all law-abiding. I nodded to the cook and said, "Police. This man is wanted."

There was a phone on the wall and I punched 911 and told the dispatcher to get a police car over right away. I gave her my full pedigree, Reid Bennett, police chief Murphy's Harbour. It would cut down some of the dumb questions I'd be facing when the uniformed guys got here.

The divisional headquarters is about three hundred yards up the street and there were two cars at the door in thirty seconds. The uniformed men were first, then the detectives who had been in their office when my call came in.

The bluecoats were young and keen and anxious to make a name for themselves. I just flashed my Murphy's Harbour badge and told them I wanted the detectives. They came pounding in a moment later. I explained all that was necessary. "This man is wanted on suspicion of the homicide last night, Tony Caporetto. Please keep a close watch on him, he's a kung fu expert and can be dangerous. And notify homicide; they're looking for him."

Detectives never trust anybody's account of anything. These two were professionally cynical about what I'd been doing. One recognized me from my stint on the force but the other one was more excitable. I could see he was ready to investigate the whole case from scratch. I told him, "Later. First off, get this kid to hospital. I think his leg is broken."

"Did you do that?" he fussed. "That's wounding, I guess you know that."

"I'm not going anywhere, we can discuss this later," I told him. "Please do as I ask or else the supersnoopers are going to get very annoyed with you."

He opened his mouth to argue but the first one took over. "Sure thing, Chief. Do I need the cuffs on this guy?"

"Just watch him, he's seen too many of those chop suey movies."

Behind him, the boss was coming into the kitchen. He looked anxious; I guess he was wondering how I'd known he was lying about Wing Lok's not being there. I decided it was time to make myself a friend. "Thank you for your help, Mr. . . ." I let it dangle and he supplied the name eagerly, "Lee." I nodded and turned to the detectives, gravely. "Mr. Lee has been very helpful," I told them.

The younger one surprised me. He stood up and shook

Lee's hand as if this were some kind of award ceremony. "Thank you," he said politely. "We appreciate the help."

Lee was formal. "Any time, off'cer. Everybody should be good citizen."

I watched the whole charade carefully. It looked to me as if the police knew Lee. He was a wheel in Chinatown, somebody to treat with special respect. That was fine. But it didn't jibe with the fact that he employed grifters like Wing Lok. I wondered if they realized that, but I kept my questions to myself. At best they would make me look antisocial, and I didn't need policemen pegging me for a Neanderthal. So I said nothing and went with them to where my car was parked.

"I'll follow you to the hospital. Call homicide on the radio and tell them I'll be in emergency with this guy."

"Sure thing," the helpful one said, and this time his partner added a respectful, "Right, Chief."

# 20

THE homicide detectives took an hour to reach the hospital. In the meantime Wing Lok had been treated for a broken tibia and collarbone and was not likely to harm anybody new for a couple of months. I had also been treated to a torrent of verbal abuse from a large Jamaican nurse who had called the department to protest my brutality. On the face of it she was right, a six-foot-one storm trooper beating a defenseless little man. But she hadn't seen Lok kicking that coffee table out of my hands and knocking me colder than mutton with a casual backhand.

The supersnoopers looked in on him first, telling the uniformed man not to leave the room until relieved by another policeman, and then came to find me. There is nowhere private to chat in Emergency at Toronto General, casualties are coming and going all day and night. So they asked the sister if they could speak to me in the chapel. I guess she was a good Catholic, she gave permission as long as nobody used any bad language.

We sat down in two of the pews, the detectives behind me so that I had to turn to speak to them. They were both bushed. Cooper kept yawning. Homicide wears out policemen faster than any other duty.

"So what happened?" Hooper asked me. I told them, starting with my arrival at the Palace Gates.

"Like, you just happened to fancy some chow mein and picked the place where this guy works. Right?" Cooper said.

"I heard that he was a buddy of the guy who hit my house last night." This was the piece of information I had not wanted to part with, but there was no way around it.

"And who gave you the information?" Hooper asked. It seemed they slipped in and out of one another's line of thought as smoothly as a man and wife, there was never a duplication, never a pause.

"The kid himself. I was at court this morning and he was sprung on two grand bail."

"Yeah? Who sprung him?"

"A girl who works at a big law office down town. She's the secretary for a guy called Cy Straight. A lawyer."

"And she waltzed down there with two grand, just like that?" Hooper let his eyebrows climb towards his thinning hairline.

"I guess. She had him out of there in two minutes."

"And you went over to him and said, 'Hi, kid, no hard feelings about last night,' right?"

"Something like that."

Cooper choked off a yawn and said, "How come he understood what you were saying. Did he learn English since one A.M.?"

"The girl who came for him was Chinese. She interpreted for me."

"Kind of obliging, wasn't it?" Hooper was looking at me the way I've looked at a lot of suspects with a lot of shaky stories. I shrugged. "How else would I have ended up finding this guy?"

"Beats the hell outa me," Cooper said, then covered his mouth like a boy caught swearing. "Ooops, sorry, sister."

Hooper laughed, the genuine enjoyment of a partner's sense of humor, one of the bonuses that helps make detective work worthwhile.

He dropped the laugh and asked me, "So where was the other kid while you were putting the blocks to Bruce Lee? Didn't he try to get between you?"

"I was interrupted at the court house. He left after I'd spoken to him and the girl. I went to the Palace Gates on my own."

They bored on, taking me through all the obvious questions. Why hadn't I called them as soon as I knew the murder suspect might be found at the Palace Gates? Why did I wait until three-thirty to go over there? Why? Why? Why? All of the questions I would have asked in their place. Cooper summed it up at last.

"What it adds up to is this. You say this kid was at Caporetto's apartment last night. You say he clobbered you and took off. Now you say that a third party told you where to find him and you went over there without backup and kicked him around and brought him in."

He paused for a yawn and Hooper finished for him. "What it adds up to is you could be framing him for what you did last night. If you weren't a cop yourself we wouldn't listen to you for thirty seconds. Instead, we'd be charging you with assaulting the kid."

From the way he said it I knew they didn't intend to. It was still a test. They wanted more from me, had to have more, before they could take the case to court. But they were beginning to believe that I was telling the truth.

I shrugged. "It's what happened. I know it sounds crazy but the truth generally does. Surely you've fingerprinted the apartment. He opened the door for me, his prints are all over that inside doorknob."

"There were some unidentified prints on the doorknob, and on a lamp and a picture frame in the deceased's bedroom," Cooper said. "However, we don't know if they match the prints on young what's his name upstairs."

"They will, I'll bet you," I said triumphantly. "And, hey, while we're talking prints. Did you print that money I gave you?"

"Come on," Cooper said. "What the suffering Judas Priest are you smokin'? You know 's well's me that printing money is like tryin' to get prints off a whore's hind end."

"Very poetic," I said and we all laughed, and I relaxed a hairsbreadth, we were all policemen together. I was out from under the worst of their suspicions.

The same tough old sister looked in to tell the detectives that a gentleman was waiting to see them. They thanked her and we all trooped out, leaving her alone in the chapel. The gentleman was a small, neat Chinese, the interpreter from the courthouse. They thanked him for coming and led him away towards Wing's room, leaving me without looking back.

I guessed that meant I was free to go, so I left and walked back to my car. It was rush hour by now and University Avenue was chockful of northbound cars. I stood on the curb and envied them. They were all heading home to wives and kids and hot suppers. I was stranded, without even the leisure I would have found at Murphy's Harbour, no chance to take the canoe and try a few casts for pike along the reed beds on the point north of my house. I debated driving over to Louise's office and picking her up for a dinner out with her kids, but decided against it. My life was getting settled into its customary solitary state and that was healthier for her and the children.

I left the car parked and walked the four blocks to the Eaton Centre. It was full of people and that felt good to me. There's another English pub in the main concourse and I went in for a pint and a review of what to do next.

It seemed I had the choice of reporting back to Su and letting her know that the kid her brother ran around with was bad news, or of thinking of some new way of trying to find the string that tied the whole bundle together. I pondered how to do this over another pint and worked out that my only unfollowed lead was Bojangles at the race course. So I went down to the fast food area below and picked up a burger, then reclaimed my car and headed for the track.

It was early when I got there and only the diehards were present. I didn't see Bojangles right off, so just to kill time I picked up a form sheet and picked out a couple of bets. Neither one came in. I was about to quit when I caught

# Introducing the first and only complete hardcover collection of Agatha Christie's mysteries

Now you can enjoy the
greatest mysteries ever written
in a magnificent
Home Library Edition.

# Discover Agatha Christie's world of mystery, adventure and intrigue

Agatha Christie's timeless tales of mystery and suspense offer something for every reader—mystery fan or not—young and old alike. And now, you can build a complete hardcover library of her world-famous mysteries by subscribing to <u>The Agatha Christie Mystery Collection</u>.

This exciting Collection is your passport to a world where mystery reigns supreme. Volume after volume, you and your family will enjoy mystery reading at its very best.

You'll meet Agatha Christie's world-famous detectives like Hercule Poirot, Jane Marple, and the likeable Tommy and Tuppence Beresford.

In your readings, you'll visit Egypt, Paris, England and other exciting destinations where murder is always on the itinerary. And wherever you travel, you'll become deeply involved in some of the most ingenious and diabolical plots ever invented . . . "cliff-hangers" that only Dame Agatha could create!

It all adds up to mystery reading that's so good . . . it's almost criminal. And it's yours every month with <u>The Agatha Christie Mystery Collection</u>.

**Solve the greatest mysteries of all time.** The Collection contains all of Agatha Christie's classic works including *Murder on the Orient Express, Death on the Nile, And Then There Were None, The ABC Murders* and her ever-popular whodunit, *The Murder of Roger Ackroyd.*

Each handsome hardcover volume is Smythe sewn and printed on high quality acid-free paper so it can withstand even the most murderous treatment. Bound in Sussex-blue simulated leather with gold titling, <u>The Agatha Christie Mystery Collection</u> will make a tasteful addition to your living room, or den.

**Ride the Orient Express for 10 days without obligation.**
To introduce you to the Collection, we're inviting you to examine the classic mystery, *Murder on the Orient Express*, without risk or obligation. If you're not completely satisfied, just return it within 10 days and owe nothing.

However, if you're like the millions of other readers who love Agatha Christie's thrilling tales of mystery and suspense, keep *Murder on the Orient Express* and pay just $9.95 plus postage and handling.

You will then automatically receive future volumes once a month as they are published on a fully returnable, 10-day free-examination basis. No minimum purchase is required, and you may cancel your subscription at any time.

This unique collection is not sold in stores. It's available only through this special offer. So don't miss out, begin your subscription now. Just mail this card today.

# BUSINESS REPLY CARD

FIRST CLASS     PERMIT NO. 2154     HICKSVILLE, N.Y.

Postage will be paid by addressee:

The Agatha Christie
Mystery Collection
Bantam Books
P.O. Box 956
Hicksville, N.Y. 11802

sight of him, betting at the ten-dollar window. He didn't see me until I stepped from behind a pillar and said, "What happened to Baby Lou, Bo?"

He jumped around with a TV sized double take, put his hand on his heart and gasped. "Geez, Mr. Bennett, I bin lookin' all over for you. You won. Paid fourteen eighty."

"I hope you had a fin on it." I held out my hand and he counted out fifteen dollars from a healthy roll.

"I done more than that. I put the whole eight bucks down. Figured you had to know somebody. What're you doin' t'night?"

"Tonight I'm asking questions, Bo." I said. I detached the five dollars and pushed it into the top pocket of his ratty suitcoat. "One question, anyway. Ready?"

"Sure am. Waddya wanna know, Mr. Bennett?"

"Just one thing. Who gave you the message I should go over to Tony's house last night?"

He looked at me, wide-eyed, and swallowed nervously. "Hey, yeah, I heard that. Somebody iced Tony last night."

"For keeps," I said. "So who told you he'd be sitting home waiting for me?" I watched him, cranking up the silent pressure while he swallowed, dry-mouthed and licked his lips.

"Wasn't nobody. I made that up. Honest." He ran a forefinger around the neckband of his shirt. I grinned at him, the soul of friendliness.

"Why'd you do a thing like that?"

"Jus' friendly," he scrambled. "I din' figure he'd be home an' I thought you'd be better off not seeing 'im."

"If I want somebody to take care of me, I'll put myself up for adoption," I told him. "Now who paid you to send me over there?"

"I'm sorry, Mr. Bennett. I went lookin' for him, like. George, the buddy of mine 's knows Tony. He seen you waitin' and he gave me a sawbuck to send you over to Tony's place."

"Then the guy I should be talking to is George." I kept my voice breezy, I wanted him relaxed. "No hard feelings, Bo. I just need to see George. Is he around tonight?"

He licked his lips again. "I haven't seen him tonight, and that's the God's truth."

"So I'll settle for his whole name and a description." I

smiled at him, the kind of smile dentists give when they're about to drill. "That shouldn't be hard."

He cleared his throat. "Waddya want with him?"

I sighed. "Listen, don't worry, your name won't come up. You tell me where to find him and I'll go and talk to him and that's it. He doesn't know where I heard about him, and you're back at the ten-dollar window making the big bets."

He did a little move with his shoulders, like a bad middleweight waiting for the bell to start round one. "Well, like he goes by more than one name, Okay?"

I nodded. "There's a lot of it going around. What's his other name?"

Now he sniffed, catching his nose a quick swipe with his cuff. "Like, most of the time he goes by Kennie," he said.

I didn't let my excitement show. "What's he look like, this Kennie? Big guy, fat, what?"

Bojangles stopped and looked all around us at the crowds of bettors, none of them paying any attention to a couple of guys standing by a pillar talking form. He slackened his anxiety a hair and said, "He's small, kind of runty. Fair hair an' a whole lot of tattoos on his arms an' that."

It was my Kennie all right but I probed anyway. "Small as a jockey?"

His hand sliced the air carefully at the five-foot-five mark. "No, 'round that high. He's like thirty, been inside once or twice." He looked around again, nervously, then gave me his prime piece of news. "Like, he's mean."

"Then I'll be real careful." I nodded towards the rail where the serious bettors had lined up to watch the race. "Go and watch your horse break, Bo. And don't play games with me any more."

He was like a kid out of school. "This horse won't break. Best trained horse in the race. Won twice in a row, then four no-shows. They been savin' him for the stakes race tonight." He nodded and jogged off to the rail, skipping a couple of steps like a six-year-old.

I'd parked on a side street a couple of blocks from the track and as I walked back to the car a quick shower started, spattering suddenly like a handful of coins flung from an upper window. I ducked into the nearest doorway, a shabby entry to the walkup apartments over a grocery store. I flicked up the collar of my light windbreaker and turned to look out into the rain. Except for a few cars coming and going the street was deserted. But as I waited an old sedan, maybe a sixty-eight, mostly blue but with patches of dull primer paint on the fenders, ducked into the parking spot in front of the doorway. Before I could move the doors burst open and two men jumped out. One was Kennie and the other was Tony's chauffeur and there was no arguing with them; they both had guns pointed at my guts.

# *21*

THERE was no chance to run, they were only eight feet from me, they couldn't miss. Instead I turned and tugged at the door behind me but it was locked. And then it was too late. They were in beside me, both guns rock hard in my ribs. I might have gambled against one, but with two, I stood very still and asked, "So what's with the artillery?"

As I anticipated, Kennie was the rougher. He jammed his gun barrel under my ribs, trying to hook at the rib cage with the foresight. It hurt and I told him softly, "Pull the trigger if you've got to, but don't poke me or I'll stick that thing up your nose." Brave talk but I didn't have a hell of a lot left to lose and I've never liked bullies.

Kennie eased an ounce on the pressure but the other guy said, "Nice and easy, okay. Just walk out to the car like we was all friends, get in the back seat and keep your mouth shut."

"You got it." I was planning as I moved. If I got into the car I could kick back with one foot as I dived through and unfastened the far door. In the confusion I could have ten feet on them both before they could take a shot at me. Odds were they would miss in their excitement and I'd be free.

Both of them were wearing light jackets, Kennie's zippered, the other guy's a regular suitcoat. They drew their guns back from my ribs and held them out of sight under their coats, but I could see where they were pointing. Nothing had changed.

"Now," Kennie said. He moved out, casually, backing away as a friend might from a conversation he hated to leave. He glanced each way, casually, so as not to obstruct the passage of any pedestrian who might be ambling by. None was. He hooked his head at us and the other guy prodded me through his coat. I went ahead of him, past Kennie who was standing at the open rear door, kicked back and hurled myself through to the far side. I was scrabbling for the door handle when Kennie slid into the front seat and stuck his gun barrel against the back of my neck. "Nice try, asshole," he said. "We figured you'd try that."

I drew my feet under me and sat down carefully in the seat behind the passenger side of the car. Kennie knelt back, covering me until the other guy got in, rubbing his ribs. "You're gonna be sorry you done that," he promised.

I already was. If you're going to make a play it's best to have surprise going for you and mine was spent now. They would watch me every second from here on. Now he sat half turned towards me, his gun pointing at me, rock steady. I could see now that it was a smallish automatic, a Beretta I figured, only 32 mm caliber but as lethal as necessary from three feet away.

Slowly Kennie relaxed into the front seat, slipping his own gun into his waistband, on the left side of his pants so he could draw across the body in a moment. He paused to look back over his shoulder. "Okay to go?"

"Sure," the other guy said softly. "Nice and easy. Don't run no lights or nothin'. Keep it cool."

"Ten four," Kennie said and chuckled. He started the noisy old motor and pulled out, signaling first as if this was his driving test and I was the guy who could stop his getting a license. I sat back in my seat, noting which way we were headed, eastward up Kingston Road towards Scarborough, and then checked the inside of my door. There was no door handle or ratchet to wind the window down. I was locked in for keeps.

That left me the choice of going with them, on what looked like it was going to be a one-way ride, hoping to find some way to break free as we got out of the car, or else distracting this mean-eyed little man next to me. I concentrated all my power into trying to will a police car to come up by us at one of the lights, but none did. Whatever happened from here on was up to me.

Kennie drove out of the city and into Scarborough, the suburb to the east. There are some fancy homes in the borough but the whole Kingston Road ten-mile strip is urban sprawl, gas stations, chicken joints, little plazas and motels. He drove carefully and no police car came in sight. At last we reached the highway that led to the 401.

It's the main artery for the whole of southern Ontario, from the border with Detroit right over to Montreal. I began to wonder if they had a rendezvous set up along the highway—if I was to be transferred to some other car so my disappearance would be total. It would be easy enough to arrange. There's three hundred and fifty miles of the highway between Toronto and Montreal. Much of it follows the lake shoreline where there are plenty of places to make a man vanish. All it takes is a bullet in the head and a few minutes to dump the body into one of the swamps along the lake shore, weighted down with an old engine and dropped out of a motorboat. I shuddered and tried to get my head around a plan of escape. Locked in as I was, with that pistol trained on me, I was stuck, until they made me get out of the car. When that happened, I would have to make my move.

Twenty minutes clear of the suburbs, Kennie pulled off, up a major north-south road, Brock Road in Ajax. It's the main access regional road, down to the 401 from the rolling land that the government expropriated in the seventies for an airport that died on the drawing boards, killing the area with it. Now the abandoned farmsteads are falling down. The land is farmed by renters, men who move their machinery about as needed, living elsewhere. It's a favorite spot for lovers, and for people who want to do things quietly. I thought I knew what that meant for me.

I made another try. As Kennie pulled sedately across Highway Two, I glanced to my left, over the head of the guy with the gun and shouted, "Watch out!" covering my face as if a car were coming at us through the lights. But he didn't buy it.

"Put your hands on your knees or you're dead," he said

softly. So I did it. Then Kennie spoke, over his shoulder like a talkative cabbie. "Don't shoot the bastard yet. I got a better idea."

My watchdog wasn't impressed. "Jus' drive," he said. "I know what we gotta do."

Kennie took us five or six miles north and turned west down a concession road. I was starting to get desperate. If a police car came along these roads once a night it would be a miracle. I was on my own and I had only a few minutes left to live.

A mile or so over he pulled in to the gateway of an abandoned farm. In the headlights I could see that the house and barn were still intact. Then he cut the lights and cruised up behind the house. I braced myself, this was the only chance I would get. If they were sloppy now I might be able to run for it. But they weren't. Kennie stopped and put the handbrake on, then switched on the inside light. He turned around to kneel on the seat, but far back on the edge where he would be able to get a shot off even if I dived at him. He drew his gun and pointed it, grinning the way he had grinned that very first night with the two-by-four in his hand.

"Back out, George. Keep your gun on him, he's slippery." The other guy opened the car door with his left hand and slid out and stood six feet away, gun trained on me. "Now you, bigshot," Kennie said and grinned.

I guessed they planned to shoot me and stuff me in the trunk of the car. My heart was racing but I moved quietly. I had no chance inside the car, perhaps a prayer once I got out. But Kennie robbed me even of that. As I came out of the back door, he came out of the front, smoothly covering me the whole way. Then he surprised me. "In the front seat," he said.

I hesitated but there was no chance to hit him. With both their guns on me, a move would be suicide. I played my luck out down to the wire, hoping for the microsecond's carelessness they hadn't yet shown. And the first crack appeared.

The other man said, "That's not the plan. You know what we're s'posed to do." But Kennie ignored him.

"Get round the other side and open the door," he ordered and George walked around. I could see him shaking his head but Kennie never flinched and the muzzle of that pistol was only four feet away. When George was in place Kennie told me, "Okay, now I want you behind the wheel. Okay?"

I got in and he said, "Now push your left hand through the steering wheel."

George interrupted without taking his attention off me. "Fer crissakes, Kennie. We're s'posed to ice him and put him in the trunk. You know that."

Kennie cackled. "He'd like that, nice and painless. But him and me go back a ways. I owe him."

I tried for some sympathy. "Listen, Kennie, didn't I stop that punk Willis from beating on you?" It was a long shot but I had no others.

"He wasn't beatin' on me, you turkey," Kennie said impatiently. "He's in this thing with us, right up to his ass."

The words jolted me like a cattle prod, but they hit George even harder. "You dumb bastard!" he shouted. "You got the biggest mouth I ever seen."

"Relax," Kennie assured him. "This guy's a dead man." He crouched so he was looking in at my eye level, his gun trained on my head. "Get in the other side and cover him like this, George, you're gonna like this."

George swore but he did it. I turned my head to tell him "Don't get in any deeper," but he just slammed me in the temple with the barrel of his gun. It was the same side the Chinese kid had hit me the night before and the pain put all my lights out for about twenty seconds. I slumped there in the seat, hearing Kennie laughing, feeling something happening to my hands. Then slowly, as if I was coming up from the bottom of a black pool, I shook my head, making the pain jangle around in a way that woke me to full consciousness.

Kennie was laughing harder. "How's that for size, tough guy?" he asked me and I became aware of my hands, one inside, one outside the steering wheel rim, tied together at the wrist. I tugged but they were tied to stay.

"That's right. You're in good," he jeered. "Can't even get any leverage to snap the steering wheel rim when you start to fry." I glanced around at the other man. He was outside the car crouched where he could look at me. His gun was no longer pointed my way. He was grinning the kind of grin you see on kids who pull the wings off flies. "Now what?" he asked Kennie.

Kennie didn't answer at once. First he stuffed his gun into his belt then he said, "Get the car outa the barn, George, I got me a couple things to do here." And then they both walked away, I could here them chuckling to one another as I struggled helplessly to free my hands. But it was no use. The cord was tight enough to cut off circulation completely, too strong to be snapped, too restricting to let me grip the rim of the wheel and try to work-harden the metal and snap it off. I was stuck tight and my hair prickled as I thought of what he had said. He was going to set fire to the car.

He came back with an armful of hay, just as the other car rolled down from the mow of the barn. He waved at it. I saw his shadow, unnaturally huge, flickering like black fire over the interior around me. Then he threw his hay into the back seat.

"I figure it'll take two minutes to get hot enough to blow the gas tank," he said, breathlessly. He was moving like a man on the brink of an orgasm, taut and shortwinded. His voice was as brittle as fingernails on a blackboard. "You got time maybe to say your prayers, maybe not. Then you'll be fryin' in your own fat."

"You can still hang for killing a cop," I told him. I didn't expect it to change his mind but I had no other cards to play.

"Save it, dead man," he said, and lit the match. Twisted round in the seat I saw him drop it on to the hay and slam the door. Then the hay took light, catching and spreading the fire in its tips first, like jewels in a crown, then redder and deeper as the flame penetrated into the full depth of the pile. I swung around, in time to see Kennie's laughing face at the side window, then he was gone and within seconds the headlights of the car rolled down the driveway and on to the road.

I struggled to bring my body across the seat, then got my legs over the seat and kicked at the burning hay, but it was not controlled enough. My pants caught and smouldered and all I did was scatter the fire further. The car began to fill with smoke and I felt fear pouring through me like icewater. I swung my feet back over to my own seat and lay there. If I kicked the windows out, the fire would burn faster. I had to risk the smoke. And in the meantime, what could I do?

The smoke filled the interior completely. First it was fragrant, the sweetness of burning grass on a summer's day, but within seconds it was overlaid with the ugly plastic stench of the car seats. I had less than two minutes before losing conciousness, but perhaps that was a blessing.

And still I worked by hands back and forth through the steering wheel, until I could clench the rim in the crook of my elbow. I tried to bend it, throwing all my weight against it, but it was too strong for me. Then, in a sudden burst of clarity, I knew what to do. I pushed my hands all the way through the wheel and felt along the dashboard for the ashtray. Above it was the homely nub of a cigarette lighter. I pressed it in and held my breath until it snapped back out with a tiny pop. Clumsily I bent over until I could put the end in my mouth. Then, holding it like a cigar I pressed it to the cords on my wrist and blew through it, feeding its tiny glow with all the oxygen I could spare. I knew I had just this one chance. I could never find the hole again to replace it. I sat there exhaling the very last of my breath until I felt the marvellous agony I was praying for. The cord was on fire. I drew in a quick gasp of smoky air and blew some more and as the pain savaged my wrists I could see the fibres on the cord glowing and popping. I was going to win, if I didn't black out first.

As the pain grew more intense I started twisting my wrists, careful not to crush out that fragile fire, but trying to loosen the fibres so they would burn more quickly. And all the time the smoke grew thicker and the smothered glow of the burning back seat grew redder. I had about ten seconds of clarity left.

And then I felt the first jolt of release as a cord snapped, then another strand, and then my hands were free and I was rolling sideways out of the car and on to the grass, choking and coughing and trying to gather my weak legs to run and dodge.

But nobody shot at me. And as I drew in a great lungful of clear night air and coughed, I turned and stumbled away, heading for the angled up ramp of the barn and the shelter it could give from the blast that was coming. I found it and collapsed behind it, safe from the blast if the car blew up. I didn't bother moving further. I was too close to the end of my strength. I'd achieved a miracle and I lay face down on the sweetest smelling grass I have ever known, sobbing my starved lungs full of oxygen until suddenly the night erupted in a flash and a boom that carried away my sense of sound.

I didn't move, slowly gathering strength while the blaze colored the barn wall orange above me. Then I sat up, working my jaw, popping my ears until they were suddenly filled once more with the rushing roar of the fire. I had a sudden shocking visual replay of a napalm attack in Nam. The captain had called in air support and they had dropped their cannisters that burst with the same deadly rush of sound, the same wave of torturing heat. And afterwards, when the woods cooled and nobody was left to fire on us as we picked our way into the ambush area we had found four Cong, their arms and legs drawn up in death in the burn victim's classic pugilist stance. And the guys had laughed and pointed and called them crispy critters. And I had managed not to vomit. And now it had almost been my turn.

I poked my head up, half expecting to be shot at, and checked that nobody was waiting for me to breeze out into the open. Then, using all my strength I ran ten yards, dived, rolled, ran again and dived and rolled the other way until I was level with the lilac bushes at the back of the farm house. From there I stood up and moved carefully, as carefully as ever I had in Nam on a night patrol. I went down the fence line to the road, checked each way and saw nothing was coming. I guessed what had happened. Kennie and George knew the explosion would light up the whole sky. They had left before it happened so they would not be seen coming away from the site by a police car or firetruck racing to it. Isolated locations have dangers of their own, when you're planning spectacular executions. I was glad they had thought it through so carefully. In the meantime, I expected somebody would be coming soon. Fires are a farmer's greatest enemy. Somebody would report this one that lit the world behind me. And when the fire reels came, so would the police cars. I would wait for them before I came out of hiding.

There was a foot of cold water in the ditch beside the

roadway and I bathed my burned wrists in it until the police car arrived. When I saw it driving towards me, red light flashing on the top I jumped out into the roadway and flagged it down. It stopped fifteen feet from me, headlights on high beam as I stood there, a scorched clown. Then a young, confident voice called out. "Police here. What the hell happened to you, fella?"

I held my hands up, keeping the pressure off my burned wrists, but at the same time making a gesture of surrender.

"It's a long story," I called out. "But you're just the guy I want to tell it to."

# 22

HE was suspicious, but no more than I would have been if I'd come across a smoldering scarecrow on my own patrol. He put me in the back of his car, in the cage, and drove me to the hospital. He had already radioed and their sole detective was there ahead of us. I told him I needed the homicide guys from Toronto and after enough of an investigation to make him feel that he wasn't being jerked around he called Toronto and Hooper and Cooper headed out to see me.

They found me in a treatment room, sitting on a gurney. The second-degree burns on my wrists had been treated, smeared with some gunk which took the sting away completely, but I was feeling punchy. It was a long time since I'd been as close to dying painfully as Kennie had brought me. And the rules were different in Nam. Here I wasn't at war with anybody, except, it seemed, for Kennie and his band of brothers.

I gave the story to the homicide guys, and they listened, carefully. Hooper stepped out once, to call the Toronto dispatcher and put Kennie and the other man on the air, wanted for attempted murder, then he came back and the pair of them sat sipping coffee and trying to work out what the hell was going on.

"From what you say, this Kennie and another guy beat up the security guard at that building site in TO," Cooper said patiently.

"Then this guy Willis turns up, makes like he's going to assault him and gets you to investigate," Hooper finished.

"Yes, and from what the two guys, Kennie and Hudson, told me, I figured that the assaults had been done for Tony Caporetto. I followed him, and then Kennie and his chauffeur tried to beat me up. It didn't work, and we were all taken to the station," I explained.

Cooper continued. "So you follow up Tony and he puts you on to this lawyer, what's his name, Cy Straight." I nodded.

"You see him, next thing you're getting envelopes of cash delivered at home."

He stopped to blow in his hot coffee and Hooper went on, in almost the same tone of voice. "You follow up, and you find some Chinaman in Tony's place. He cools you out and you wake up with Tony dead and you in trouble." He shook his head and took a little peck at his own coffee. "The way trouble follows you around we're gonna have to start calling you Dark Cloud," he said cheerfully.

"Then don't forget the Chinaman who tried to take me out at the restaurant. I figure he hit Tony. Did you find any prints of his up there?" I was aware that my head ached and my hands and legs were sore from the burns. Even the dressings on both wrists had not made me comfortable. I wanted a stiff drink and a good night's sleep. But it was not coming yet.

"I still don't see any pattern that'd stand up in court," Hooper said, ignoring my question. "If this guy Willis is up to no good, it's likely some scam about robbing warehouses that Bonded is looking after; that makes sense. But there's no connection between him and Tony Caporetto. And from what you say, these two guys who tried to torch you worked for Tony."

We sat and looked at one another and mentally chewed the last of the meat off these dry bones of information. The door opened and a pretty nurse came in. "Your room's ready now," she told me brightly. "Doctor says you should stay overnight."

Hooper and Cooper were weighing her up, the way all policemen weigh up all women young enough. They hadn't heard what she said. I grinned and told her, "Thanks, but no thanks. I've got a dog at home, been stuck inside the place since noon. He'll be in real misery by morning."

"Then phone somebody up and let him out," she said briskly. "You need the rest."

I didn't bother explaining that nobody could get into that house without killing Sam. It was too complicated. Instead I just shook my head again and thanked her. "These big handsome policemen are going to take me home. I promise not to do anything rash before morning."

She wagged one finger at me. "You be sure and don't," she said and left as if all the Matrons in hell were after her.

"You wanna go home?" Cooper asked. I nodded. He stood up. "C'mon then, Hoop. See if we can find this greasy little rounder Kennie."

"It's not even our goddamn case," Hooper grumbled but he stood up as well, tossing his coffee cup into the waste container. "Come on then, Dark Cloud, let's go home."

They drove me to Louise's house. I must confess I was asleep for part of the ride. It's a reaction I've seen before, in Nam. You run on nerves for just so long and after that you can't keep your eyes open. I was glad when they reached the house. But they didn't just tip me out. "Listen, after last night, we'll see you're alone," one of them said. I was too sleepy to notice which one. So they came with me as I opened the door and whistled one low note. Immediately good old Sam was there with me, tail wagging. "It's Okay, nobody's been here," I said. "Come in if you want, but there's nothing happening."

They had been detectives long enough to come in anyway. I offered them a drink and while they sipped I took Sam outside to get comfortable and then ran with him to the corner of the block and back, maybe a fast quarter mile altogether. It felt good to have cold air rushing against my face after the smoke and fear of the interior of that car.

They refused seconds on the rye and went on their way. I

was too whipped to ask if they were going to check on Willis. All I wanted to do was collapse into bed and sleep the clock round. When they'd gone, I fed Sam, let him out again briefly and then posted him on sentry duty, this time commanding him to "Keep," which meant he was to raise the roof if anyone came in. Then I poured myself a stiff belt of Black Velvet and took it upstairs. It was just daybreak when the phone woke me.

It was Simon Fullwell. As soon as I said "Hello," he said, "What's been going on, Reid? The homicide guys say that punk from our job site tried to murder you."

"No lasting damage done, except maybe to Willis's reputation." I yawned. "Was he around when they came?"

"No, he was out at one of the sites, so they went out there to talk to him. Then he came into the office about ten minutes ago, madder'n a wet hen. What's up?"

I gave him the comment Kennie had made and he whistled. "Doesn't surprise me," he said. "Of course, I shouldn't say anything on this phone but our party lives in a very swank house, must've cost him three hundred thousand anyway, just south of Forest Hill. I figured he had family money because I know what he gets paid and it's not that kind of bread."

"Well, there's nothing on him but Kennie's say-so and that doesn't mean a damn thing, except for the time and place where he said it. Lying wasn't important to him right then. And besides, the other guy came alive and chewed him out for careless talk."

Fullwell sighed. I guessed he was pumping away on one of his everlasting cigarillos. "So where do we go from here?" he asked.

"Well, for me, it's back to bed. But it might make sense if you were to take a look at Willis's file. Find out where he comes from, what his background is, any connections anywhere that might make sense of the allegations. Then if there is, maybe you could have a word with that suit who runs your place. But don't expect much sympathy. He'll probably think I made it up to spite you guys for cutting me loose."

"I'll soon change his damn mind about that," Fullwell said angrily.

"Don't count on it," I told him and went back to bed. It must have been an hour later, as the first of the neighbors drove out to go downtown that Sam started to bark downstairs. It wasn't his real "Keeping" bark, just a friendly warning that somebody was moving around outside, but I was rested enough to get up and slip into some clothes and head downstairs to check.

He was glad to see me, but he insisted on barking so I opened the back door and let him out, he scooted around the front and I followed, staying way back in case it was somebody who meant business.

I could tell from the way Sam grew more fierce that someone was out there. As I came around the corner of the house I heard a high, nervous voice saying, "Good boy. Easy boy!" over and over like a prayer, to which Sam wasn't responding.

It was a woman, maybe thirty, lean and pretty in a businesslike way. She saw me and called out. "Mr. Bennett, will he bite?"

"What do you want?" I asked her. She was backing up to the edge of the lawn, trying to stand tall as far from Sam's teeth as she could reach. I told Sam, "Easy," and he relaxed, falling silent but staying in place, ready to move again as ordered.

Now she grinned and stuck out her hand, unafraid of Sam. "How do you do. I'm Phyllis Henderson. I'm a friend of Lou's, we were in the same writing class at university."

I held up my bandaged wrists. "Excuse me if I don't shake. Louise is away for a few days. I'm not sure when she'll be back."

She grinned again. She had a nice, lean-faced grin. "I know, I spoke to her on the phone last night when I heard the news."

"What news?"

She cocked her head pertly. "About your adventures."

I groaned. "Was it on the radio, mentioning me by name?"

"It sure was. So I came right round here, as soon as it was light. I don't meet many celebrities."

"You still haven't," I told her. I stooped and rubbed Sam's head. "What I am is tired. So, excuse me, I'll tell Louise you were by. I guess she has your number."

I smiled and turned away but she persisted. "You're not going to send a girl out on the streets without a cup of coffee?"

There was something too bright about her for my mood that morning so I just shrugged and said "Sorry," and kept on walking. But she followed me. "Please. Can't you tell me what happened?"

"It's all under investigation," I said. "That's all there is to it." I waved good-bye over my shoulder but she kept talking.

"I need to know," she said seriously and when I didn't stop she shouted at me. "You're a hero, dammit. Can't you spare me one lousy minute of your time?"

That stopped me cold. I turned and asked, "Are you with a newspaper?"

She did her grin again but it wasn't charming this time. "Right in one," she chirruped. "I'm with the *Sun*."

"Well tell them I appreciate their sunshine girls. Good morning." I matched her grin and went on to the back door but she didn't give up.

"You have to talk to me," she insisted, and then, as I reached the door, "The people have a right to know."

I waved and went in. She came behind me and opened the door and walked into the space at the head of the basement stairs. "Come on, please. I haven't had a chance at a real piece of news in months. Nothing but council meetings and school estimates. Can't you give me an exclusive, for Louise's sake."

I stood four steps above her, looking down into the bluest eyes I have seen in a while. "Look. There's nothing to tell. If you want to print something, tell people I sicked my dog on you and he chased you off the property, because I don't want to talk to you or anybody else about what happened. I have no comments of any kind. Now, would you like that cup of coffee?"

I thought it might soften her up so she didn't report anything at all but asking her in was a mistake. She wouldn't sit in the kitchen. She walked from room to room, exclaiming at the house, then she admired my coffee, and she pressed me for details until I was tempted to fling her out with her coffee still in the cup. But I didn't, and bit by bit she won me over. Not to talk to her about the case—I've

been a copper too long to talk to anybody, especially press
people, but I found out a bit about her. She had been a
reporter for seven years, first in the sticks, then, because
she was bright and chirpy and youthful, with the *Sun*,
which is the Toronto tabloid, big on popular attitudes and
pretty girls.

When I finally kicked her out, she still hadn't learned
anything but I was wide awake again and ready for
breakfast. She offered to stay and make it for me but I didn't
feel like fencing any more so I said no and prepared my own
bacon and eggs. I switched the radio on and listened to
country music until news time. And that was when I got my
first surprise of the morning; there was no mention of my
name. The report was that a car had been burned up in the
sticks but there was no mention of me or of anybody having
been threatened with burning to death. And that got me
forgetting the eggs and reaching for the phone to call
Louise, breaking the rule I had set myself earlier of staying
separate from her.

Her friend answered, sounding as if she was about a
quart of coffee short of being ready for the day's disasters.
She brightened some when I said who I was. I figured Lou
must have told her I was single. That brings out either the
maternal or the mating instinct in a lot of women. Louise
came on, bright as morning orange juice and asked how I
was. I told her fine, no need to give her any worry, she had
some client's cough medicine and somebody else's pantihose
to worry about that day. Then I slid in the important
question.

"Met a friend of yours, says she was in college with you,
taking the same writing course."

"Writing course? I never took any writing course. I took
straight English and history, with one psych credit," she
said, and my hackles began to tickle.

"Well, maybe I didn't listen carefully enough. Anyway,
she's a lean-looking blond girl, around your age, got really
blue blue eyes, like you hear about in Irish songs. Calls
herself Phyllis Henderson."

Louise laughed. "Policeman of mine, you've been sold a
bill of goods. I never knew a Phyllis anybody in college. I'd
have remembered, I don't think I know anybody my age
with that name."

"Then I guess I got her confused with somebody else. I met a few people last night."

"That's nice," she said brightly. "I hope you had a tremendous time and found yourself somebody worth knowing."

"I did," I assured her. "A couple of real sweethearts."

And that was the end of it. I promised to let her know when things had cooled out enough for her to come home, asked after the kids and hung up.

I didn't enjoy my breakfast. I was wondering about my visitor. On impulse I phoned the *Sun* and asked for Phyllis Henderson. The switchboard girl told me there was nobody of that name working there. I gave a sketchy description, said she was a reporter, the woman thought about it and said no again, there was no reporter of that description with the paper.

When I had finished eating and washed the dishes, I rang Bonded Security. Fullwell was in and he sounded eager. "Let me take this on my own phone," he said. "In fact, better than that, I'll go across the street and call from there."

It took three minutes. He was bursting with news. "I was just heading over here to call you," he began. "I managed to get through to the head office computer in New York and check Willis's file. He's a very interesting guy."

"In what way?"

"Well, he's older than he looks, must be in his fifties. He's Canadian, not American, as I thought. He was in Korea with the Princess Patricia's Light Infantry. His outfit was shot to hell somewhere and the whole company got an American Presidential Citation which is on his record."

"Yeah, so he's a hero."

"There's more than that." Fullwell was crammed with news and it poured out of him, almost too fast for me to take it in. "He came home in 1953 and stayed in the army for another two years, working as a military policeman. He was in the Provost, which was an unusual switch for an infantryman to make. Then in '55 he quit, with the rank of Sergeant, took his Veteran's grant and went to college."

"Come on Simon, you're holding out on me." I was anxious to hear the facts that focussed all this background.

"Well, he took law courses, criminology and, are you ready?"

"After last night I'm ready for just about anything," I promised him.

"Yeah, well he also took a language, something which wasn't done by a lot of people with that mix of subjects."

From his tone I knew what was coming. "Don't tell me. He majored in Chinese."

Fullwell's excited laugh filled the phone. "How in hell did you guess that?" He laughed again. "It was the last thing in the world I ever expected, he never told me that and I've worked with him for a year. I've never even heard him order egg rolls."

"And then what did he do? Take a course in leg-breaking?"

"No." Fullwell grew sober again. "No, then he went legit, he quit college without a degree and joined the police department in Hamilton."

"He wouldn't have needed his Chinese there," I said. "That's a steel town, they hardly speak English, most bars I've been in there."

"I know. It's a tough town." Fullwell said. "He put in a year and a half on the beat, walking tall and sorting out fights. And then, guess what?"

"He joined your company?" I didn't believe it but it speeds conversations along if you take an adversary position once in a while.

Fullwell played his ace. "No. What he did was volunteer as a policeman overseas."

I was about to ask where but he rode in almost at once. "In, of all places, Hong Kong."

I whistled. "And then suddenly we're investigating a bashing at a site controlled by Hong Kong money. We move out a little and find ourselves faced with hoods who kick holes in people with kung fu and talk Cantonese, which is the way Chinese is spoken in the colony."

"Right. Right, right on the money." Fullwell almost crowed. "We find ourselves in a situation where a man with a Hong Kong background might be considered a suspicious character. And then to top it off, some little rounder with nothing to gain accuses him of being crooked."

We were both silent for a moment, then I said, "I've got to talk to this guy, very, very soon."

## 23

WE discussed it a little longer. Fullwell was still surprised that the homicide guys hadn't taken Willis in. I wasn't. I knew better. The facts I had given them didn't make a case. All it gave them was hearsay of hearsay connecting Willis to a nonfatal beating, not a murder. So, unless he had come unglued and started confessing they wouldn't have had anything to lock him up for. It was normal and legal and expected, but it didn't change my mind that he was behind the whole chain of events.

"I think I should head up to his place and talk to him. He'll deny everything and raise hell, but maybe I can put a bit of pressure on where the police couldn't," I said. My wrists were hurting this morning and deep breaths still brought up memories of the smoke in that car the night before. I would be a while getting over this particular case and I wasn't as concerned with law as I was with finding out who was behind it all.

Fullwell grunted. "Good idea. I'll come with you."

"No. I don't want you booted out of your job for running interference," I told him. "This is kind of personal. I'll keep it that way."

I thanked him and hung up and set Sam on guard in the house. Then I took a taxi to where I'd left my car and spent a few minutes looking for devices that hadn't been put in place by General Motors. These people, whoever they were, played for keeps and I didn't want sticks of dynamite leaving souvenirs of me all over the scenery. But the precaution was unnecessary; there was nothing around the motor or under the car. I didn't even locate a bug of any kind, so after a second check I put the key in and started up.

By now it was eight-thirty and the streets were full of commuters, headed down where the dollar bills grow.

I didn't envy any of them. It was good to be alive and moderately independent, out on a fishing trip with some hope of wrapping up this entire mystery within the next hour or so. I wasn't even sure what I was going to do when I found Willis, but investigations have a dynamic of their own, like stage plays. They usually start abruptly, then slacken while you race around looking for leads. And then things start to come together faster and faster, leading you to an arrest and the inevitable slowdown. I figured I was there now, just ahead of the arrest. If I had to lean on Willis a little to get cooperation, that was fine by me, I wasn't a policeman on this case, just an injured citizen. I had the same rights as everybody else, including the right to get exercised when people tried to set fire to me.

I found his house, in the south end of Forest Hill village. It's a primarily Jewish neighborhood, full of beautiful homes with Mercedeses in the double garages. This far down, close to St. Clair Avenue, it starts to shade off into more down-to-earth places but this house looked like three hundred grand's worth.

I pulled my Chev into the driveway, went to the door and rang a few times but nobody answered, so I knocked until my wrists started hurting again, but still got nothing.

As far as I could tell there was nobody looking out at me through the neighbors' lace curtains but I went into my fallback routine, walking back to the car and opening the trunk. I have a shovel in there, part of my emergency gear for winter driving in Murphy's Harbour. I didn't think anybody watching would know a shovel from a spade. They would never lay hands on one for themselves. Holding it made me some kind of workman, a nonperson as invisible as the postman in that Father Brown story.

I took it and walked back around the edge of the house onto a good stone patio in the shade of an oak tree that had been there before they dug the foundations for the house. It screened me from any of the houses behind and I spent a few seconds checking the back door and windows. I was in luck; one of the windows was open a touch. It was a casement style and there was no fly screen so I was able to hop over the sill and into the house inside ten seconds.

I found myself in a large room, decorated in the way that says "Money" loud and clear. It made me uneasy. I was ready for a confrontation with Willis, but I wanted it on my own terms. Right now, I had broken in, and that made me illegal. I slipped out to the front door, opened it and stood on the mat calling up the stairs, "Hello, Mr. Willis," in the kind of voice that Avon ladies might use. Nobody answered but I stayed nervous; it was only two days since I'd walked in on Tony's corpse. I didn't want to find myself framed, or worse yet, ambushed, one more time. I kept calling as I made a quick spin through the downstairs.

The ground floor was deserted but there were no signs of trouble, the place was neat, there was food in the fridge, including a fresh quart of milk, so it looked as if he was still in residence, unless he'd skipped out this morning. If so, he must have had a real pile of cash on hand; he hadn't bothered to pick up the valuables. There was a set of silver in the dining room that had cost a year of my pay.

One thing was certain, I decided: the man wasn't living on what he earned at Bonded. A house like this needed an income well into six figures. But I didn't have much time to theorize. I had just come out of the kitchen and reached the stairwell when the front door was kicked open. I spun to face it, trying to compromise between a fighting crouch and a look of surprise. My right hand had gone into my jacket pocket to grip my only weapon and I was prepared to rush anybody who threatened me. But there was no need. The man in the doorway was Elmer Svensen, still wearing his hat, grinning now as if he'd won a doorprize.

"Police work a little slow, Bennett?" he jeered. "Taken to B and E, have you?"

I kept it casual. "Hi, Elmer, what brings you here?"

He kept his grin on like a conventioneer's nametag. "You do, asshole," he said happily. "I've been wondering when you'd step over the line and today's the day. Breaking and entering."

I walked towards him, elaborately casual. "Get real, I'm just visiting my old workmate, Henry Willis. D'you ever meet him, he works for Bonded Security, I'm working with him."

"In a pig's eye," Svensen said. "They kicked you the hell off the payroll yesterday, don't try to tell me different."

I was beginning to sweat, he was mean enough to take me in unless I was very careful and I had worn out any credibility I brought into town with me as a small-town police chief.

"Where'd you hear a story like that?" I asked him. "I don't think it made the newspapers."

He chomped his chewing gum and grinned. "I hear things all over," he said happily.

"I've noticed. Every time I turn around on this investigation you're there. It gets a man wondering just who your friends are, Elmer."

He shrugged. "You know the score, a copper's only as good as his information. I get around. Now suppose you give me some information about what you're doing in Willis's house when he's not even home."

"We're good friends and this is a social call."

"Sure," Svensen said. "And I'm Miss Toronto." He reached around his waist for the handcuffs on his belt. "Hold your hands out."

"Are you kidding?" I stuck both hands in my pockets. "I'm here at his invitation. I called him earlier at the office but he's left. He told me yesterday to come up and see him."

Svensen didn't believe me but his confidence was fading as my own grew. I put myself right into the part. And it worked. "Great house he's got, eh?" I wandered off, hands still in my pockets, staring around as if I'd paid a buck admission.

Svensen said, "Don't give me that crap. I got a phone call saying a man was breaking in here. I come right up and here you are, bold as brass."

"Of course." I laughed. "I told you, he invited me. He said if he was out the front door would be open. I tried it, it was, so I came in."

He was weakening. I sensed it and let my own thin shred of confidence tug me back into the dining room where I had noticed a decanter on the sideboard. "This guy really knows how to live. Come and have a look at this dining room. That table looks like it's older than Canada." I picked up the decanter and took the stopper out. "Wow. That's real gold braid booze, just sniff it."

I thrust it towards him and saw him swallow convulsively.

It would have been easy to overplay it and offer him a drink but instead I put it down and stuck the stopper back into it. "If you want to wait for him, maybe I can find the coffee," I said. "I guess it's in the kitchen somewhere."

I walked through to the kitchen and started banging cupboard doors. I was getting more and more tense. If Willis came back and found me here with Svensen it would be easy for him to turn me in. I had to get out or get Svensen out right away.

I found a kettle and filled it and put it on the gas stove, then walked back through to the dining room. Svensen was standing by the window but I could tell he had taken a half inch of liquor out of the decanter. I decided to press in. I had to scare him away. "I guess you won't want coffee now," I said innocently.

He turned and stared at me through narrow, angry eyes. "You disgust me," he said in a low voice.

I shrugged. "I seem to annoy a lot of people but it comes with the job. I mean I go around being suspicious all the time. I ask myself questions like, why is a detective from 43 division answering phone calls about suspicious characters in Forest Hill, which is about eight miles out of his area?" I let that one dangle while I walked over to the decanter, picked it up and wiped it with my handkerchief. "And I wonder why a man from 43 division is over in the west end of Toronto in the apartment of a crummy little loan shark who's just been wasted?" I turned to stare at him. "What's on, Elmer, are you turning into a Guardian Angel for the whole city?"

He didn't answer but his anger was building and I knew I would get a reaction very soon, perhaps even the truth. That would be pleasant for a change.

"On top of that, I wonder why a good copper gets a monkey on his back and starts sucking up the rye all day, every day?"

"Who're you talking about?" he roared suddenly. He walked over towards me as if he was going to take a roundarm swipe at me but I didn't flinch. He was too slow for me the best day he ever saw, and this wasn't it.

"I'm talking about you, Elmer. You used to be able to take whatever crap the job threw at you. We've had a lot of laughs. And now suddenly you're turning into a snotty-tempered rummy who comes running whenever anybody with a bottle snaps his fingers."

He was ready to hit me but defeat was too deeply ingrained into his soul. "What makes you so goddamn smug?" he said. "Just becuase you've been trained better'n I ever was to tackle guys with guns, that don't make you special, it just makes you lucky."

His pace was slowing. I didn't answer him. I knew he was still living with that few seconds when those guys had gotten the drop on him. It was a play he sat through every time he closed his eyes. What would have happened if he had refused to hand over his gun? And if they had shot him, would it be any worse than this endless reliving of the moment, over and over? I wanted to comfort him but all he wanted from me was distance.

"I've had the same thing happen, more than once. It happens if you're a copper, some bastard gets the drop on you sometimes. Don't let it stick in your craw."

He swore at me, a dull, tired word. Then he pulled up his sleeve and checked the time. "I've got to be going," he said. "I'll tell Willis next time I see him that you were here. If he wants to press charges, you're going inside."

There was nothing to say so I waved one casual hand and walked back out to the kitchen while he clumped over the polished parquet and slammed the front door behind him.

I debated what to do next. Willis might be home at any moment, I had no time to waste if I was going to check the place out. But on the other hand, I had nothing special to look for. All I wanted was a conversation with him, an honest talk this time, a chance to find out what was going on, and remove myself from it so that Louise and her children were out of danger.

In the end I took a quick spin through the upstairs portion, finding one beautiful master bedroom with Oriental screens and silk sheets and an embroidered dressing gown laid out on the bed and a couple of other rooms, one made up as a spare bedroom, the other containing a pair of double bunks with blankets on them that smelled of sweat. It didn't jibe with the rest of the furnishings and I began to wish I could let the homicide guys share my information. It was starting to look to me as if Willis boarded out wetbacks, possibly Chinese illegals. That would have fit the evidence

I'd found, anyway. If he was doing it from his own home, they must be very special people, possibly killers like Wing Lok, guys he didn't want out of his reach. It was all very suspicious and I wished I could find him.

I came down to the front again and prepared to leave. I would head out and search for him, starting at Bonded Security with an interview with his boss. And this evening, when the homicide guys came back on duty I would share my information with them and see what we could do from there.

I was at the door when the doorbell rang, a timid ring, just the faintest chink on the gong, then a pause, then a repeat, just as brief.

Moving as if I owned the place I went to the door and opened it, expecting to find the paperboy or some delivery man there. Instead I found myself looking down at the bent form of Cy Straight, the lawyer. I opened the door wide.

"Well, hello, counsellor, come on in," I told him.

# 24

ONE of the illusions you lose early as a policeman is the thought that people will collapse and confess when you bring out the evidence of their crime. Most don't. Either they're psychopaths who don't believe they've done anything wrong, or they're cool professionals who know how to keep a straight face. If Cy Straight was involved in this case, he didn't show it. He looked at me for a moment or two, as he might have done if we'd been introduced at a cocktail party and asked, "Is Mr. Willis in?"

"'Fraid not," I told him. "I'm waiting for him now, if you wanna come in." I grinned at him as if all his secrets were known to me, a brothel-keeper's grin. He ignored it.

I wondered at the way he was dressed, blue jeans and a

soft sports shirt that looked handmade to cover his hump. It was a weekday morning, I would have expected gray flannel, if he was heading for his office. The only professional touch was a briefcase, one of the old concertina leather variety that looked stuffed with papers. "I didn't know lawyers made housecalls," I said cheerfully. He turned away, not answering. It seemed to me that he was moving fast and I guessed he was angry.

I called after him. "You wanna leave a message?" He said nothing and I loped out of the door and confronted him. He stopped and faced me, calmly, the quiet strength of a man who recognizes his own frailty and ignores the evidence.

"You're in my way," he said quietly.

"I've got a feeling you're in mine, too," I told him. "Everywhere I go on this case, you turn up. Tony tells me about you and he's found dead. I find that Willis is up to no good and when I come to see him, there you are again."

"A lawyer has many clients," he said.

I nodded slowly, knowing for sure that he was involved. "But if this one wasn't a rounder of some stature, you wouldn't have bothered reminding me of that, would you, Cy?"

He looked into my eyes unblinkingly, then pursed his lips and stepped around me, down the drive to his DeLorean which was perched there with the door up, like a gull with a broken wing. He ducked under the wing and pulled it closed. He was facing me now and I waved and grinned a big hammy grin. "See you later," I called. He ignored me, backing out without turning his head to glance over his shoulder.

There was nothing left to do at the house but wait for Willis to come home. Maybe that would have been the right thing to do, certainly the place should have been staked out by somebody, but I was too impatient to sit there myself. I had a hunch he was running scared, he might never come back here. And so I decided to go looking for him. Which left me the question—looking where?

I closed up the house, retrieved my shovel from the back patio and drove away, slowly, checking the driver of every car I passed until I was clear of the area completely. I didn't see Willis. And so I drove aimlessly, still churning the case over in my head. I knew that he had left work at Bonded, hours ago. There was no sense heading down there to look for him. So what else could I do? Maybe the best place to look was the address Hudson had given me for Kennie.

It wasn't brilliant, but it made sense. Most petty criminals don't think things through with any care. They don't leave their home turf easily, even when it's too hot to hold them. There was a chance Kennie was still there, and if he was maybe he could direct me to Willis.

But I dropped the thought. The police were looking for Kennie on a charge of attempting to murder me. There was no way he was sitting around his mother's apartment watching TV. The place had been shaken down already and was probably being staked out by some unobtrusive plainclothesmen. When they found him they would ask him all the questions I could think of and more. No, I needed a fresh connection to Willis.

And that was when I finally faced the truth that had been niggling at me since I heard Willis and Hong Kong mentioned in the same breath. Where, I wondered, did Yin Su fit into this puzzle?

I turned north and east to her apartment. I felt disloyal heading there. It bothers me that my work spoils every relationship it touches. Yesterday I had been intoxicated and delighted by her. The same thing would happen today, the moment she opened her door to me. Only today it wouldn't last, I was going there as a policeman. She would be happy to see me and I would have to watch her become first puzzled, then angry as I asked her what she knew about her boss's most important client, the man with the Hong Kong connection.

This time I did stop on my way over, picking up the little four-rose posy from the hippie girl at the corner of Eglinton and Yonge and phoning Cy Straight's office to check if Su was there. She wasn't. Miss Anorexia told me that she was away from the office for the balance of the week. I thanked her and drove to the apartment.

The lobby entrance was unlocked so I let myself in and rode up to the fourth floor, carrying my roses head down, out of the back of my hand so they wouldn't be too obvious. I tapped on her door and waited a moment and then there was a faint movement inside, slow and deliberate and a voice that seemed too low called out, "Who is there?"

"Reid Bennett." I tried to make myself sound loose, relaxed, but I backed off two paces and moved to the left, away from the door so nobody could launch himself out at me in a straight line. And I slid the roses further through my hand, butt first so the stems made a crude dagger. I was as ready as I could get. There was a little scraping sound and then the door was opened slowly. It was Su but she was moving like an old, old woman, and the silk sheath dress, the cheongsam she was wearing had been ripped completely up one side. There was blood on the front of it. She looked at me sightlessly.

"What happened?" I let the flowers drop, ignoring any chance of danger, stepping forward to cup her elbows in my hands. She slumped into them like a rag doll. "Mr. Willis was here," she said. I moved her back a step into the apartment, pushing the door closed behind me with one foot, checking around for anybody else present in the room. There was no one. "What happened?" I asked her again, lowering her on to the couch.

She looked at me, slowly bringing me into focus. Her face was bruised on the left side. I noted it, remembering in the same instant that Willis was right-handed. I reached out to touch the bruise and she blinked like an injured child. There were tears in her eyes now. "Oh, I am so ashamed," she said in a whisper.

"You have to tell me." I touched her unbruised cheek, filled with an anger so powerful I could barely breathe. "What did he do to you?"

She lowered her eyes and as I bent to listen she whispered it. "He raped me."

## 25

I could hardly breathe. I wanted Willis there, in front of me, so that I could hurt him, could transplant some of the agony from my heart into his body.

"Su, I will find him and I will make him sorry," I promised her. She said nothing, quietly overcoming her horror and shock, gathering her resources as only a woman can. I moved my head down closer to hers, brushing her cheek with my lips as I held her like a baby. "You have to go to the hospital."

She stiffened suddenly and I slackened my hold and moved back almost to arm's length from her as she composed her face and pulled the tattered cheongsam around her. "I do not wish anybody to know," she said.

I leaned down and kissed her on the forehead, a spell to disperse the demons. "He must go to prison," I told her. "To do that, you must charge him with assault. You won't be named in court."

She looked at me out of eyes filled with ten thousand years of wisdom. "Many people will know my shame," she said.

I kissed her again. "All right. You don't have to charge him. I'll find him and show him you're angry." I said it very formally, making it a sentence, pronounced by a judge. "But first, you must tell me whatever you know about him and then I will take you to the hospital for treatment. You won't have to tell them anything you don't want to."

She looked at me for a long, slow moment, then she said, "I will do it."

"Good." I patted her on the shoulder, wanting to do more, wanting to bury her head against my chest and hold her until the hurt went away, but knowing better as a policeman than a lover what had to be done. "Now can I ask you to forget that we're friends and that I'm a man. Please let me see what he's done."

She said nothing but lowered her eyes and covered them with her left hand in a gesture so graceful I could have wept.

Gently I moved the torn cheongsam aside. She was wearing a brassiere but no panties. The insides of her thighs were stained with blood. The sight made my pulses hammer, drowning out everything else until I got control of myself and drew a long breath to cool myself out. When I knew my voice would be calm I asked, "What happened, Su? Tell me everything."

She was more calm than I, dignified as she told me a story I have heard in different versions perhaps a hundred times before. "I stayed home today. Mr. Straight said he would not be coming to work and I could have the day off if I wanted. So I stayed here. At nine o'clock I hear a knock on the door. I think it is you because you have not called me since yesterday. So I open the door and it is Mr. Willis."

I waited, saying nothing and she composed herself and went on. "I have seen him before at the office. He's a client. But I am surprised to see him at my house."

"Did he push his way in?" The scene was playing itself out in my brain. Willis, the criminal, betrayed by his own man, looking for ways to avenge himself on me. Maybe afraid to tackle me face to face, coming here and assaulting this girl. My voice was too thick to continue and I stopped and waited for Su to go on.

She nodded first. "Yes, he take me by the arms, here." She indicated a spot high on her biceps. I noticed there were bruises on both sides where fingers had pinched in, agonizingly, just above the bone. "Then, the next thing he say, 'Bitch, you tell that bastard Bennett where to find Wing Lok.' I tell him, What are you saying? but he hit me. He threw me across the room. I fell here. Then he said, 'Bitch, I'll teach you a lesson.' " Her voice stopped and she sat very still. My blood was roaring in my ears but I waited until she went on, only keeping a gentle pressure on her fingers with my own, letting her know she had a friend. At last she said, "And then he tear my clothes. He tear off my underwear. He cover my mouth and he . . ." her voice failed her. I just sat and stroked her hand. "I'll find him. Su, I swear it. Please try to remember anything that might tell me where to look for him."

She said nothing and I sat almost without breathing as I waited, feeling her tremble as she wept, silently. My head was ablaze with hatred for Willis. I remembered every word he had said in my presence, his readiness to hit my prisoners, his comment when he saw me with Su, the easy way Kennie had betrayed him as an arranger of beatings. And now this. I waited perhaps a minute before I spoke.

"Did he say anything at all, after he had, after he'd hurt you?" My arms were around her shoulders and she had let herself mold to my shape, but now she stiffened and stopped crying. She looked around blindly and I pulled out my handkerchief and gave it to her. She wiped her eyes and handed the handkerchief back to me, slowly drawing in a long breath.

"After it was finished, he say to me, 'Tell your friend Bennett that I will do the same to him when I see him again. Tell him he is nothing.'"

I patted her back and waited. She was recovering well. She didn't need a cross-examination; she needed space in her life so her own strength could bring her through the shock. After a moment or so more she went on. "Then he stood up and closed his trousers and said, 'Remember me, doll-face. Remember me to Bennett.'"

The policeman portion of me took over. "Did he say anything to let you know where he would be? Did he say he was going home?" I had an image of him driving the opposite direction from me as I came away from his house, perhaps passing me on the same street. I wanted him but I kept all the anger out of my voice, I was only a conscience, prodding to be heard. "Anything at all."

I waited again, and slowly her head came up from her chest and she looked up at me. There was the beginning of animation in her face as she spoke. "He said, 'I've got work to do. I've got a business to run.'"

That made me frown, it was an unusual choice of words and I guessed it meant that he was still involved with crime as a business, but which crime? I forced myself to stop thinking about Su and concentrate on what crime Willis might have been talking about. And then I remembered the warehouse robbery. Maybe he was talking about disposal of that truck full of liquor. Which meant he might be with it right now. The question was where.

She pulled gently out of my arms and stood up. "I will take a bath," she said. "I was going to when you came."

I touched her arm. "Don't, please, not for another minute or two, I'll take you to the hospital as you are."

She looked at me, then down at the floor, embarrassed. I held back from putting my arms around her. It was time for something constructive. Sympathy is only the first step in any investigation. And then she slowly looked up at me, her face lifting as gracefully as a flower turning to the sun. "I remember," she said and her voice trembled with excitement. She walked over to the low table and picked up the tiny tabletop phone that stood flat on it. "He used this telephone."

I came over and took it out of her hands. It was a custom phone, the kind they sell for twenty bucks in grocery stores, the kind that has no cradle but lies flat on the tabletop. No doubt Su had chosen it because it was small and had an attractive ring. But it had one other feature as well.

"This redial button. Is that the one that remembers the last number called?" I could hardly speak for excitement.

She nodded. "Yes, it remembers until you dial a different number. To call again, you just have to press the button."

I glanced around. She had a ballpoint pen and a scribble pad on a shelf below the phone. I brought them out and punched the redial button. The numbers clicked and tumbled in my ear. I counted and scribbled, stopping the phone before it rang the last digit. It took me five tries but at last I had the number. By the look of it the source was up north of Toronto, in the area called Agincourt, the area immediately north of the warehouse that had been robbed.

I thought about it for a few seconds and made my decision. This wasn't Murphy's Harbour. I couldn't go it alone. I had to call in the local guys. I needed their firepower for one thing, and on top of that I had no police rights beyond those of any citizen. Toronto was not my patch. If I picked a fight with Willis I would end up in jail. I made up my mind what to do.

I turned to Su who was standing, holding her side, studying me. "You must go to the hospital. It's important.

You're hurt." She lowered her head, but I didn't back off. "There's nothing else for it, Su. I'll call the police and they'll bring a policewoman in and you can talk to her and meantime you get the treatment you need. He hurt you, you're hemorrhaging."

She did not answer but I waited, agonized, helpless but determined to do things right for her. I wanted to catch Willis and break him, but her welfare came first. At last she looked up.

"I will go with you, but you must not wait. I would like you to find Mr. Willis for me," she said.

I patted her shoulder. "I will. Believe me Su, I will." I was acting as soothingly as a nursemaid but inside my mind was racing, forming the plan that would catch and keep Willis, even if Su refused to press charges. One of the details in my head was the way she was dressed. Her appearance had to be preserved so the examining doctor would see what had happened, but she could not go out on the street without a coat. I went to the closet and dug through it until I came up with a raincoat. "Put this on over your cheongsam," I told her. "You must keep those clothes on until you've been to the hospital."

She looked at me and then away, a sad glance. I patted her again and helped her into the coat. She stood, like a guest at a party, reluctant to be the first to leave, and I touched her elbow and steered her to the apartment door. Then as she stood there I went back and looked around the room, checking over the floor until I found what I was looking for. It was a pair of bikini panties, torn almost beyond recognition. The sight of them was the final evidence of the rape. As I bent to pick them up a jolt of animal ferocity raced up my arms from my fingertips and seemed to explode inside my brain. In that instant I wanted Willis dead. But I did not say anything. I rolled the piece of ragged nylon up small and pushed it into the pocket of her raincoat. Then I led her down the stairs and out on to the street.

We were about ten minutes from the hospital. In the time it took to drive there, Su said nothing. She sat staring ahead in a daze. I kept glancing across at her but there was nothing I could have done beyond what I was doing. She was in shock and needed help. Willis would have to come later, and so would sympathy and a slow readjustment to the fact that not all men were brutal, not all of us cause pain.

I parked in the circle at the side of the emergency entrance. Some fussy little East Indian guard came rushing out to tell me to move but I told him, "Emergency." He didn't take the hint but jogged after me into the reception area.

"I am sorry. You cannot stay there," he said fussily.

"I'm sorry you're having so much trouble understanding me," I said. "This lady is hurt. I will move the car in a couple of minutes. For now, make yourself useful, get her a wheelchair."

He opened his mouth to protest but I turned and smiled right down his eyes until he bustled to get a chair. A Chinese nurse caught sight of us and came over, anxiously. She looked sternly at me and fired off a clatter of Cantonese at Su. Su answered in the characteristic singsong and the nurse took her arm. Su turned to me and with a frightened little smile said, "I will be looked after. Please find him," and went away through double doors with no glass in them.

I looked around for a phone and saw one on the wall in one corner. I went and fed it a quarter and called the Metropolitan Police Department. I had to speak to four people in all before I reached Irv Goldman.

"Irv, this is Reid Bennett, looking for help, and offering you a nice pinch."

"I give at the office," he said automatically and when I didn't laugh, "What's up, Reid?"

"It's a rape case. I need a make on a Toronto phone number. Do you have the 'somebody called you' book?"

"Right here." The phone clattered on a desk and I could hear the echoing activity of the detective office. Typewriters were clicking, people were talking, a door slammed. And then Irv was back. "What's that number?"

I told him and he checked the backwards directory. "Yeah, it's a body shop on Sheppard Avenue in Agincourt, close to the intersection of Kennedy. What's it mean?"

"I promised you a pinch." I said, "I'll fill you in later, but for now, that's the probable location of that hijacked truck disappeared from the Bonded Security warehouse the other night."

His voice was gentle. "Where does the rape fit in?"

I cleared my throat. "The guy I want, name of Willis, he attacked a girl called Yin Su, at her apartment. I want him inside."

Irv was professional. "This Yin Su a friend?"

"Yes." I didn't have to draw any pictures.

"So okay, what I'll do is get the plainclothes guys up in that division to stake the place out till we get there. Then I'll pick you up somewhere and we'll go in. Tell me, this guy Willis, what's he look like, in case he tries to leave while the guys are watching the place?"

I gave him Willis's description, then remembered to add, "Thanks Irv. Don't let them show any uniforms up there, and don't move in on this guy until I get there. Please."

"Where are you?" was his only answer.

"I can be up at that corner waiting by the time you've made your calls and got there. Can I see you there? I've got a blue two-year-old Chev."

"Northeast corner," he said, and hung up.

I worked in Toronto for nine years as a policeman and I know the city like the back of my hand. In less than five minutes I was crossing the Bloor Street Viaduct, heading for the Parkway. I glanced north from the viaduct to make sure it was clear, then accelerated down on to it and north to the 401. As I drove I went over what Su had told me. It all fit. Willis was rattled. Kennie had blown his cover completely. His career with Bonded was over, as soon as they could mount a proper investigation. If he was into organized crime, he was now all in. Nobody else would hire him for legitimate work. He was alone and angry and his first thought had been to lash out. He must have realized how things stood when he saw Su with me in court the previous morning, or perhaps he had been talking to her brother since then. If he had worked in Hong Kong it was a cinch he knew enough Cantonese to carry on a proper conversation with him. He knew the way to hurt me was through her.

I was at the rendezvous ten minutes ahead of Goldman and I waited impatiently, wishing I had asked him for the address so I could have staked it out. The thought of Willis getting away was an agony. I wanted him locked up, if I could keep from breaking him in half in the process of arresting him.

Irv pulled in behind me and blinked his lights in my mirror. I was glad to see he was alone in the car. I jumped out of mine and went back to slide in beside him.

"Just like old times," he said cheerfully and I had to stop and program myself to grin. Irv was a policeman. He didn't deal in vengeance, he dealt in policework and this was just another case. He would solve it and head home to help his kids with their math homework. That was the kind of guy he was.

"Yeah," I said.

He glanced over at me. "Is she hurt?"

"She was hemorrhaging," I told him. "I want that bastard inside, Irv. She's a straight, pretty, fragile little thing and he's a headbeating sonofabitch with a grievance with me that he took out on her."

Irv drove, nodding, until I stopped. Then he asked, "You carrying?"

"No. My gun's in the station up at Murphy's Harbour."

He nodded again. "Good," he said. "I don't want to have to lock you up for plugging this guy, good or bad, right or wrong. He has to go inside or I'm not playing. Okay?"

"My first choice would be to put the bastard in traction," I said savagely. "But I know the rules. I'll settle for having him inside. That okay?"

He reached across with his right hand and said, "Welcome back, I've missed you."

The body shop was closed. There was a sign outside, crudely painted in red undercoating that had been applied with a spray nozzle. "Gord's repairs, closed until September 20th."

Irv looked around. "No sign of the locals," he said. "Unless they're out the back waiting." He took the key out of the ignition, shaking his head wearily. "You never can tell with these bastards in the sticks. They wouldn't realize the guy could come out the front door just as easy as the back."

He got out of the car. "So let's go see if anyone's home."

I followed him to the front door. It was glass, set in a glass-windowed office, the typical automotive or gas station setup. The inside door to the work area was closed. Irv tried the door. It was locked. Then he leaned forward and pressed his ear against the glass. "There's somebody inside," he said. "Let's try the back."

We walked around the back, not hurrying, not looking at all concerned, not policemen, just a pair of guys ambling aimlessly. At the back we found a single small door, locked. Irv tried it once, quietly, then put his ear against it and listened hard. "They're awful quiet in there. Maybe they heard us out front and are keeping their heads down." He straightened up and we looked at one another for a moment, then he said, "The smart thing to do is for you to stay here and pound hell out of this door while I go around the front. If they're up to anything, they'll bust out that way."

"Just don't let them get by," I said softly. "Okay, you head around there. In thirty seconds, I start hammering."

He bumped me on the shoulder and strode off. I watched him go, concentrating on him, not Willis, thinking how he had put on weight since we last worked together. I hadn't, but then I didn't have Dianne at home cooking for me like he did.

The thirty seconds stretched on into the next century but I used it well, finding a metal rod on the ground and using it to jam the door so it couldn't be opened. That made it time and I started hammering, shouting "Police, open up!"

I kept it up for almost a minute, before I heard Irv shout from the front, and then the sound of a shot. I left the door and sprinted around to the front. Irv was standing there, his gun drawn. "Stand back, they're shooting," he called. And then the crazy bastard slammed his foot through the front door, shattering the glass in a rainbow of sound. He reached in lefthanded and opened the door and then we were in, him first, me behind him, picking up a stamp machine and a distributor cap full of pencils off the desk, missiles of my own in case Irv went down and I had to face somebody with a gun.

There was another door inside and I knew it was the Rubicon. Whoever was inside would be covering it. We had to open it and we had to face fire to do so. Irv didn't even hesitate. He crouched low, turned the door knob gently then threw himself inside to the right away from the door. I heard a ripple of shots one after the other, so close I couldn't tell who had fired them. But I didn't wait. I caught the door as it was about to click closed, launched myself against it and crashed through, throwing the machine to my left, the distributor to my right and shouting loud enough to make my old Marine instructor proud of me.

Two shots slammed my way and I rolled farther, under the side of the tractor trailer that was standing in the bay. From there I checked the terrain all around. I couldn't see anybody's legs at my level, but Irv Goldman was lying collapsed against the wall beside the door. He was alive, I could tell that from where I lay, but he was badly hurt. His gun was in his right hand, which was lying on the floor two feet from the trailer. As I glanced at him he saw me. He took a big, gasping breath and nodded imperceptibly to his right and high. Then, with the guts I had always admired in him, over years together, he flicked his gun under the trailer to me. I grabbed it, as the shot rang out above me, then rolled out the other side of the trailer, Irv's .38 in my right hand. I glanced up. There was some kind of loading platform at the rear of the trailer. I guessed the gunman was up there. He was probably edging to my side now, ready to snap a shot down the side of the trailer at me. I did what I'd been trained to do. I made for the high ground. Darting to the front of the trailer I clambered onto the roof, treading softly, training my gun ahead, watching for the gunman.

As I inched forward he fired again. The echoes filled the whole workspace. I could not judge where he was, but I guessed he had come to the side I'd been, and snapshot without looking. I ran forward on tiptoe to the end of the trailer and looked down. Kennie was below me, holding a pistol. I took careful aim, before he knew I was there, but I didn't shoot. This isn't Nam, I'm a copper here, not a grunt. I said, "Drop it!" in a clear voice and waited while his eyes came up and then the muzzle of the gun. And that was when I fired, into his right arm, smashing it above the elbow so that he roared with a pain bigger than anything he had ever known before and the gun slammed away from my shot, back on the ramp, skidding across it to fall with a clatter into the well of the shop.

I darted across the top of the trailer and checked the ground on both sides before I vaulted down on to the loading ramp. Kennie was on the floor, clutching the compound fracture with his left hand, rolling back and forth in blind agony. I grabbed him by his good shoulder. "Where's Willis?"

He turned his face to me but he didn't recognize me, nothing mattered but the reality of his pain. I know, I've been there. I shook him again and this time he said, "He isn't here."

I left him then, jumping down into the pit to pick up the gun and stuff it into my belt before running around the other side of the trailer to where Irv was lying slumped against the wall. All the color had drained out of him and his eyes were closed but he opened them when I spoke. "Get him?" he whispered.

"Yeah. Where are you hit?"

He made a vague swoop with his left hand towards his shoulder. "Up here, I think. It's numb."

I glanced around again, checking there was no one else there. There wasn't. I pinched him, on the inside of the thigh. "Can you feel that?" His eyes narrowed with pain. "Yes, what the hell was that for?"

I patted his good shoulder, not speaking. His spine was intact, that was the good news. The bad could come later. I ran out to the car and called in an emergency. They crowded me for details but I just told them, "I'm alone with the injured officer, send help," and went back to Irv.

He had not moved but his eyes were open and he tried a grin. "Check the back," he said hoarsely. "I thought I could hear somebody out there."

# 26

I gave him Kennie's pistol. He tried to hold it but the weight was too much for his injured arm and he let it clunk to the floor under its own weight. "If you hear me holler, get the gun up and stand by to use it," I told him. He nodded and I went back to the end of the truck and up on the loading ramp again.

Kennie was lying there, numb with pain. He looked at me dully but did not move or say anything. There was no menace left in him. I checked around. There was a door to one side of the ramp, leading out to the back area inside the rear exit, I guessed.

Moving carefully, carrying Irv's gun in my right hand ready for use, I opened the door and jumped through it. Something crashed against the wall behind me, and as I dived and rolled away from the door it fell with a clatter onto the concrete.

I snapped off a shot in the general direction of where the wrench had been thrown from. I've been under fire enough times to know it was necessary. I didn't expect to hit anybody, just to teach him a little respect for my firepower. It might even shock him into surrendering.

I rose into a fighting crouch, facing an empty oil drum with a pile of cartons behind it, still flicking glances all around me, searching for whoever had thrown the wrench. And then Yin Su's brother jumped up with a scream and advanced on me, straddle-legged, ignoring my gun. I shouted at him, "Hold off or I shoot," but he kept coming. I took the time to gesture with the gun, wordlessly, letting him know I was the equal of any martial artist. But still he came, like a kamikazi pilot, oblivious to the weapon. And at last, when he was ten feet from me, I aimed, two-handed, for the meaty part of his upper leg, on the outside where it would not smash his thigh, and fired. And the hammer clicked closed on an empty shell. I fired again, twice, while he stood taller, knowing he could win. Desperately I hurled the gun at him, hard enough to smash his head, but he batted it out of the air without looking at it and it fell with a clatter against the oil drum. Then he composed himself into a tighter stance, coiling himself for maximum power and began to stalk me.

I was too far from the door to make it before he leaped. I saw his face crease into a tight little grin. He had me. Now I would pay for the shame Sam had worked on him. In those seconds, he was a cocked weapon and I was a man about to die, except for my one hole card.

It had sat in my pocket, round and flat and harmless,

since I purchased it the day before. I had already opened the lid a time or two, now I reached into my pocket and loosened the lid again before bringing it out, concealed under my clawed hand.

I knew it would give me a moment, no more, and then only if I timed it perfectly, so I concentrated on the fighter while I opened the lid totally, working with my fingertips, out of his sight, and waited for him to advance.

He was playing with me. He could have launched himself across the space and hit me at will but he was too angry. He wanted revenge, wanted to be close, to savor my fear.

We circled, about eight feet apart, for maybe fifteen seconds. By now the container was open in my hand and I was poised to make my move waiting for him to decide when he would kill me. I was still praying for the door to open behind me and a big uniformed copper to come in and blow the little guy away, but that wasn't going to happen before I was dead. So I waited, holding my hand loosely until he made his move. I saw the flicker in his eyes, fast as a camera shutter, and in the instant he advanced I uncoiled my clenched hand and threw the contents of my tin into his face. He ducked instinctively but not far enough. A fine cloud of English snuff filled the space around him and before he could stop himself he had breathed and was sneezing.

As his eyes closed reflexively, I was there, slamming my full weight down my left leg and against his right shinbone. I heard it snap in the same second he sneezed convulsively and fell. Then I backed off while the cloud of snuff settled to the ground on top of his writhing body.

He was almost too tough, he was back on his feet, in his stance again, before I could find something to hit him with, but the snuff was too much for him. He could control everything, the pain, his balance, everything except the automatic closing of his eyes as he sneezed. And as he did, I hit him hard on the right collarbone and it was my game.

I stooped for Irv's gun, picking it up and checking the cylinder. All chambers had been fired, he must have shot four times before I got hold of it. I looked down at the dazed kid on the floor, still blinking and sniffing, rubbing his eyes with his good hand.

"Unlucky for you I remembered my father's bad habits," I

said cheerfully. Then I picked up the snuff can, a 25 gram container of Top Mill #1, the kind my father had carried with him down the mine every day, joking that if they ran out of blasting powder, he could help. There was a thin crust still clinging to the bottom groove of the can and I ran my finger around and assembled a good pinch which I took, not sneezing but feeling the immediate buzz that makes this the best way there is to enjoy tobacco. Then the door opened behind me and a young policeman in uniform sporting the standard moustache was standing looking in. "What's your name?" he asked me sternly. He was just a baby, fresh from writing parking tickets around one of the shopping malls, suddenly confronting his first crime.

"Reid Bennett," I told him, and spelled it out. "Did the ambulance come for my partner?"

# 27

ALL I wanted to do was find Willis. The local police, when they came pouring into the place, were caught up in the obvious situation, two men shot and a stolen truck. They were set to plod through their investigation at the normal speed, but I was anxious to leave and go on looking for Willis. I owed him a further grudge now. Irv Goldman was a friend, and it hurt to see him suffering. I had taken a look at his wound. It was high in the shoulder, not bleeding much; possibly it had smashed his collarbone but he would recover, I was sure of it. I've seen enough bullet wounds in my time to know, but it was another reason for finding Willis.

I helped the medics load Irv on the ambulance. He was coming out of the initial shock, showing some of the chutzpah that had made him a great partner. "For this I gave up my lunch hour," he said, and winked at me. I patted him on his good arm and stood back.

"Now you owe me one," he said, pointing a finger as the doors closed on him. And then they were gone, with the siren howling, and the crowd of passersby growing thicker around us as the cars stopped on the highway and people jumped out, hoping for excitement. A second an.bulance had been ordered for the two injured rounders and while it was coming, I was overlooked by the local police and went to find Kennie again. He was holding his arm, his left hand cupped around the break, tugging impatiently on the handcuffs that connected him to Yin Chang. Chang himself was ignoring us, lying like a sick animal, not looking up, not generating any vital force at all. Even when I came and crouched next to Kennie he didn't look up. Kennie did and anger blazed in his eyes.

I said, "Where's Willis, Kennie? Tell me where he is and I'll do what I can for you in court."

He looked away, then back at me, stoking up the hatred that he would live for, back in the pen. "I shoulda shot you last night."

"Don't feel bad, it's been tried before," I said. "It's not you I want, it's Willis. Where is he, do you know?"

I waited for about thirty seconds while he stared down at the floor, then he raised his head and spat, trying to hit me in the face but his mouth was dry from shock and he just dribbled on his chin. "I wouldn't help you if it meant hangin' not to," he said.

I took out my handkerchief and handed it to him. "I admire your balls, Kennie. Where you're going, you'll need to hang tough."

He wiped his mouth and gave me back the handkerchief. There was respect in his eyes, but it didn't change his mind about what he should do. Mentally he was already in the pen, telling tall tales of how he'd made me beg. I didn't begrudge him the dream. He would have very little else to groove on.

In the end I went back to the local station with the detectives. They were young and aggressive, busy playing games with one another, finishing one another's comments, laughing loud and long. They were in no hurry to take a statement from me. One of them said, "You sure seem to attract a lot of bad asses, fella."

I nodded and waited for the other Bobbsey twin to take over. "Yeah, kind of makes a guy think you may be part of this bullshit." They both laughed, hard, loud, meaningless laughter. Then the first one said, "Waddya say to that?"

That was my cue. I told them, in a very few words. "You're a pair of amateurs who ought to be out writing parking tickets. If you're not going to do anything productive, call the Metro Homicide squad. Otherwise let me out of here, you're wasting my time."

One of them said, "Now just a minute, fella," and I cut him off.

"You call me Chief or Mr. Bennett. I was a detective while your mommie was wiping your nose for you. Face up to your limitations. Let me talk to a real policeman, right away."

They blustered some more but neither one of them could meet my eyes and when clown A made a joke, clown B didn't laugh. In five minutes I was free of them, giving a statement to a sergeant who was old enough to see what was happening.

It took half an hour and then I was dropped back at my car and I sat there, trying to work out what to do next. By now Willis was listed as wanted, his description circulated by teletype and radio. Any policeman might find him and I wondered where I might look. He hadn't been at the rendezvous point. Where else did that leave? He might have headed home, but a detective would have been sitting across the street, waiting to talk to him. It made no sense to go there. But where else was there?

The only contacts I could think of were Cy Straight and Su. At the thought that he might go back to her apartment I felt rage break over me with almost physical force. I could see her face again, dazed with horror, as it had been at her apartment and in that instant I could have killed Willis, barehanded.

I shook my head, that wasn't the answer. I had to find him and he would not be at Su's apartment. One place to look might be in the company of Cy Straight. They had something going between them, otherwise the little man wouldn't have shown at Willis's house. It was thin but I hadn't talked about Straight to the police. He was all mine, for whatever that was worth.

First I called the law office and found that Mr. Straight was not in. Fine. Next thing was to look for his private address. He must have had a clear conscience because it was in the phone book, Cyril Straight, barrister, and an address in Rosedale, which turned out to be half a million dollars' worth of house. It deserved to sit in five acres of private park, but instead was stuffed into a row of others, just the same, behind a narrow green lawn with century-old hard maples growing in it.

I parked a few doors away and considered my approach. There was no way I could bully Straight into helping. He knew the law and would stomp all over me if I started suggesting deals for help. No, it would have to be more direct, I would have to bring some moral pressure on him, coupled with a suggestion of physical threat. Basic terrorist tactics that would have made me vomit if I hadn't been looking for the man who had raped Su.

I checked the driveway as I walked up to the house. Straight's DeLorean was parked out back. He was home. The big thing was getting past the front door to see him. I rang and waited and after a moment a tall fair woman who looked as if she should be in a diamond advertisement opened the door for me. She was a step above me, which made her tall enough to look down her nose slightly. "Yes?" she said.

I was all charm, I smiled and nodded amiably. "I have an appointment with Mr. Straight. My name is Willis."

She frowned and I wondered if I'd blown it, that Willis was already inside and this would trigger her alarms. But all she said was, "He told me he wasn't to be disturbed."

"I imagine he meant during our meeting," I volunteered, and she frowned again. By the lines in her forehead she did a lot of it.

"You could be right," she said in a voice you could have used to write on slate. "You'd better come in, I suppose."

I followed her, through a hallway bigger than my living room and on to a library. It had a good, used look. These books were friends, not wallpaper. She went to a door in the far side and tapped. A faint voice said, "Now what is it?" in an angry hiss.

"Man called Willis, for you. Has an appointment." Her own voice hadn't changed. I could see there wasn't a nickel's worth of affection in that whole million-dollar household. No wonder the books looked so well cared for. They were all the company Straight had.

A chair scraped and the door was opened by Straight, his face eager. He saw me and tried to shut the door but I was too quick for him. "Hi, Cy, good of you to see me." I held the edge of the door and beamed a big stupid smile at his dragon lady. "Thanks ma'am. What I have to tell your husband is legal, confidential."

He was trying to speak but I overrode him as I moved into the room. "I really appreciate your seeing me at short notice, Cy." I closed the door and raised one finger at him, like an admonishing mother. "You're in real trouble."

He said, "I want you to leave," but he didn't open the door, and I knew he was whipped. I let him sweat for a moment while I looked around. The office was a copy of his downtown place, only smaller. There were a few rows of legal books but no file cabinets. On the desk were a couple of big manila envelopes. He sidled towards them as I looked around but I moved faster and picked them up. He grabbed but I just looked at him sternly and he pulled his hands back, like a greedy child caught reaching for the cookies without leave.

I glanced into the top one. It contained photographs and as I reached in to see what they were I caught a flash of pure anguish in Straight's eyes.

I pulled them out, glanced at the top one and realized what was going on. "How long has he been blackmailing you?"

He sat down behind his desk and put his hands over his face. I felt sorry for him, but that wasn't going to do anything for either of us. "How long?" I asked again, my voice toneless.

"Two years," he said through his fingers. "Ever since I went to Hong Kong. I was there for a convention. He was a police officer."

I laid the pictures down on the desk top. They were the

standard stuff of blackmail, grainy, badly composed snapshots of this bent little man on a couch with a girl of about eleven, a Chinese girl. I spread them out with one fingertip. "Is pedophilia big with you?" He said nothing. I could see tears running out between his clenched fingers.

He shook his head. "Just one time," he said croakily. "It wasn't as if she was a little innocent. She was a tart. Her father sold her in infancy, I guess."

"Who took the photographs—Willis?" The rest was unimportant. The girl was ten thousand miles beyond my ability to help, an indentured prostitute in Wanchai, keeping 10 percent of her earnings, if she was lucky, another nameless casualty, out of reach. I needed Willis.

He nodded again, and then took down his hands and looked at me out of his tearstained face, like a mourner. "He got hold of them, I'm not sure whether he took them."

"He's the man I want," I said. "I'm not interested in your past. Willis attacked Yin Su this morning."

Straight flinched. "No." He mouthed it, almost silently. "No, not that."

I hate the delicious horror so many people feel about rape. They shudder but can't let go of the thought, toying with it, fantasizing about it. "She'll be fine. I took her to the hospital. Now I want to know where he is because . . ." I read the look in his eyes and I let the sentence dangle. I had been about to say, "because he's going to jail," but I could see hope in his face. I would kill Willis, would take the menace away and let him live in all the peace his handsome, hateful wife would allow him. His thoughts were vivid in his eyes.

"I don't know. He was supposed to come and see me this morning. When he didn't arrive, I went up to his house."

"Did you have money for him, what?"

Straight sniffed, a long, deliberate noisy breath that calmed him. "It's not important," he said at last.

"Look." I leaned down on both hands so my face was close to his. "Unless you help me, I'll pick up those photographs and take them down to a friend of mine who knows where to have them circulated. Now I don't want to. All I want is information, I don't want your ruin on my conscience." It was brutal but I had to know everything I could find out about Willis.

Straight made a half-hearted snatch for the photographs but I leaned my weight on them and he pulled his hand back. "I helped him with some contacts," he said quietly. "There were people he wanted to deal with, people he didn't want to reveal himself to."

"What people?" Now I was getting warm. Maybe one of these contacts knew where he was, now that he was running.

Straight took out a Kleenex and wiped his face, scrubbing it, trying to remove the tear marks. "Tony Caporetto for one."

"He's dead. Did Willis do that?"

Straight shrugged, a gesture that made his bent spine even more pitiable. "I suppose so. It said in the newspapers that he was attacked by a martial artist. That fits, Willis knew lots of Chinese. Not the usual law-abiding ones, the troublemakers, including some enforcers."

"Let's handle this the easy way." I sat down on the edge of his desk, something I knew he would hate. Office-bound people all hate it; their desks are their egos. "Suppose we stop fencing and you just tell me everything you know about Willis."

He opened his mouth and I knew he was going to make the "By what authority?" kind of speech so I tapped the envelope. He dropped his eyes, cleared his throat again and began.

"It started after I got back from the conference in Hong Kong. I was in my office, he made an appointment in the normal manner, then came in, shut the door and showed me these."

"When was that?"

"Two years ago next month. I remember because it was just one month after I got home."

"And what did he want, in return for silence?" I was filled with a hunting lust. Once I knew this man's pattern I could find him.

Straight squirmed his back. I wondered if it hurt or if he had the itchy tension that comes with interrogation. "He wanted me to work for him, making contacts with people whom he wanted to impress."

"Names?" I snapped it out but he shook his head at me.

"They wouldn't mean anything to you, they were people in Hong Kong."

"Why would he have to blackmail you to get that kind of help?"

"He wouldn't have needed me if his aims had been legitimate, but they weren't. He was extorting, trying to take over a space that had grown up among the Chinese gangs in Toronto."

"You mean the Triads?" I asked impatiently.

Straight looked at me in surprise. "I'm astonished that you've heard about them. It's not common knowledge."

"Where does Willis fit in?" I kept the pressure on him, no point explaining that I'd found out about the Triads the hard way, just a day before. Let him talk. I could always go back over the facts for explanations if they were needed.

My comment didn't speed him up any. He just nodded and said, "You understand the Triads hold the real power in the community. They exist by extortion, exclusively of Chinese businesses. Their methods are similar to those used by the Mafia. They provide services such as cleaning or advertising, at extortionate rates. If you don't pay, your restaurant burns down."

"Tell me about Willis. What void is he trying to fill?" I kept the pressure on in my voice, forcing him back to the reality of why I was there.

The thought of Willis brought a frown back to his face but he went on in a calm voice. "What has happened recently is that some Viet Namese groups have moved in. They have started extorting. Under the old, Triad deals, restaurants and gaming houses paid their money under the heading of 'protection.'" He allowed himself a smile at the thought. "Well, the Viet gangs started wrecking places that were supposed to be protected. And as a result, these places stopped paying tribute to the Triads and they lost face, lost prestige, and most important of all, lost money."

He paused, as he might have done in his summation to the jury, but I pressed him. I didn't want him taking control of the conversation. "So Willis decided to become some kind of warlord."

"More than that. He wanted to break new ground, to reach the companies that were coming into Canada from

Hong Kong. He had contacts in the Crown colony so he could apply pressure back home if they gave trouble here."

"And where do you fit into all this?" I phrased the question crudely so he couldn't hide behind his legal credentials.

For a moment he looked at me, going pink in the face, then he realized I was there to stay so he explained. "I think Willis must have been involved with crime in Hong Kong. What he did was give me the names of people to contact there. I put some carefully worded suggestions to them without revealing the identity of my client."

"Did any of the people you contacted make any comments, try to bargain, or did they roll over and play dead, what?" I wanted to find how much power Willis had. It sounded as if he was some kind of WASP figurehead for Triad activity in Toronto. And yet he was cunning enough to hide himself behind Straight. Obviously he was a man with a lot of people at his command. If he decided to take me out, I would be killed, no question. I had to find him and either kill him or put him away for keeps.

"Nobody said a word in protest. I was to ask for the money to come in under the heading of insurance and they all paid, heavily. One company, opening a restaurant here, paid five thousand dollars a month. That must be close to the profit they'll make for the first few years."

"And the Heavenly Lotus corporation refused to pay?" It figured, I just wondered if he would remember that it was the outfit which owned the construction site and so far it was the only one in trouble.

"Yes." He nodded. "They sent me a letter stating that the insurance companies they have in Hong Kong could provide all the protection they needed."

I said nothing, just thinking things through and he blurted, "I had no choice. I had to do what he told me. One mistake, and he owned me."

He was going to continue but I held up my hand. "That's enough. A guy like Willis would have kept some cash for emergencies. Maybe we can get him by finding out where his deposits are and staking them out. Did you have any ideas about that?"

Straight shook his head. "He told me nothing more than

what I had to know. He received money, a lot of money, but where he put it I couldn't tell you."

I stood up, grabbing the envelope of photographs, spilling them into my hand. I heard him gasp but went on riffling through the shots as if they were family snapshots. I have seen too much crime to be sickened by them. I just wanted to remind him of the hold I had over him. I would never have used it, but he wouldn't believe that. His guilt was choking him.

"Okay, I need help." I put the pictures back into their envelope and tucked it under my arm, like a commuter with his morning paper.

He looked at it, hungrily. There was more than fear in his eyes. I realized it as I watched him. He wanted his pictures back. That practiced child, a miniature woman, smaller and more frail than he was, she had made him feel invulnerable. He wasn't whipping himself for his guilt when he riffled through those pictures. He was reliving the one time his life had matched his fantasy. It was something else to use in my own struggle to solve this case. I put away the threat I had been contemplating and promised him, "You get these back when you're through helping me."

He flushed and I knew he recognized my knowledge of him. That was a start. Now he had to help.

"You must have had fallback plans with Willis. If he had you by the short hair, he wouldn't have bothered coming here to your office. You must have seen him. The question is, where?"

He answered automatically. "I went to his house usually."

"But that wasn't all, was it. Where else did you see him?"

He stared at me blankly. He looked catatonic. I guessed it was some kind of trick he used on witnesses in court, lulling them for a second before lashing out with the exact question that tripped them up. He spoke at last in a soft voice. "I used to meet him, by appointment, at the Palace Gates in Chinatown."

I stood up. It was coming together. Willis's enforcer worked there. It must be one of his points of contact with Chinatown. And besides, Lee was an important man. That could mean he had the clout Willis needed to get things done in Hong Kong. It wasn't likely but there was at least a

possibility that Lee was in the scam with him. I shoved the
telephone to Straight. "Call Lee and tell him you want to
talk to Willis."

He flinched. "That would be irregular, I've never done
that."

"These are highly irregular times. Get on with it."

He didn't have to look up the number. He dialled from
memory and a moment later said, "Mr. Lee, this is Captain
Hook. I would like to reserve a table with Dr. Smith." He
looked up at me, over the phone, just as blankly as before
and waited for about half a minute. Then he nodded. "I'm
sorry you are so booked up. I will wait for your call."

He hung up and I put my hand on his wrist. "Now what?
It sounds like you've done all that a lot of times before."

"Only as necessary." He was coming to life, still as frail,
but his eyes were burning with excitement. Whatever else
crime did, it certainly gave him something to live for. He
looked up, a bland, self-assured lawyer's expression. "Now I
wait and Mr. Lee calls back and tells me where the meeting
will be."

# *28*

WE waited for the call, me in the only comfortable chair in
the room. Straight at his desk, turning the envelope of
photographs over and over in his smooth little hands. At
last I pretended to close my eyes and he slid the shots out
and went through them slowly. There was a sensuous hiss as
he rustled them and I could feel his excitement in the air
like the tension that grows before a thunderstorm.

When the phone rang he sat up quickly but pushed the
photos away before answering "Hello." I had my eyes fixed
on his and he held up one hand in a gesture that meant "Be
quiet." Finally he said, "Yes, I'll be there," and hung up.

He stood up and reached behind him for a cardigan jacket that was hanging over the back of his chair. "We have a meeting," he said. "At 1:07 P.M. That gives us thirty-two minutes."

"We'll take my car." I reached for my keys as I got to my feet. I didn't want him driving. I wanted Sam with us, and he wouldn't fit into that metal seagull of Straight's.

"If you insist," he said fussily. "But I think we'll have to take the subway. We're meeting inside the Eaton Centre."

"Fine." The subway ran within four blocks of Louise's house. We could be down to the Eaton Centre in twelve minutes from there. I had just enough time to get Sam.

I didn't bother picking up the photographs. Blackmail is beyond me and a lawyer as shrewd as Straight could read that in my eyes. Besides, I needed his cooperation, not his fear.

I opened the car door for him, and, as he got in, I caught a whiff of some lime aftershave. It seemed pathetic on a man who could never be anybody's sex object.

"There's a pair of dark glasses in the glove box, put them on," I told him.

He blazed at me. "You think that will disguise me? You think a pair of glasses will straighten this back?"

"You're going to be a blind man," I told him softly. "The help I want to take with me isn't allowed on the subway except with a blind man."

He didn't understand and started to say so but I cut him off. "I'm in your corner and I know this murderous sonofabitch better than you do. Please put the glasses on." He pulled an angry face, but he did as I asked. They were a very dark pair, clumsy and large on him. I had found them at the site of an accident in Murphy's Harbour. They had outlived their previous owner and I had picked them up and kept them. I don't wear them, but the occasional passenger does. Now it was Straight. They added to the pathos of his crooked back. I knew that nobody but a true bastard would give him any hassle when he took Sam on the train.

I turned north on Yonge Street before I noticed the blue Datsun in my mirror. I had seen it come out of a side street as I drove away from Straight's house. It could have been a coincidence but I watched it as we drove north. There were two people in it and it stayed behind me, two cars back, moving legally. I didn't act immediately. After all, Yonge Street is the most heavily travelled street in Canada. Then, as an experiment, I turned without signalling, just cutting left between a couple of cars and heading down one of the side streets that have been fitted with anti-speeding bumps. I kept the Chev moving fairly fast and we bottomed on the springs as I rolled over the first set of bumps. I slowed, checking the mirror, and saw the Datsun careen around the corner behind me, moving at my speed.

Straight was holding on to the dashboard, his mouth open to protest. "We're being followed," I told him. "Don't look round." He flicked a glance at me but in the same instant I hit the second set of speed bumps and settled with a scrunch that had my rear end dragging sparks off the roadway.

The Datsun wasn't as reckless. I gained twenty yards on him at each of the bumps and was half a block ahead by the time I turned on to Avenue Road. I swung north and stuck to the curb lane. Balmoral Street runs off to the west again but just north on my side there was a one-way street much closer. I broke the law and wisked into it the wrong way, causing an oncoming Mercedes to swerve and honk but not loudly enough for the Datsun people to hear.

Straight said, "What the hell are you doing?" but I ignored him. The road curves fifty yards from the corner with Avenue Road and I pulled around there and backed into the nearest driveway, all the way up behind the house. I waited for a minute, time enough for the Datsun to have missed us and head west along Balmoral. An elderly man, frosty enough to be Straight's father-in-law, came out of the garage and said, "I say," in the kind of voice you hear in twilight-of-the-empire movies. I beamed at him and said, "No hablo Inglese," which made him open his mouth in astonishment, then I drove out and up to St. Clair Avenue, still against oncoming traffic. Fortunately there was no policeman around and all I had to put up with was waves and abuse from outraged senior citizens obeying the law on the street where they lived.

In eight more minutes I was outside Louise's house. I

told Straight to sit tight and ran in to get Sam. He came easily so I knew there was nobody prowling in the house. I gave him thirty seconds to himself and then whipped the rear door of my car open and he jumped in. I have a leash in the car. It's not necessary for Sam, I could take him to a dog fight and he wouldn't look sideways until told to, but I keep it there for use in places where dogs are not supposed to be.

I snapped it on to his collar and told him, "Good boy," then drove back out to Yonge Street and down to the nearest subway station at Davisville. I abandoned my car at a meter that was magically vacant just when I needed it and with Sam and Straight jogged over to the subway entrance. Outside I handed Straight the leash and told him, "Say nothing, just make like you're following Sam." Then I stepped in front of Sam and told him, "Heel," and led the way into the station.

The Korean at the ticket window looked at Sam and frowned, but before he could speak I cut him off. "Me 'n my buddy are from Sudbury, that's his guide dog. What's the fare?"

He told me and I put the coins in, then made a show of helping Straight through the wicket. Still leading the way I went down the stairs and headed for the southbound trains. It was ten to one. We had just enough time.

Straight was behind me and I stopped against a wall so he pulled up there, not looking around. There were a couple of people at the station, a businessman with a briefcase and a girl pretty enough to be a model, carrying one of those leather cases that contain photographs. The businessman looked us over, the girl ignored us. I said to Straight, "You're doing fine. When this is over, you can take up amateur acting."

"Yes," he said curtly. "I'll be a natural for Richard the Third." The train came into the station and I moved forward, with Sam behind me and Straight behind him. There were lots of spare seats and I took one facing the door. Sam curled at my feet and Straight sat beside me, looking dead ahead, being serious about his part. I could tell that Sam's training was reassuring him, he wasn't sure what was going to happen, but he felt better equipped with Sam along.

When the train started he leaned towards me, whispering. "Who was that following you?" I didn't speak for a moment and he went on nervously, "Did they follow us on to the train?"

"No. Relax. Whoever it was is long gone. Now what I need to know is, what's the meeting place?" I was recapturing the interior of the Eaton Centre in my mind, trying to plan what to do. It was a good choice of rendezvous. It's a three-tiered shopping plaza under a glass roof. Tourists love it, it's replaced Niagara Falls as our most visited tourist attraction. At this time of day, out of tourist season, there would still be five thousand people in there. Willis would be able to hide in the crowds and melt away without being seen. He had a choice of ways to escape. The subway had two stations right in the place. He could jump on to a train and vanish. One stop up or down the line would put him beyond reach of a search party. Or, he could have his car in the lot, ready to race. Or he could flee on foot. A hundred men searching would be no guarantee of finding him, and all I had was me, and Sam.

Straight confirmed my guess. "He wants me to come to the foot of the escalator on this level, close to the subway, Lee said."

I nodded, although he was pretending he could not see me. "That figures. He can stand one or two levels up and check that you're clean. Then he'll come down on one escalator and take you up on the other so that you can't be followed."

Straight half turned his head to me, then realized he was out of character and checked the motion. "Have you done this kind of thing before?" he asked and his voice was almost respectful.

"Security is a big part of police work," I told him. "I figure he'll be on the far side, above you, so he can get the best possible view past you down towards the subway. If he sees me, or anybody suspicious, he'll be gone."

Straight sighed, a quick nervous uptake of air to calm his nerves. "What can we do?" he asked and I could almost see all the cogs turning in his mind, churning out the questions, like why am I here?

"What we do is this. You take off those glasses and walk

out there and wait. Make a point of checking the time, look impatient. That will make him think you want to get away. I'll get off at Dundas and go through the bottom level with Sam. I'll be there before you are. What I want you to do is hang in, at the bottom of those steps. If he tries to call you up, pretend not to notice him. He has to come to us or we'll lose him. Okay?"

He nodded. "Okay," he said quietly. Just to be sure he understood, I made him go over it again and he did, word perfect. And then we were at the Dundas station with two minutes to go before his stop. We both stood up and he took off the glasses and handed them to me. "I hope you know what you're doing," he said.

I didn't tell him otherwise. I didn't let him know I was running on instinct. Sure, Willis was wanted for investigation on charges relating to the finding of the hijacked truck. But he was wanted on the strength of my say-so. Any lawyer could get him off in a flash by saying I had set it all up out of vengeance. And the fact that somebody had followed us had me tense. I wondered who, and why, but I hid the facts and clapped Straight on the shoulder.

"Trust Sam," I told him, "he'll keep you as safe as a church." I put the glasses on myself and took Sam's leash. "When the train comes in, get out fast and head for the nearest exit," I told Straight. "I'm on my way. Just stick to the plan and this guy is off your back." He nodded once and turned to the door, gripping the post hard as the train pulled to a stop.

As always there was a crowd of people waiting at this stop. I made a show of being blind, letting Sam move ahead of me, out to the turnstile and into the concourse. Now I took the glasses off and unsnapped the leash from Sam's collar.

You have to go down a flight of steps to the bottom level of the Eaton Centre and I pattered down with Sam behind me like a shadow. He was so well behaved that nobody noticed us although no dogs are allowed inside the building.

I moved quickly through the basement of the Eatons store and on into the concourse. There's a fast food area there with all kinds of take-out food and half an acre of chairs and tables. Away on the far side of it I could see Straight, like a rock in the river of people that swirled around the bottom of the escalators. He was using his head, concentrating on looking around him, not up. That meant he couldn't be called up, out of my sight and beyond Sam's and my power to help him.

I moved closer, taking care to stay far enough back that I could not be seen from the gallery above this level. The escalators flow out into the floor space in the center of the mall, directly under the big glass roof, against a fountain where some kids who should have been in high school were leaning down to scoop out coins. There is an orange-drink stand close by. I moved in to the far side of it, using it as cover while I waited. A bright little girl with red hair came around inside it and asked if I wanted a drink. I shook my head and waited.

Suddenly I saw Straight stiffen, glancing up. He looked around, didn't see me, and licked his lips nervously as he moved closer to the foot of the escalator.

I hissed at Sam and came up under the escalator, moving out far enough to see Straight as he waited, obviously, for someone to come down to him.

He took a couple of steps to the left, out of my sight. I flicked a glance above me, making sure nobody was looking down on top of my attempt to hide, then moved around the foot of the escalators, through the torrent of people pouring down, nonstop, from the floor above. Straight was at the foot of the escalator, talking to Lee, the boss of the Palace Gates Restaurant. I saw him shake his head while Lee smiled and talked and smiled and waited. I saw Straight lick his lips again, then finally he nodded and went ahead of Lee on to the up escalator. I swore, under my breath. I could lose them both. Willis might be waiting at the top of the escalator. If I stepped out, he would see me and be gone before I could reach the second floor.

Impulsively I took off the glasses that Straight had been wearing. The merest trace of his lime aftershave clung to them. I held them down to Sam and he nosed them while I fussed him and told him he was a good boy. I let him take thirty seconds, then I told him, "Track," and he took off around the corner, nose to the ground.

The Eaton Centre isn't the best ground for tracking. Half the men in Toronto wear some kind of cologne. Sam must have been teased by a thousand sniffs that could have been Straight's scent but he followed true. After a second's hesitation he ran up the escalator, moving among the people as if they were trees in the bush up north.

I sprang after him. People exclaimed and tutted but they moved back as I hissed "Police" at them. I was watching Sam and he took off to the left towards an Olde Englishe type pub. I gave a short, sharp whistle and he stopped in his tracks, nose twitching, following the trail in the air. People were commenting, calling out to one another. I thought Willis would be inside the pub, waiting for Straight to be brought to his table. He wouldn't see Sam. But I was wrong.

Ahead of me, beyond the short row of stores, there was a second balcony. And there stood Willis, his back to the rail, Lee at one side of him, Straight in front of him. And as I came closer he saw me.

I saw his hand go for his pocket and I pushed Sam, racing forward and shouting, "Fight!" Sam covered the distance in a moment, hurling himself at Willis's arm, pinning him while he writhed and roared. All around, people were screaming, backing away. I sprang in and grabbed Willis in a headlock. "Put your hands up," I told him. He squirmed against me, but suddenly went limp and slowly raised his free arm. I took hold of the other one and told Sam, "Easy." I pulled the hand out of his pocket and put my own hand in. There was a gun in there but before I could take it out he reversed his position and locked me in a hold, head down. I called to Sam, "Fight!" and he slashed into action, gripping Willis by the leg. Willis kicked at him and swore. Sam hung on, I knew he was watching for a chance to grab Willis's arm, but he had them too high, holding me in a full nelson. He was strong and the pressure on my neck was insupportable. I knew he would kill me in a second if I gave up. So I struggled back, and when he was braced as firmly as he could, I dug the inside of his calf with my heel, scraping down past the nerve center on the inside of the shin so he went weak in the legs, then kicking his foot out from under him so that we fell and Sam was on top of us, grabbing him by the arm in a hold that could not be ignored.

I felt his hands slip from my neck and I wriggled out from the loose hold and stood over him while Sam, my precious, life-saving Sam, hung on keeping a steady pressure.

Now I glanced around. Lee had gone. Straight was still there and I told him, "Phone the police and vanish," and he went towards the pub in a rapid, hobbling stride. I didn't take the gun out of Willis's pocket. If anybody saw me with it, the case would be confused beyond belief. Instead I did the old gypsy trick of pulling his coat off his shoulders so that it pinned his arms back. Then I sat on his back and told Sam "Easy."

Sam stood, panting, and I sat while the police came. It took them only a couple of minutes but in that time the crowd had swelled to a couple of hundred people. Tourists were taking photographs, teenagers were climbing on top of seats and garbage containers to look at Sam and me. I was glad to be against the railing where nobody could come up behind me. Crowds are fickle. If somebody thought Willis was being abused they could turn on me in a moment.

The policemen were young and handsome, with the little dark moustaches that seem to come with the uniform these days. I told them "I'm a police officer. This man is wanted for hijacking and he's armed. He has a gun in his right coat pocket." I stood up and pointed down at him, turning him over to their care.

They didn't ask any more questions. One of them got out his handcuffs while the other dug in the coat pocket for the gun. He got it out and broke it open to check it for load. That was a mistake. Willis gave a shout and rolled on to his back and kicked the first one in the testicles, then smashed the second with his elbow, got up and ran into the crowd, along the edge of the railing around the balcony.

I yelled "Track" and Sam followed him but before he could reach him, Willis stopped and grabbed a baby out of the arms of a woman coming out of a store. She screamed and flapped at him but he pushed her down and turned to face me.

"Shoot the dog or the kid goes over the railing," he shouted. He meant it. His face was sweating red and his eyes were blazing with fury. The mother got to her feet, screaming, reaching for her child past other people who held her back. She was pretty and black, maybe thirty years old and her scream was out of a nightmare. Her baby was wailing too, and all around us people were yelling and my beautiful dog was waiting like an unexploded bomb for me to give him the order to bring Willis down.

Willis adjusted his hold on the baby, moving his fingers through the fabric of its woolen jacket. As he did it the wool slipped up over the round little belly and the baby dipped in his hands. The sigh from the crowd was a gust of horror. Willis did not even look at the child. He kept his eyes on me. "Shoot the dog," he said.

"Then what? You're going to have to face this crowd. They'll tear you to pieces. They won't need any dog."

"Don't waste time," he said again. "I've got the kid and I'll kill it if anybody gets in my way. The first thing is, shoot that dog."

Sam must have known we were talking about him. He adjusted the set of his head, cocking it sideways as he stared at Willis, wondering why my command to fight him was so long in coming. In the same view I could see him, puzzled, waiting and see the screaming, terrified baby, hysterical with fear. I heard his mother whimpering "Please, please, please," over and over.

"I'll need a gun," I said.

"Get one offa one a the cops." He nodded towards the policemen. One was on the ground, rolling around silently, holding his testicles. The other was sitting against the railing, holding his smashed face. They were out of it.

"What happens after that?" I wasn't going to kill my dog while I could still argue.

The mother of the baby was screaming and wringing her hands. Willis looked at her and grinned a tight little snicker. "Ask her what you gotta do."

All she could say was "Please. Please," like a prayer. I went over to the policeman with the injured testicles and unsnapped his holster. He made a move to stop me but was frozen with pain and I took the gun. Willis had moved closer to the rail. "Shoot the dog now or I hang the kid over," he said.

And then from out of the crowd came a roar that drowned all the other voices. It was the roar of a powerful man and as

we all turned, even Willis, a big black man came out of the
crowd and grabbed Willis by the throat with one hand as he
grabbed the child with the other. He moved so fast there
was no time for anything else to happen. I saw Willis let go
of the child and I leaped to take it as Willis's hand went
down to gouge at the other man's eyes. I shouted "Fight,"
and Sam caught Willis's hand again. Then the baby's mother
grabbed her child and next we were buried under an
avalanche of helpers as man after man piled on top of the
struggle. I called Sam off, and when he was free, slipped
out from under the mass and went back to the policemen.
They were recovering now. The one with the injured
testicles was sitting, holding his groin, his face like chalk.
The other one was fingering his broken teeth. I handed the
gun back to the man on the floor and he put it away. To the
other one I said, "You've got yourself a good pinch,
attempted murder of the child." Behind us the fight went
on, like a rugby scrum, people seething in to land a punch
or kick on Willis. I was hoping to slip away while the police
made their arrests but as I turned, with Sam at my heels,
three more uniformed men came running up and the man
with the hurt face told them, "This guy's a copper. There's a
guy on the bottom of that pile who had a gun."

## 29

THEY booked Willis into Toronto General, short a few teeth.
People in Toronto are more law abiding than you find in
most places but you can't fool around with a baby and
expect to have the crowd on your side. The doctors also
found facial cuts, broken ribs and a dislocated wrist. Willis
was too tough to act sorry for himself but he was plenty mad
at me. He had the brass to complain to the Metro

detectives that I had set him up. As the senior policeman at the scene I should have controlled the crowd better.

Hooper told me about it, after they questioned Willis and laid charges of attempted murder for his episode with the baby. They still had nothing on him for conspiracy in the Bonded Security extortion caper that had brought me into the case, nor on the murder of Tony Caporetto. But Hooper told me they were working on it. And he gave one of his rare grins as he said it. They were well pleased with progress.

For now, they had Willis to themselves for as long as they liked, nobody was going to grant bail to a man who menaced infants. No righteous lawyer could make a case for releasing him. He was staying inside without bail. I was glad of that. He might or might not have been a criminal mastermind but he was a mad dog, and it was comforting to have him behind bars where he couldn't try to avenge himself on me or on Louise and her children.

When the homicide men had finished questioning him, and as a special favor, "Because you started this goddamn mess," as Cooper put it, they let me have a private minute with Willis. It wasn't confidential. The standard issue shiny-faced young constable was on duty in one corner of the room, but at least he didn't know the story of the case and he pretended to be doing the *Globe and Mail* crossword while I spoke to Willis.

I had only one question for him. I no longer cared about Bonded Security, that was Fullwell's job. He could take the evidence I'd uncovered for him and use it as he saw fit. I was concerned only with Yin Su, so I asked Willis why he had attacked her.

He glared at me over his Band-aids. "What're you talking about?"

I repeated the question, not changing my words or the inflexion. He glared at me some more and then, slowly, his face split into a grin. "Hey, yeah. I forgot. You're big on her, right?" He stabbed his unbound hand at me. "That's right, eh?"

"Why did you attack her?" I asked again.

He didn't answer for a few seconds, just kept up his grin, luxuriating in it, tasting its sweetness in his cut mouth. "Yeah, I forgot about you having big eyes for her."

I leaned a little closer. "If you need reminding, I can always give that bad hand a twist, just to get your attention," I said, and smiled so sweetly that the policeman looked up from his crossword puzzle and beamed at us both like an indulgent mother with two saintly children.

Willis sniffed, contemptuously. "You could," he allowed. "But I've been worked over by experts. I was a prisoner in Korea; you couldn't show me any new tricks."

My anger boiled up inside me and I snapped out the question again. "Why did you rape her?"

I was expecting rage, pride, anything except surprise. But Willis put his head on one side and looked at me for a second the way early birds look at worms. "Rape her?" he almost whispered it. "Rape her?" I thought he was going to deny everything but instead he threw back his battered head and laughed, loud and crude and strong. "I don't have to rape her. She's mine. She does what I say. You wanna lay her, I tell her lay down, you lay her."

My fists clenched convulsively but he suddenly dropped his laughter and leaned forward to hiss the words at me. "She's mine, body and soul. She's bought and paid for, right in Hong Kong."

Before I could stop myself my hand lashed out but the brain outstripped the reflex and I pulled the punch, an inch from his laughing face. He ignored it, laughing again, safe and sound with the years of prison ahead of him. "Bought and paid for," he said again. "If you got the hots for her, tell her I said it was okay."

I stood up and nodded to the young policeman. "Keep this bastard safe and sound, it's dangerous for him on the streets."

He pushed the pencil back into the tab of his notebook and folded the paper shut around his uncompleted crossword. "Sure thing, Chief," he said and pulled out a fresh stick of gum.

Cooper was standing outside the door, drinking coffee and admiring the bottom on a big blond nurse. He heard me come out and asked without looking around, "Learn anything?"

"Enough. Thanks. You need me any more?"

He turned reluctantly away from the nurse who was

bending over the counter at the nursing station, projecting the line of her panties through the tight white uniform. "Yep," he said amiably. "One more time through the whole screwed up story, from top to bottom. Shall we go down to the station?"

It was eleven at night before I got out and went to collect my car from the pound where it had been towed during the rush hour. I got a dispensation from the homicide men to avoid paying the nintey dollars in towing charges. The old time-serving copper in charge was impressed. "Don't get many guys getting away with it like this," he told me.

"Special rates for visiting police chiefs," I said. He laughed politely and even went to the trouble of waving as I left, with Sam sitting up beside me in the front seat.

The drive let me unjangle my thoughts. It was a painful process. I didn't believe anything Willis said, about Yin Su or anything else. He was a chronic liar. But I was uncomfortable. She was just too close to the source of the action to be entirely legal. For one thing, she had a brother who was working for Willis as a thug. And even if he was not her brother, she had claimed he was, so the connection was there. And she was strategically placed in Cy Straight's office, close to whatever dealings Willis was conducting with the people he was trying to pressure. No matter which way you looked at it, she was not the girl I had thought she was. That was no fault of hers, just a mistake in my judgment, but it saddened me. I'm getting a bit long in the tooth to find true romance but she was the most exciting woman I had met in a long, long time. I wanted to trust her. And besides, the attack this morning had been genuine. I had seen her injuries myself, the bruises, the blood.

I switched on the car radio, drowning out my personal thoughts with a cheerful blast of country music. John Conlee was twanging away at "Rose-colored glasses," and I sang with him, no closer to the melody than I ever get. Sam glanced at me, then ahead, the way a weary wife might have done and I laughed and scrubbed behind his ear with my free hand.

The song ended and the DJ broke in with the usual time-filling patter they use to dilute the music in the evenings when there are fewer commercials. He rattled away about the Eaton Centre incident and quoted the man who had overpowered Willis as saying, "I just lost my head. I was dumb, I should've waited until somebody was in place to catch my baby. I believe the policeman was right." I nodded approval, a little smug. And then the DJ gave the kicker: the man, who was a rookie linebacker with the Toronto Argonauts, had added, "But it was sure good to get my hands on the sonofabitch." It was perfect and I laughed along with the DJ, remembering good buddies from the South Bronx who had fought beside me in the monsoon mud and leeches in Nam, angry black men who just wanted to kick ass and get home safe.

Then in his patter, the announcer made a comment that catapulted me right back into the middle of the case I thought was over. "Sad news tonight for the legal fraternity in Toronto. One of the most respected lawyers in town, Cy Straight, died suddenly at his Rosedale home. Not many details, but the police report says that Mr. Straight was cleaning the family shotgun when it accidentally discharged and caught him full in the chest. A member of the law firm where he worked said his death will be a tragic loss to a number of provincial and national organizations for crippled children. Apparently Cy Straight was a tireless worker for them. One of his partners described him as a small man with a big heart. A real loss for Toronto." He paused and then gave the time and announced the next record.

I stared at the radio in disbelief. This case was supposed to be over. We had Kennie and Willis and the two Chinese hoods in the slammer. Who else was there to have driven in to Straight's big driveway and fed him his own shotgun at short range? I didn't think he could have done it himself. Maybe, out of guilt and shame and the knowledge that his secret had passed into my hands. But he must have known, when I told him to get lost after helping me, that he was clear. He could have dealt with Willis from strength, acting as his lawyer at the trial, plea bargaining for him. He was safe, except for some unknown person or persons who were proving to him and to me that the case was not yet closed.

The light on Davisville turned red and I sat there through two changes, blind to everything but my worry about who could have killed Straight. I knew it wasn't suicide. He wasn't the type. He'd lived with a handicap all his life, with a bad marriage for however long that had been, with shame since Willis first walked into his office. He hadn't killed himself now.

A car came up behind me on the green and blew me away with a long hard blast on the horn. I let in the clutch and drove on, still wondering. I had been over the whole case with the guys from homicide. I had told them about Willis, about Kennie and the Chinese youths. I had told them my suspicions of Lee, the oh-so-important restaurant owner who employed hoodlums in his kitchen and served as a clearing house for Willis, the man pressuring the Hong Kong developers. They knew about everybody involved, even the unimportant bit players in the case, guys like George, Caporetto's chauffeur, and Hudson, the nebbish who had been with Tony the first night. As I drove on, slowly, I wondered who was left.

The only connection I could thing of was Yin Su. The idea hurt me, but I gave it full and fair consideration before dismissing it. Maybe Willis had been telling the truth when he said she was his possession, but if so, she was a doll, a plaything, not a moving force. Even though that was a painful realization, I could handle it. I'm a second-hand man myself and don't expect to be the first or even the most important person in some woman's life. How's that for pragmatism? It comes easy when you've just heard somebody say things about your girl that you might otherwise read on a wall in a garrison town. But it still hurt me, so I kept on thinking about the case instead of myself.

And then I remembered the one other name that had cropped up too many times to be pure coincidence. When I thought of him I slapped the wheel and let out a bellow. Elmer Svensen. Of course. He had turned up wherever this case had taken me. And I hadn't even mentioned him to the detectives.

I turned at the first cross street to head back downtown but even as I did, I realized what my priority had to be. If I was right and Svensen was clearing up loose ends on the case, the next one he reached would be Yin Su. I had to keep her safe. I could call the detectives from her apartment.

There was a phone box on the corner. I went in and dialled her number. She picked it up at once. "Hello."

"Su, it's Reid Bennett. How are you?"

I expected a pause, and the remote, detached tone of a survivor, the chill that takes over when the tears stop. I thought it might be intensified in Yin Su. She would have the polite remoteness of her race. Instead she responded like any anxious Western girl. "Oh Reid," she said, her voice full of despair.

"I'm in the neighborhood. That's why I phoned. Is it too late to come up and see you?"

"No." She snipped out the syllable so promptly I wasn't sure whether she meant "No, don't come" or "No, it's not too late." Then she explained. "No, it is not too late. I would like it."

"Five minutes," I promised, and hung up.

Sam was lying in the front seat and I bumped him on the back and told him, "Make yourself comfortable, old buddy. You may be there a while."

I still had all the questions in my mind, I remembered all of Willis's comments, but there is a part of me that has never been a policeman, the young part, and it wanted to be with Su, to comfort her and keep her safe.

All the street parking spots close to Su's apartment were taken up but I stuck my car against a fire hydrant, leaving the window open on Sam's side and telling him "Easy." That relaxed him and meant he wouldn't wake the neighborhood if some drunk stopped to tell him he was a good dog.

The inner door of her building was unlocked and I went through to the elevators and rode up to her floor. Somebody had picked up the roses I had dropped there but a petal lay trampled in front of her door. I stooped to retrieve it, then tapped her door. Her voice asked "Reid?" softly.

"In person," I told her and stood back. She opened the door and stood, formally, smiling. It was the most courageous thing I had seen in years.

"Come in," she said gently.

I nodded and stepped inside. Her radio was tuned to some soft classical station and there was a smell of flowers. I glanced around. Part of me, the cynical policeman function, wanted to check the bedroom and bathroom to be sure we were alone, but I took another look at her and knew there was no need. She was wearing a soft silk dress, not long like her cheongsam. It was peacock blue and it made her hair as rich as jet. She had circles under her eyes and there was a sadness in her expression, even though she smiled at me. "It is good of you to come," she said.

I have seen my share of rape cases and I know how victims react, shying from contact of any kind with a man, so I didn't reach out to her. I just smiled and said, "If there's anything I can do, I'd like to hear it."

She pointed to the couch and I went over and sat down. It had its back to the wall so my inner cop relaxed a little. She said, "I was going to have some tea. Would you like some?"

I nodded and she went out to the kitchen. I heard the gas pop then she came back in and said, "Two policemen came to see me."

"Was it about your going to the hospital today?" I couldn't bring myself to put it any more bluntly.

She shook her head. "No, Reid. I hope you will not be angry. I could not do what you said. I told the nurse what had happened and she gave me precautions but she did not report it."

I sighed. "You should have gone ahead. What he did was a crime. And what the nurse did was wrong. She should have notified the police."

"She is like me. She understands," Su said. "This man is in prison now. It does not matter that he is not there because of me."

I held up my hands. "It has to be your choice, Su. I respect that, but tell me, who came to see you?"

"Two men called Hooper, something like that." She moved back towards the kitchen door and checked the kettle. She kept her back to me as she spoke. "They say that he is saying I am his girl."

I stood up and went over to her, aching to put my arms around her, but instead only standing close enough that I could speak in a voice that was almost a whisper. Somehow it made the words less bruising. "He made it sound as if you belonged to him, Su."

She said nothing, for a moment and her shoulders bent a

little as if she was about to cry. Then, without turning, she said, "And you believed him. Is that why you came?"

"I've never heard one word of truth out of the man, so why would I believe him about this?" I said.

She turned to me, and when I raised my hand, to touch her cheek, she intercepted it with her own and pressed it to her face.

We stood like that for a moment, then she said, "You must understand. I am from Hong Kong. My father is a powerful man there but he has family here. He knew Mr. Willis and when he came home to Canada, my father asked him to take me. My father wants me to live here because he is not sure what will happen in our homeland."

I nodded; I've heard the endless discussions about the future of Hong Kong after the British contract ends. That's why so many Chinese have come here. When I said nothing, Su went on.

"Because I am a woman, my father thought I would need a protector. I have no uncles here and my brother is young and does not speak English. He did not even come when I came here. And so my father asked Mr. Willis to protect me."

"And this protection, what did it entail?" I knew the information might be painful but I had to know.

"He helped me to find this apartment and to find work in a law office. I was trained, in Hong Kong, and Mr. Willis knew a lawyer here. He said Mr. Straight owed him a favor." She was looking at me calmly, there was no deception in her eyes and as we stood, holding hands, I felt more peace than I have known since the month in my life when I was with Li in Saigon.

"Su. I have to ask this, forgive me for it, but it's important. Were you under any obligation to Willis?"

She gave a tiny frown and I expanded the question as far as I was prepared to. "Any sexual obligations."

She shook her head, puzzled. "Not at all. That is why my father asked him to look after me. He does not . . ." she paused and waved awkwardly. "He does not get excited over women. He prefers young men."

I had a sudden recollection of the looks that had passed between Willis and Kennie in the construction site shack.

They had been charged with reciprocal power and fear, I thought. But perhaps Kennie, the jailhouse victim, and Willis, the strutter, had a relationship going already. It could have been. But a more important question was still unanswered. "What happened this morning? Can you tell me now?"

She stiffened and let go of my hand, moving into the kitchen. I did not follow, I can tell when people need space. She spoke at last, again it was over her shoulder, in a voice so low I could hardly hear it. "Today it was different. He was excited. He said so. After he had . . ." she paused and waved one hand low at her side, a gesture of defeat. "Afterwards he said that it was not bad, perhaps he had found a new thing."

My fists clenched and unclenched. I wished I hadn't pulled that punch at Willis. I wanted to go back to the hospital and pound his face, as I had once wanted to track down the man who killed Li and kill him, over and over again.

Su turned and gave me a tiny smile. "Sit," she commanded, "I will bring the tea."

I sat, staring sightlessly at the screen across the other side of the room. A guy I knew when I was first a policeman in Toronto was a Tai Chi expert and he taught me the secret of breath control, for inner peace. At the time, just back from Nam and with the anger over Li's death still burning in my memory, I had thought him naive. But, over a few nights in the patrol car, I had practiced with him and found it worked. Now I tried it, slowing my breathing down and counting each breath with an inner mantra. I am breathing in, in tranquillity. I am breathing out, in tranquillity.

When Su joined me, carrying the tray, I was calm again. She sat on a low stool, across the little table from me and poured tea into two tiny cups. She handed one to me and I raised it to my lips in the same instant that the window shattered.

I dropped the cup and sprang to my feet, batting Su behind me with one flick of my left hand. And then Elmer Svensen reached through the broken pane, opened the casement and let himself in off the fire escape.

"Hold it right there," he said, and his service revolver was rock steady in his hand.

"Listen Elmer, it won't wash. Give it up right now," I told him but he just laughed, the same square-mouthed, mirthless laugh I had seen every time we met.

"You stupid sonofabitch," he said. "When are you gonna wise up. I got no beef with you, it's her that's all the trouble. One sip of that witches brew and you'd've been tits up in the bay."

"What the hell are you talking about? Are you drunk?" I looked back at Su who was straightening herself, slowly. She was as bewildered as I was.

"Take a look in the kitchen, behind the spices on the lower shelf of the rack. You'll find the bottle that I'm taking with me down to forensic," Svensen said. He was beaming happily and I could detect no trace of booze in the air around him.

I looked at Su, and back at Svensen, and turned towards the kitchen just as the bedroom door opened and a man charged me.

I reacted automatically, side stepping and slamming out a straight right hand that caught him high in the chest. He reeled back and I jumped for him as I heard Svensen swear behind me. My man fell on his back, bracing to kick me away. But I stood back, out of range of his feet, grabbed a wooden chest from the table top next to me and slammed it down at his face. As he covered himself, catching it, I kicked hard at the side of the right knee. He howled and I dived and smothered him, lying over him, cracking his head side to side with elbow smashes to the chin. It took three before he quit struggling and then the bullet slammed past me into the floor a foot from my back.

Without looking I rolled sideways, towards the bullet, figuring the next one would correct on the other side, and scrambled to my feet. Su was standing over Svensen who was holding his stomach, retching. She had his service revolver pointed at my head. I saw the hammer go back as she pulled the trigger and I dived under the muzzle, knocking her feet from under her and bringing her down in a tangle on top of me. She kicked and as I turned face up to grapple with her she beat at my head with the pistol but I didn't hesitate. I sank a solid punch in under her ribs and she went limp.

I turned to Svensen. He was dead white. "I'll call the ambulance."

"Later," he whispered. "Cuff that bitch first. She's a black belt in kung fu."

I reached around his belt for the handcuffs and snapped them on Su's wrists. She was powerless, winded, but the hatred in her eyes was vivid enough to etch metal.

Then I reached for the phone, calling emergency for an ambulance and police backup. When I turned back, Svensen was looking a little less ghostlike.

"Damn you, Reid Bennett," he said. "Am I never going to get straight with you?" But he was grinning.

# 30

I had hardly hung up the phone before the knock came at the door. I was cagey enough to take Svensen's gun with me when I answered it, keeping the piece out of sight behind my back but ready to shoot first if I had to.

Outside I found the woman who had come to Louise's house that morning. I waved her in, using the hand with the gun. "I've been wanting to talk to you, lady. Step inside and tell me just who the hell you really are."

She laughed, then whisked out an ID card. "Policewoman Harris, Metropolitan Toronto police," she said. "Elmer's my partner. We're in Intelligence."

"Intelligence?" I shot a look around at Elmer who was managing a weak grin. "So that's why you were hanging around, every which way I turned on this case. You're working on organized crime."

Elmer nodded, and spoke, painfully. "Investigating the Triads. That's what bugged me about you. I figured you'd spent time in Nam, you had to be part of the operation. It made me sad to think my ex-partner was à grifter."

I shook my head a couple of times. Then, acting automatically, we both stuck out our right hands and shook like a pair of kids who know they've been dumb. "Once a copper, always a copper," I said. "Sorry I got you worried, Elmer."

"Sorry I didn't trust you," he said.

The policewoman was looking around the apartment. "And I'm sorry about giving you that line of bull this morning. I wanted to get a bug on your telephone. It's not kosher, but I figured you wouldn't mind. It was for your own good so we could keep tabs on you if these guys sucked you in with some story." I started to say something but she wasn't listening. She was bending down to get a clear look at the man I had stopped.

"Lee Hop," she said to Svensen. "Right again, Elmer. It's Mr. Nouveau Riche Chinatown himself."

Svensen sniffed. "I always knew he was Triad. Sonofagun arrived from Hong Kong and takes over Chinatown in a year. I knew he was bad." Moving painfully he stood up and went over to Lee who was lying dazed, trying to move his jaw. I think it was unhinged from my elbow work and he was learning something new about injuries. I hoped it would discourage him from getting back into the pain business.

Elmer administered the caution, on a charge of conspiracy to murder me, and then sang the new Charter of Rights song for him and Lee ignored both and went on counting his teeth so Elmer did the same for Yin Su who lashed out at him with her foot. Then we all sat and waited for the ambulance.

More detectives arrived, but Policewoman Harris took charge of the situation like a veteran, handcuffing herself to Yin Su for the ride to Headquarters. I went with them and she gave me the rest of the story on the way. It wasn't what I wanted to hear, but I've been hit with bad news before so I said nothing.

Lee Hop was from Hong Kong. He'd been a sergeant in the police there, and was the kingpin of the local Triad. Yin Su was his mistress.

Somehow that hurt me worse because she was so classically Chinese than it would have if she'd been some gum-snapping blonde. It didn't dim any of the emotion I felt for her, it just dulled the whole way I looked at life. In a different way I felt as bereaved as I had done over the death of Soon Li. But I'm older now and my heart isn't on my sleeve any more so it wasn't so hard to cover up. It wasn't her I'd seen die, just my outdated illusions. There are people around who still find that kind of action a real hoot.

Back at Headquarters for what they promised was my final questioning, everyone was kind to me and didn't step on my soul any more than was absolutely necessary. It took an hour and at last I was free. I drove home and poured myself a long shot of Black Velvet and watched some TV movie until dawn. Why, it was practically painless. Until I woke up again, anyway.

# *31*

THE next morning I called to tell Louise she could move back into her house again, then spent the day doing chores and watching the TV and reading the papers when they came in, with photographs of some of the people in the case. Yin Su looked like a princess from some Asian legend. And Elmer and his partner both looked a credit to the basic blue they wore.

I didn't think anything of all this, but that evening over dinner out with Louise and her kids she said, "Why don't you have a barbecue for everyone? It would be nice to see them all socially now this case is closed." Innocence itself, nobody would have known she has a black belt in match-making.

The following Saturday evening saw me with a barbecue fork in one hand and an open Labatt's Classic in the other, standing over the steaks. Fullwell was there with his wife,

Barbara, Irv Goodman, with his arm in a sling, along with his wife, Dianne, who was exchanging crab dip recipes with Louise. Elmer Svensen was there, holding a class of orange juice.

Fullwell had a beer on the go and we were all standing around the barbecue while Elmer filled us in. I couldn't tell if he was a touch high already, or whether he had recaptured the good spirits he used to have back before he was jumped that time. Anyway, he was holding forth.

"It's coming out, a bit at a time as we talk to all these clowns, but the pattern seems to be that Lee Hop came over from Hong Kong a couple of years ago. He had papers, they could have been phony, but the amount of clout those Triad guys have at home, they could be real. Anyway, he had no problem getting into Canada. And with the money he had along, he soon finagled his way into being the big wheel in Chinatown."

"He took over the restaurant right then?" Fullwell asked. "I remember that place has been there for years."

"Yeah, seems he made the owner an offer he couldn't refuse," Elmer said and we all laughed. "Anyway, there he is, all legitimate and starting to assemble a gang of roughs to enforce the Triad extortion nonsense here in town."

Goldman said, "That must've been kept pretty quiet, I never heard a thing about it, except at work, off the record."

"That's because we were on top of it," Elmer said with a touch of real pride. "There were incidents, remember, suddenly there were murders happening in Chinatown. One guy found with his throat cut down there on Spadina Avenue. And that club shooting."

Louise chimed in then. "I remember that one. Some men were robbing the place. They shot the owner and then an off-duty policeman saw them and nailed one of them."

"Shot him dead," Elmer said cheerfully. "Only he wasn't off duty, he was one of our guys, acting innocent, just happened to be there on cue. We knew there was going to be trouble, a Triad robbery, but we nipped that one in the bud." He stopped and took a sip of his orange juice, a small one. I liked that. He didn't have the driving thirst for any fluids that you find in a lot of ex-boozers. I figured he might stay dry.

I pitched in a question, to keep things rolling. "Where did Willis fit in? Was he part of Lee's gang, what?"

Elmer nodded, glad of the chance to hold center stage. "That's the way it looks. He was inspector at the station in Hong Kong where Lee was a desk sergeant. That was the way it worked—the white guy had the rank, the Chinese had the real power. Anyway, the pair of them quit Hong Kong at the same time and came to Canada. Maybe Willis was going to go legit. He didn't really need any more money. He'd made a pile in graft in the Colony. But Lee got in touch with him and suggested a way to make some extra money."

"Extorting money from Hong Kong people coming to Canada?" I asked, turning the steaks.

"Right," Elmer said, finishing his juice with something like relief. "Lee Hop knew he had to break out of the Chinatown circuit if he was going to make the real money, the way the Mafia makes money. So he had some kind of a grip on Willis. It could have been just the old Hong Kong connection, but we figure it was Willis's thing for guys that made him vulnerable. Sure it's legal but a security firm executive doesn't want to be known as a fairy. And Willis liked working Security, it gave him a chance to set up robberies."

"Is that why Willis was tied in with Tony Caporetto? or did Lee set that up?" Fullwell asked, finishing his beer and reaching down for another from the cooler beside the table. "Anybody else?" he asked. I nodded and he looked at Elmer's glass, which was empty. "How about you Elmer, want to switch?"

I watched Elmer but he didn't even hesitate. "Not me." He checked his watch. "I had my last drink three days and eight hours ago, a mouthful of smooth cognac that tasted lousy when the Boy Scout here came back into the room." He waved his empty glass in my direction. "You did me a favor, Reid."

"You did it yourself, Elmer." I winked at him. "Good luck with the new routine."

He grinned, awkwardly. "Yeah, well so far, no pain. And I've already joined AA so we'll take it one day at a time."

I raised my beer to him and he winked. We went back a

long way and it was good to see him on the rails again. He turned to Louise, "How's the juice jug holding out, Louise?"

"Stay right there. I'll bring it out," she said. She turned away and I gave Fullwell the fork, asked him to turn the steaks while I got some water to splash on the coals, and followed her in. I caught up to her in the kitchen, getting the juice. "You've got a fan," I told her.

She looked up and beamed. "I noticed and I'm glad. He's kind of cute. But the real reason I suggested this was to bring his partner over here."

I groaned. "When will you give up? I've told you before, I'll screw up my own life without help, thanks."

She laughed. "I took the trouble to read up on her in the *Star*. She's a university graduate, master marksperson, if that's the term, and she lives with her widowed mother."

"Never mind lining me up, I have my dog to give me all the devotion I need," I told her. "You just look around for a replacement for that horse's neck who walked out on you."

"Bossy," she said and got more juice concentrate out of the freezer.

I went back out with water in a beer bottle to splash on the blaze that had sprung up around my steaks. Elmer was going on with his tale.

"The way I read it, Willis got antsy. He wanted a piece of the action for himself. They'd given him the big house and all the Chinese boys he could handle, but he wanted the kind of clout he'd had in Hong Kong. So he got connected with Tony and was going to get into the more legitimate kind of crime—straight, honest-to-God theft from warehouses, he liked that."

"Well why was Tony killed?" Goodman finished his own beer but shook his head when I offered him another. "I've had two already," he said.

Elmer was enjoying himself. Untangling a case is the best part of it. When all the facts are known, you're still not sure how they fit, and finding the connections is often the key to getting the conviction. "They all got tangled up in a web of politics," he said. "Willis advised Lee to do his enforcing with local hoods, to keep the kung fu crowd out of it. He figured that would be something the Hong Kong people couldn't handle. They were dealing with Cy Straight, a Westerner. Their trouble was coming from Western-style heavies. They wouldn't know where to put the pressure on to stop the problem. It was a good move."

"Right, so Willis asked Tony to get him some heavies. Which he did. The only thing was, Tony got to think he was important. He started getting greedy for more of the action. So Willis had to put him away. The only question was, how to do it without leaving any mess."

Elmer nodded. "That's why Willis set up the phony investigation. He didn't want the police in on it. And when he heard you had killed a couple of guys barehanded, he figured he could kill Tony and get you suspected of the murder."

Fullwell finished one of his cigarillos and was about to drop it on the charcoal when he saw me looking alarmed. "Ooops. Sorry about that." He walked to the flower plot and forced the butt out of sight in the dirt. When he came back he said, "It all makes sense. He got Kennie to give you Tony's name, looking reluctant. We chased Tony and there was that fight. It established both contact and some kind of motive for Tony's killing when it happened later."

Elmer nodded. "I think that's right. But before that could happen, Tony got cute. He figured it should be him who was getting paid by the Hong Kong companies. So he got smart, he thought, and told you about Cy Straight."

Dianne Goodman tutted. "I'll see if Louise needs a hand in the kitchen. This is too complicated for me."

She left and Irv immediately helped himself to another beer. "The way I see it, Reid, he figured you would pressure Cy Straight right out of the game and leave a neat little space for him to fit into, collecting those enforcement payments from Hong Kong."

The coals were cooling and I gave the steaks a final flip.

"Could be. I think that was why he sent me the Triad payment. He was trying to involve the Chinese everywhere."

Now Elmer Svensen laughed. "Right on, that's what we saw. And because we were already working on the Chinese angle, we naturally got interested when you appeared, Reid. That's how come we started chasing you around."

At that moment, Louise came out, carrying a tray of juice

and some cans of soda water. "I figured your juice might be more interesting with a splash of soda," she said, and Elmer agreed it might and they spent a friendly minute mixing him a new drink. I looked at him and hoped, seriously, that orange juice would stay satisfying enough to keep him off the booze. I didn't want my sister in any more emotional jackpots.

Fullwell took over the musing. "It all makes sense to me. Willis was acting just like you say, from the beginning. Wanting to investigate that first beating internally. Then when he heard your reputation, he figured he could find a way to fix Tony's murder on you, because Tony was for the high jump as soon as he started getting big ideas."

"Right." Elmer lifted his glass to Louise, they exchanged smiles and he sipped and went on. "I figured you were set up that night at Tony's apartment. If he'd wanted to, that kung fu kid could have taken your head right off the hook."

"Tell me about it." I rolled my head loosely on my neck and we all laughed. "So I guess they were covering their tracks when they iced Cy Straight and went after me. We were the only witnesses who had any information that could harm them in the investigation of Tony's murder. Sure there was lots of suspicion, but nothing solid except for Straight and me who could testify we had seen Lee with Willis in that kerfuffle at the Eaton Centre.

"Exactly," Elmer said. "That's why your welfare is very important to us for the next little while, until the case comes to court." He glanced up, over my shoulder and then called out, "Hey, come on in, Beryl." He waved and we all turned to see his partner coming in, carrying a bunch of carnations. She handed them to Louise and then came and took a beer from Fullwell and I took the steaks off the fire and we all settled down to eat, with Sam under my feet trying to look as if he was too well trained to lust for a scrap of meat.

By some magic it worked out that Elmer and his partner were at one table with Louise and me, while the others were in the other group. We talked about the case some more. Beryl had the details from Yin Su about how she had tried to get me killed, once I was released without being suspected in Tony's killing. She had set me up with finding Wing Lok. He would have taken me but I got lucky. Then she had arranged for me to find Kennie at the truck hiding place. She figured I was so angry about the alleged rape that I would rush right in and get myself killed.

Beryl was careful how she told me about the rape but the truth was, the story was all phony. Beryl had followed through at the hospital. The nurse there said Su had taken a cab straight home. The bruises on her arms were self-inflicted. The blood came from a piece of meat in the fridge. She had thought it wouldn't matter, by the time she came back from the hospital, I would be dead, up there in the body shop where Kennie was waiting. But I had kept on surviving and at last she had decided to kill me herself, to please Lee Hop who was angry at me both for getting close to his organization and getting next to his woman.

The upshot was, I felt midly foolish and said very little, but after a while the talk about the case dwindled and Beryl asked me what I was going to do next.

"I'm going home on Monday. Then I'll take the canoe and head into Algonquin Park. By the time you've portaged in about two lakes from the road you won't see another person for days at a time."

"That sounds so nice," she said wistfully.

"It will be." I was too empty inside to follow up the implicit invitation in her tone. Maybe one weekend in winter when I came into Toronto with a prisoner or just to see Louise and buy books, I could call Policewoman Harris. But for next week I had some healing to do and it would happen faster in the open air with the mist on the lakes at first light and the sky blazing with sympathetic stars all night. A week alone would enable me to bury the memories of Yin Su in the same graveyard that covered Soon Li. It had to be done before I could look another woman in the face. But when I did, I would like it to be this one.

"I'll be back in Toronto to give evidence at the trial," I said. "Maybe we could meet then."

She looked at me, nodded slowly, and said, "I don't see why not."

## ABOUT THE AUTHOR

TED WOOD was born in England and emigrated to Canada in 1954. He served on the Toronto police force for three years and later was a copywriter and agency creative director for a Toronto advertising firm. He has written radio and stage plays, TV dramas and documentaries, magazine articles, and short stories. He is also the author of two previous Reid Bennett mysteries, *Murder On Ice* and *Dead in the Water*, which won the 1983 Scribner Crime Novel Award. Wood now lives on a farm north of Toronto.

# MAX BYRD PROMO: CALIFORNIA THRILLER, FLY AWAY JILL AND FINDERS WEEPERS

## By Max Byrd

☐ **A CALIFORNIA THRILLER** (26179-7 • $2.95)
Mike Haller is hired to hunt down George Webber, a journalist for the San Francisco Constitution. Carlton Hand, Webber's robust editor, is sure that his reporter's suffering from a mid-life crisis and is off on a fling with a woman. So does Webber's wife—he's done it before. But Haller's search reveals a truth more sordid than an extramarital fling. A truth that turns the peaceful Sacramento Valley into a death trap for Mike Haller.

☐ **FLY AWAY JILL** (26178-9 • $2.95)
Mike Haller's second mystery sends Haller on a mission to England and France to find Caroline Collin, the missing daughter-in-law of a very rich California businessman, Carlo Angeletti. But Angeletti wants to find more than Caroline. She has disappeared deliberately, it turns out, taking with her the plans of her father-in-law's international drug smuggling operation. Haller tracks Caroline through Europe, tangling with hoods and hired killers as he untangles the secrets of the drug network's chain of command.

☐ **FINDERS WEEPERS** (26177-0 • $2.95)
Private eye Mike Haller gets deeply embroiled in a case with a lot at stake. There's money—nearly a million dollars—and a strange beneficiary, prostitute Muriel Contreras. There's self-respect, as Haller is deprived of his license by a cop who's itching for revenge. With little more to go on than a photograph of a woman in a black bikini, Haller embarks on a journey that takes him through the kinky underside of San Francisco, into the boardroom of a superlawyer, and forces him to make the worst choice a man has to make—between the woman who can clear his name and the woman he loves.

Buy these novels wherever Bantam books are sold, or use this handy coupon for ordering:

# Special Offer
# Buy a Bantam Book
### *for only 50¢.*

*Now you can have an up-to-date listing of Bantam's hundreds of titles plus take advantage of our unique and exciting bonus book offer. A special offer which gives you the opportunity to purchase a Bantam book for only 50¢. Here's how!*

*By ordering any five books at the regular price per order, you can also choose any other single book listed (up to a $4.95 value) for just 50¢. Some restrictions do apply, but for further details why not send for Bantam's listing of titles today!*

*Just send us your name and address and we will send you a catalog!*